AN
AESOP
IN
BROKEN
GLASS

ISBN 978-1-312-34318-4

Acknowledgements

To Staff Sergeant Edward E. Rivera,
whose expertise and support helped make this novel possible,
and to all of the friends and family who saw me through it.

I.

It's a rare man who isn't blind.

But forgive me: if there's one thing I've learned, it's that you can't understand the future, or even the present, if you don't understand the past. You deserve an honest account. God knows I've wanted one. It's a hard thing to give, but I'll do my best. I think you can wait that long.

When the Grand War ended, I was just old enough to understand, but not yet old enough to care. I remember sitting on the couch with my parents, watching the television as a brave reporter from Candor Network strode over the blood and corpses of the last battlefield, toward the sea of crimson and gold. Our boys. The grand North Licenian military, with their colorful coats—it was the first color broadcast—relieved faces, and shiny new machine guns. A detachment were gathered under the flag of the lion, while the rest were out hunting down stragglers.

The imperialist forces of Greenwood had finally been defeated; after attacking South Licenia, they were treated to the full brunt of our expanded military budget. The latest innovations in death and destruction: wall-to-wall carpet bombing, light machine guns, improved tanks—it was a show of military power unrivaled by any we'd ever seen, and hopefully, any we'll have to see again. But that's not the way of things, is it? Somebody's always got to have the edge. Somebody always needs more power. Don't they?

Forgive me. The reporter was making his way across the battlefield, when he nearly got bowled over by an officer. Big guy, compared to the reporter; bigger in his red greatcoat and golden lion's mask. The reporter grabbed him by the arm before he could run off, and asked, "Excuse me, Captain: if I can have just a second of your time, what would you say was the turning point in the war?"

He paused for just a moment to think, then replied in the voice of a man who hasn't slept for a few years. All gravel and tin, echoing slowly out of that helmet. "The turning point was when they threatened us," he said. "They made the mistake of rousing the lion. And like lightning from Heaven, we made a mountain of their patriot dead." Just like that, he was off again. Not another word, not a name. Another faceless man in the midst of a long, long war.

The reporter didn't exactly know what to do with that. He sort of looked after the guy for a moment, then turned to the camera and said, "And there you have it, ladies and gentlemen: one of our brave servicemen gives his perspective on the winning of this grand war. It's been a long, hard fight for all of us, and we should all be very proud of our patriots' sacrifice to keep safe our way of life." He must have felt like an idiot, standing up there and smiling for the camera, talking about how hard the fight had been for us—for him—when he had just heard that man speak. I would have, at least. At any rate, he didn't have anything else to say: just the same sign-off as the last few years. A red backdrop with a golden lion's head, and "This Grand War update was brought to you by your friends at Candor Network. Stay safe, stay strong, and stay patriotic."

Everybody watched Candor Network. Simple reason, too: they were willing to send their reporters out into the thick of battle to get front-line news, commentary from the soldiers. They skirted the edge of legality to get into parliamentary sessions that nobody else could, and hear what was really being said by our representatives. Everyone was a part of the government: they couldn't help it. Everybody watched the news, breath bated, waiting to know whether or not we'd drive the

Greens back to the hole they crawled out of. And everybody knew what it was the government should be doing, of course.

But over the next few years, we lost our interest in politics. When you haven't got a bunch of men about to die, you don't care so much whether or not Resolution 17-A-72 passes. We were tired of war: we wanted a return to the comfortable conservatism of our older years, when TV was all comedy or dramas. But fake dramas, where you can turn off the television and know that your son's safe at home with his beautiful wife, not getting killed in a foreign war. Even with our massive bombs and unstoppable infantry, it still took a while to push the Greens back: they had footholds, and they knew the territory. And war isn't clean, no: it's a messy, sordid affair.

Candor Network had its fingers on the pulse of what we wanted. Didn't it always? It could feel our interest waning, and it adapted appropriately: less features on the aftermath of the war, less features on the latest government sessions, and more on our favorite movie stars. There were movies about war, sure, but movies about war aren't the same thing. You've got the hero who saves the day from the evil oppressors, and nobody ever has to think about how, "Hey, that guy looks a lot like me." They're just uniforms shooting uniforms, rag-dolls crumpling to the ground. I watched them like any other kid, and I wished I had been a little older, so that I could have fought in that Grand War. Everyone wants the glory without the sacrifice.

When I turned twenty, not so very long ago, I packed my bags and headed out to try my fortunes in Priius. Licenia's new capital, Candor proudly proclaimed. The city of their headquarters would now house the seat of government. It had been growing steadily under Candor's influence, and the economic boom showed little sign of stopping: even as it consolidated the smaller networks into itself, it expanded in its own right, needing more and more employees. And so, I—a poor boy from the eastern farmlands—made my way to the big city, to work as a janitor. Almost storybook. Except that storybooks don't tend to mention the whole "working your ass off and living paycheck to paycheck" part.

I hope you don't mind my apparent cynicism too much. I'm not a cynic; I'm really not. But it's a hard thing to look back on your own failings, and the failings of a country—a goddamn country—and not feel just a little bit bitter. But I have faith. Faith in humanity: a rare commodity in times like these. I truly, honestly believe that we can improve. If it weren't for that... Well, I don't believe I'd be here today.

II.

I hitchhiked from Dalton to Keller to Barbier, where I stayed for a while and worked as a shop hand, to replenish the scant earnings I'd brought with me. I ate one meal a day, most of the time, and drank from water fountains. I had one set of "city clothes," and three pairs of work clothes; I slept nude when I could find privacy, and in the day's clothes when I could not, which was most times. There's little privacy on the road, and less as you approach the city. My clothes were washed in rivers, hung out to dry in the woods, when I could.

It took little enough time for me to reach Barbier, but it doesn't seem like that when you're keeping one eye on the holes in your slacks and the other on the holes in your wallet. Though my new job helped the first, a bit, my wages were enough to feed me and patch my clothes, but precious little else if I wanted to save up enough to be able to make it in Priius for even a month. I had worked odd jobs as a boy, but spent most of my time on the farm, where you work all day long for a plateful of food and the scorn of society. Suffice it said that the merest scrap of linen for the newest hole in my careworn clothes came unwanted.

It doesn't escape me that my life story might bore you. But that's what this thing is: my life's story, from the moment I woke up, to the moment I closed my eyes, and back again. And as conceited as it may sound, I believe my life has had a rather significant impact on events, of late: history is the story of the masses, but it takes individuals within those masses to spark events. Wars are won by soldiers, to be sure; but they are begun by men of some sort of power. And our actions, I've heard, are shaped by even the most minute experiences in our lives. For you to understand what I'm about to do, you have to understand what I have done. I ask no pity, mind. Not out of some stubborn pride, but for the simple reason that I do not believe I deserve it. Most people's actions are the result of where they came from, whether or not they had money, that kind of thing. But I'd like to think that what I did wasn't anybody's fault but my own. Maybe I'm just generous that way.

My beard and skin grew darker as winter gave way to spring; the season had been gentle, thankfully, which gave me fears for summer. For the first time in my twenty years, I saw the spring's first robin alight on a guard rail rather than a fence post. A strange experience, that. Walking over to the parking lot of the shop where I worked—it was a small enough town that I could walk to my camp in the woods, an experience which seems strange and far away, now—and realizing that I was far, far from home. I stared sunward for almost a minute, wondering what my parents were doing, before I turned my mind back to the day's work and shut myself up in the store again.

By the time the next winter came, I was another year older. My figure had grown gaunt, each muscle taut against my unhealthy skin. Thanks to a careful diet, I kept most of my teeth and strength; I had forced myself to begin a more liberal allowance for food, delaying somewhat the final leg of my journey. With a few hundred in my wallet, I gathered my supplies and spent a week hitching straight to Priius. Some days, I barely slept; others, I found a ditch or a doorway, and in them, a few hours' rest before getting a nudge from the police. Only once was I threatened with vagrancy; fortunately, I had a pay stub from the last week, and managed to convince the officer that I was just stranded during my trip. I still had to move, but I wasn't hauled off to enjoy a decent meal and shelter.

Part of me is tempted to ask if you can imagine what it felt like for me to first lay eyes on Priius, but chances are, you can't.

That's not a strike against you, by any means. For most people, Priius was a sprawling, dirty city of metal, glass, and smog. For me, though, for a boy who'd grown up all his life glued to the TV and wanting to be brave like the men at Candor, it was the fabled city. God, I couldn't believe it: Priius, where all the TV broadcasts I'd watched, all the radio programs I'd listened to came from. The skyscrapers were so tall I couldn't see their tops when I stood nearby; the streetlamps, each bearing a red flag with a golden lion's head, lined every boulevard, and it seemed like a million cars were packed on the roads, all bellowing exhaust. Crowds of black business suits clopped by—being a business town, it was busy all day, and dead at night. Everyone went back home, or to nightclubs in other towns. But mostly back home to watch television.

I spent the rest of the day searching for lodging. A loiterer pointed me to Old Hampton Street, a little hole-in-the-wall part of the city preserved for "historical purposes," ostensibly. It was actually left alone thanks to its tenants being violent types who didn't take well to the idea of their homes being wrecked. Other than a few ritzy penthouses and the houses reserved for the obscenely wealthy, it was the only place to stay anywhere within walking distance of the city proper. Cheap as dirt, too, with plenty of abandoned shacks. It sounded like the perfect place for me, so I asked directions and set out.

Managing the traffic was a dangerous sport for the locals. They congregated in churning masses at each crosswalk, then hurried across in largely silent crowds, save for the clopping of shoes on pavement. The cars hunched in impatient wait for each red light, their engines growling in frustration as the herds moved by. Looking frightfully out of place, I joined in several of the matches, usually toward the outside of the group. In my tattered, cotton shirt and ripped jeans, with a week's worth of growth on my face, those who noticed me must have thought me a madman. Perhaps they were right, but I suspect I may have been invisible the entire time—I would have looked too much like a beggar.

Night quickly found its way over even the eternal suns of the city: enormous television screens adorned almost every building, lighting up the darkened sky and blocking any view of the familiar constellations. Familiar to me, at least: a man could go a lifetime in Priius and think himself alone in the universe. But I had little time to ponder astronomy; the pangs of hunger in my stomach kept me firmly grounded. With my nose pressed nearly to the glass, I scanned the bottom floors of each skyscraper, trying to look for restaurants that might be cheap enough for someone like me to eat there.

Each building was a shop atop a shop atop a shop. Were it not for the startling uniformity of the design, I would have thought they had been built independently, and dropped willy-nilly atop one another. Within the displays, mannequins modeled fine fashions designed for fine people: three-piece suits with shiny, brass buttons; dresses with trains to scrape the floor; children's clothes that cost more than my whole going-out outfit together. Pictures were set up in many of the shops, clothing or otherwise: it's really quite amazing how every family who endorses a product is upper-middle class, immaculately dressed, attractive, and happy. Their products must not have been designed for poor, ugly, unhappy people with shoddy clothes. The restaurants seemed to be reflecting that trend, and I nearly despaired of eating more than a pint of beer. Fortunately, after I slipped down an alley that intersected with Old Hampton Street, I found a handful of shops designed for the not-so-rich. They were all sandwiched in the interiors of the buildings, according to the directories placed outside. Not on the ground floor, where they draw the eye; not on the top, where they give a majestic view. Right in the middle, where no windows allow people to peek in at a display of poverty, and none of the disadvantaged are left underfoot. I don't imagine you know those places. Few enough do. But there I go, being bitter again.

Still in awe of the gilded city, I pushed my way through a revolving door, and stared in wonderment at the finery visible through glass doors. To my left, a men's clothing store: I could just see myself clad in a nice suit like theirs, rather than the wool and cotton one rolled up in my backpack. To my right, a shop where the well-to-do could buy gifts for their wives and mistresses. And before me, the largest, most ostentatious staircase I had ever seen. A staircase like that could have paid to feed my family for at least half a year. Naturally, I wound my way up with reverent delicacy, keeping my head down so as not to be blinded by those who were descending.

Painfully aware that it had been far too long since I had washed my clothes or even bathed, I slunk like a beaten dog through the finery and curios of the various shops. Stainless steel pillars, wrapped in silvery mirrors, reminded me of my disarray, while my leather boots clomped heavily on the polished tile. It was the sort of place where the people from the television might have gone ballroom dancing, in my mind. But to everyone else, it was just the hall that connected the staircase to the third-floor shops. I found only one blemish in the beautiful architecture: a solitary opaque wall, of a tasteful marble. The sign screwed above the wooden door let me know that it was, naturally, my destination.

As soon as I stepped inside, the marble became obvious as a facade. The interior was all wood: it was a small, poorly lit little tavern, with a grizzled old woman at the helm and a thin crowd gathered around. Mostly old people, hunkered over greasy food and trying to find something to talk about after forty years. A few of them looked almost as dirty as me: I was relieved as I crept to the bar, my woolen cap in hand, and asked her for a menu.

"You ain't from around here, are you, boy?" she asked, her throat a bed of nails.

"No, ma'am," I said. My own wasn't much prettier, I don't imagine.

"Got a job?"

"No, ma'am."

She nodded. "Got a house?"

"No, ma'am." I shifted uncomfortably from foot to foot, looking askance.

She nodded once again. "Then you're the usual sort. You make trouble, I get out th' fucking shotgun next time you come, hear?"

I heard, and she gave me a menu. From it, I selected a dinner of two eggs, a bit of bacon, water, and toast. I didn't want anything too rich; it might upset my stomach, after so long fasting. And besides, that was a feast, to me. The woman had me pay in advance; while she went back to the kitchen, I sat at the bar and stared into it. Soon enough, I was staring at a cup of water, which I gratefully drank. She came in and out several times over the course of making my meal, and I took a cautious study of her face. I didn't want to stare. She might get out th' fucking shotgun.

It would be trite to say that she must have been pretty once. The truth was that she was probably never pretty: just a plain sort of person, grown weathered and old before her time. Her face bore deep creases that spoke of a lifetime of work, and her brown eyes bore deep sadness that spoke of a recent pain. Her grizzled, silver hair was pulled back in a ragged bun, and she wore an apron over a grease-stained dress. It wasn't until she brought me my food that I noticed her limp. I fancied that she had danced once. Have you ever made up stories about strangers? I suspect you might have.

I ate with single-minded tenacity, left her a shameful tip, and took my leave. She said not another word to me the whole time I was there; nor, for that matter, did anyone else. Everyone ate alone together, and the couples took their leave separately, hand in hand. I had never seen poverty before, despite having grown up in it. But that was a different sort.

Having something in my stomach gave me a strange sensation as I made the last leg of my journey. The streetlights faltered and eventually succumbed, leaving only a grey blackness by the time I saw the rusted sign marking where I hoped to make my home. Through a gap in two factories, through the smog and the dark, I saw the outline of a low shack, squatting morosely in the dirt. Knowing that I had found the ruins of Old Hampton Street, I strode those last, long yards to my goal. Through luck and the wielder's careful aim, I managed to avoid the cudgel which nearly cracked my skull as I walked through.

A beast of a man, clad in a black waistcoat and white shirt, with neither tie nor jacket, bore it; his bowler came to the tops of his blonde eyebrows, while his sharp, blue eyes gave me a quick once-over. "Business?"

Not entirely sure what he meant, I told him that I was hoping to buy some lodging. He laughed a hearty laugh, called me a tenderfoot, and let me through. No flags flew here: all was abject poverty. I was noting a trend. A few ruffians, each wearing the same waistcoat, slacks, and shirt, threw pigs' knuckles over a barrel, and my new acquaintance jutted his cudgel at a shack toward the outskirts of the encampment. "You can dump your shit there, greenhorn," he grunted. "What's your name?"

I told him, and he let me know that I would be simply Jackson from then on. He was Fergus. They didn't deal much in names around Hampton. That stuck with me: to this day, if someone asks my name, I tell them that I'm Jackson. Without so much as shaking his hand, I nodded and headed to my new abode. Along the way, out of the corner of my eye, I thought I caught a flash of crimson and gold. But it was a ghost. It always was.

III.

I slept fitfully, my dreams haunted by ghosts. The faint image of my past life remained in one corner of my mind, while the future I saw before me struggled for the rest. Do you know the rush you get when you see all of your dreams within the reach of your hand? Do you know the disappointment that comes with it? There's a sense of loss, really: the realization that everything you've been striving for is in your grasp—and what does that leave you? I think it leaves you the next goal; if we ever reach true perfection, I imagine we'll be so satisfied that we won't need ambition. But until then, it'll leave that same empty ache in our gut.

Now, mind you, I'm no philosopher. But I think that deep down inside, perfection really is what we want. Those who say we don't are the ones who have given up. They lack vision. But you and I—we still have it, don't we? We're not quite so blind as they.

But I digress.

When I woke the next morning, laid out on the worn-out old mattress that was left behind in my bare shack, I knew that today, I'd change my fate forever. I took my unworn city clothes with me in my knapsack, threw on my dirty rags, put shoes on my blistered feet, and trudged out of the cabin with morning's light. Another man had replaced Fergus; he just gave me a nod as I headed toward the communal bath.

I could see why ladies didn't fancy Old Hampton: besides being a crowd of rough men, the only bathing facility was a rickety shack, hastily erected around a metal basin and a water pump. I closed the door behind me, and began working the pump, just like I had on the farm, all those months ago. It spattered down into the tub with a staccato beat; it took a while, but eventually, I'd filled the thing. I stripped and stepped inside, shivering at the icy feeling. Using a rag I'd carried with me, I scrubbed at each inch of my weathered body, watching as the road dirt was scrubbed away. I had no soap, so I just worked to get the stench off, washing away days of sweat and grime. The tub grew dark as I continued; by the time I'd reached my face, I had to let it drain and fill it up a bit again, so as not to undo my own work. Finally, I washed my hair, then let the tub drain again.

Still dripping, I pulled on my city clothes, relishing the scent of reasonably-clean cloth. It clung strangely to my wet form, nothing feeling quite right. Having been protected, the suit was soft and supple, like my newly-bathed skin. I felt almost like a new man, having baptized myself in the refreshing water and clothed myself in what was to me a rich garment. All cotton and wool, but won at the expense of my fingers and back.

I pulled the dress socks up my calves and attached them to my garters, reminded of going to town every Saturday as a child and having to do the same then. At the time, I had considered it an inconvenience; but now, without even a horn to help my feet into my shoes, I couldn't wait to finish getting into my one suit. After pulling on the waistcoat, I tucked my old clothes into the sack, and dropped them back off at my little shack before heading out again.

I wandered away from Old Hampton Street the way I'd come the night before, wandering through side-streets and alleys before finding myself in front of the tower where the little tavern I'd visited was hidden. The food was cheap and filling, and my stomach reminded me that I needed to eat if I didn't want to collapse from the lack of it. And so, back into the glass-and-steel wonderland I went, without stopping to marvel quite so much.

Now that I was properly dressed, and something approaching

groomed, I didn't feel quite so ashamed to be seen out in public. To be sure, I couldn't begin to match the splendor of even the cheaper outfits displayed on the walking mannequins I passed, but at least I didn't feel as much like an outsider. Past the glass shop displays and astounding prices I walked, making my way up the stairs to the marble facade and wooden door.

In the morning, the little bar was somewhat more lively than the previous night, though that didn't say much. A pair of old men were talking loudly about some television show I didn't watch, and a few of the couples were actually conversing with each other over their breakfast. Sitting myself down at the bar, I waited with my eyes turned to the counter for the woman who had served me the night before. She was there again, her eyes dark and sunken with a dearth of sleep.

"You came back."

Looking up, I inclined my head slightly to her. "Yes, ma'am."

"Got yourself a place? Or are you just vagabondin' it?"

"I have a... house of my own, ma'am."

"Old Hampton, then. You're polite." Her tone neither approved nor disapproved.

"Thank you, ma'am."

The entire time, she stood like stone, while I sat with my shoulders hunched, my hands clasped before me on the bar. We were like two poker players, each studying the other, though for what reason, I haven't a clue. Eventually, she shoved a menu under my nose, and walked away while I perused it. The old thing was written in ink on a piece of cardboard, probably torn off of a box. I selected a basic breakfast of a couple of biscuits, gravy, eggs, and sausage, and when she returned, quietly requested the same. I still had all my money in my wallet, which I flashed to her as a sign of good will. She looked as though she had little enough.

It may seem strange to you that I can remember with such clarity what I had for breakfast, but you must understand: all of this was a new experience to me, branded indelibly on my mind. I had never, ever ordered breakfast before: it had always been cooked up for me, or I had cooked it myself. Someone like you, surely, knows exactly how it is to sit in a fine restaurant with fine people and eat yourself a hearty plate of food, but in all my twenty years, I had never had the chance. Nor did I that day: the people there may have been good, but they were hardly fine.

When she returned with a glass of water for me, from which I fished a speck of unidentified matter, I caught her eye for just a moment, trying to get a study of her face. Her tired eyes narrowed slightly as she did the same, perhaps trying to read my intentions. Eventually, before she could retreat into the kitchen again, I asked, "What's your name, ma'am?"

She folded her arms across her grease-stained apron. "What's yours, boy?"

For a moment, I hesitated. And then, with a slight and private smile, I replied, "Jackson, ma'am."

"Uh-huh. You keep calling me 'ma'am'; don't see why you need a name."

"Do you prefer I call you ma'am?"

She rubbed at her jaw, considering that, and I watched a strand of hair pull loose from her bun. Eventually, she decided, "You can call me Mrs. Hughes."

"Yes, ma'am." I hid my amusement, but I think she might have guessed at it. She was a smart one, that Mrs. Hughes. After a moment longer, while we stared in silence at one another, I asked, "How's Mr. Hughes doing?"

She grunted. "He's pretty dead."

I'd expected it, but I don't know why I asked. And like an idiot, I just sat there for a moment, blinking at her: she was rough, sure, but she couldn't have been old enough to be a widow. Not naturally, at least. "I'm..." I began, but she waved a hand and walked back into the kitchen. I suppose that when you get to be her age, the platitudes run thin and weary.

When she brought me my food, dripping in grease and smelling of old oil, I ate in relative silence, still wondering at myself for asking that question. What business of mine was it to ask about her husband? Not exactly the way to begin a conversation with a woman who obviously works herself to the bone. He'd had to have been sick, dead, or a layabout, I figured, or she'd have something left to enjoy in her life. But she was another ghost, tending her graveyard of a tavern. I was surrounded by a million ghosts and shades, all in varying greys.

The tip I left her was slightly bigger than last night's, but still an insult: I felt the need to offer what apology I could for my awkward conversation, and left without another word.

With a full belly, I wound my way back toward the city proper, where the belching, roaring engines of hundreds of cars clogged the streets again, with frantic hordes of business suits trying to race their way to the office to do their time. I followed along with them like a fish in a stream, swimming through vast oceans of asphalt and cement, pushed along by the current of bodies. The ever-present televisions looked down on it all from above, while the office buildings on which they rested gradually swelled out with their inhabitants.

Despite my roundabout path, following the trail of red lights and crosswalks, I knew my destination exactly: Candor Tower. The highest, gaudiest eyesore in the whole skyline, sticking out above all the others with its crimson and gold banners. The televisions grew thicker, denser as I strode closer to it, the forest of sight and sound threatening to engulf my senses. But although I had grown up on many of the programs playing, I had no time for them, now: I needed to work before I could play.

Though I look back on it with a certain distaste, at the time, I thought Candor Tower was the most gorgeous thing I had ever seen. A stunning display of wealth and nationalism, from the roses and marigolds lining the path to the doors, to the lion's-head fountain roaring endlessly and noiselessly to the world. Or perhaps the trio of massive screens were its roar: when you stand before Candor Tower, in a peninsula of three great skyscrapers, you might as well stand before the ocean itself, with the rush of air and the smell of salt. Except that Candor's ocean was a rush of sound and the smell of burning gasoline.

I do believe that my heart skipped a beat as I meandered my way past the fountain and toward the grand, sliding doors that separated Candor's lobby from the outside. Within, I thought everything had been painted in gold: the walls looked like they might have been, with red carpets and tapestries hanging between every massive window. A plain receptionist—who I thought must have been an angel, in her immaculate dress—sat at the counter, and welcomed me to Candor Tower.

Candor Tower, home of everything I had ever wanted from life.

I took an application to be a janitor, filled it out, and sat in the lobby while she filed it to be processed.

For the next several hours, I sat there in the lobby of the building of my dreams.

And I watched television.

IV.

I sat there for hours, oblivious to the world. My mind was captivated by the flashing lights and chipper noises from the television, and for a few hours, I returned to innocence. The innocence of childhood, at least—no matter how I might have deceived myself, I had much left to lose. A million people could have come and gone from that lobby, and I might never have noticed, never turned around.

Every so often, the receptionist came over to check on me, as if I might have fallen asleep, or died in that tower. I might yet, but I didn't then. Each time, I smiled and nodded to her inquiries into my health, only once accepting her offer of a cup of water from the fountain. She left for a lunch break shortly after midday, but I remained in one of the comfortable seats, sipping my ounce of water and calmly letting myself get carried away by the television's comforting lights.

Evening draped down by the time I was finally considering going home; the moon's timid rays didn't stray into the lobby of that ostentatious tower, though. I had briefly fallen asleep in the chair, it being the most comfortable surface on which I found myself in over a week. I suppose they must have known me for an outsider: rough stubble, tanned skin, and that serene smile as I gazed at the screen. Perhaps they knew what it was like for me to have made the pilgrimage to the holy land: the land that launched a thousand airplanes and burned the topless towers of Greenwood. Or perhaps they thought me some poor vagabond, having scrounged or stolen a passable suit, and put in an application as a janitor in hopes of something better. Another possibility still is that they had no such kindness, and tolerated me in the way that one might a spider in the house: a pest, grotesque and yet interesting, but so harmless that its death is unwarranted.

At the chime of eight, I stood, tearing my eyes away from a trivia show. I was out-of-touch with the most recent pop culture; for my last few years on the farm, I had considered myself a "man." My areas of interests shifted from the serials and comedies of my youth, to more serious histories and classic dramas. I knew even then that I would have to educate myself: the schools had done a fair job of it, but I still lacked the fine knowledge necessitated by a life in the city. So I read voraciously when I wasn't working or watching classic films. And I realized, as my legs felt life rush back into them and my strained eyes blinked at their sudden respite, that I suddenly felt very, very detached from the city's culture.

I had gathered my thoughts, and headed toward the door when I heard a voice from behind me. Turning, I found myself confronted by a jovial, bald-headed man in a sharp suit, who waved papers under my nose. "Young man," said he, "you've got yourself a job. Can you be here tomorrow morning? Won't be much training, really; just need you to fill out some paperwork, and you'll start as soon as you're able."

I thanked him with a smile, took the papers, and promised I'd be there at eight. I decided not to mention either my surprise at my speedy hiring, nor my lack of an alarm clock; I rose with the sun, and it rose early. Besides, if I needed to know the time, I could just find one of the ever-present television screens. He clapped me on the shoulder, called me a good sport, and wandered off again, down the gold-and-crimson hallway and toward the elevator. Just once, I glanced down at the papers he'd handed me, wondering how they'd processed my paperwork so soon. With a shrug, I turned toward the door. It could be my imagination, but I do believe the receptionist may have given me a single wink.

Her kindness did not go unappreciated. I can promise you that much. She took pity on me when I was desperate, and I am not one to be ungrateful. I have the gift and curse of an excellent memory: I recall every kindness, favor, slight, and wrong dealt to me, and I pay them back. But you know that.

Just like the night before, the false darkness was a strange and ugly thing to me. Already, I missed the sight of the heavens above me; it felt like a man must feel when a prayer goes unanswered: to look up, high above your head, and know that everything you seek is hidden. There's a blindness, see, caused by the lights and splendor of Priius. You can't see the stars for the street lamps, and without the stars, you can't find your way. Do you suppose that's what's wrong with us? We've spent so long with false light that we've lost our way. It seems like the harder we look for a neon sign to guide us—religion, philosophy, politics, our heroes—the less we realize that all we need is a good pair of eyes and the world around us.

I had stayed up so late in that tower that I was among the few left awake in the city. Most of the other buildings had darkened: there remained only the glow from Candor Tower, the streetlights, and the televisions. And the cars, of course: a stream of endless light, each headlight reflecting off of each tail-light, shining through exhaust clouds. Every one of those monsters could have easily crushed me, without so much as a second thought. But all during my walk back home, I felt... invincible. I dodged and danced between metal frames, stared hungrily at the finery along the sidewalks. One of these days, I told myself, I'd waltz into Kirkmann's and buy myself a nice, gold watch. I'd put it on in my third-floor apartment, then descend the stairs to my car. After greeting my neighbor, I'd drive over to Franklin Square and sit down in one of those fancy foreign restaurants, eat food I can't pronounce, and laugh the laugh of a man whose only concern is the color of his tie.

For now, I walked past Kirkmann's, past the gold watches and the foreign restaurants. I found myself ascending the stairs of the Humboldt Shopping Center, all the way to the marble facade and the wooden door. "JOHN'S KITCHEN," the placard read.

I wondered what kind of a man John Hughes had been.

She stood there at the counter, looking as old and weary as ever, polishing a glass with a tattered rag. She looked up, then down without a word; I approached the counter and sat down, still drunk on my victory over the labor market. "I've found myself a job," I told her, though she hadn't asked. "I'm to work at Candor Tower, as a janitor."

"Good." She continued polishing the glass, staring into its immaculate interior with intense concentration. "You'll be able to keep paying for your food."

"Yes, ma'am," I chuckled, perusing the menu. We remained in silence for a few moments, until I ordered a hamburger and a beer. Not even the beer was foreign. She took down the order and disappeared into the kitchen, returning a while later with my food.

Setting it down, she muttered, "Good on you, though. Candor's a right nice place for a boy like you. Maybe you'll turn out alright, eh? Even living in a shithole like Old Hampton." Abruptly, she looked up again, half-glaring at me. "But you won't live there for long, I don't expect. I've got an eye for people, and you—you've got that look of determination."

"Thank you, ma'am."

"You just watch your ass out there, boy. I know that look. I've got an eye for people."

I was in a good mood. Most of my money was still with me; I hadn't even paid anything for lodging. For the first time in my three visits there, I gave her a decent tip, then left with a full stomach and a sort of contentment in my heart. For all my life, it was all I had wanted: to be content with who and what I am. That sort of satisfaction is hard to come by. We're always changing who and what we are; we just don't always realize.

It's not very far of a walk from Humboldt to Old Hampton, but I meandered a bit on my way up there. I tried the door to one of the men's clothing stores, but it was closed for the night, like most things in the town. Just John's Kitchen and Candor Tower seemed to operate almost all day. Soon enough, I was squeezing into the intersecting alleys that led to Old Hampton, expecting to be greeted by Fergus.

Fergus wasn't guarding the entrance, this time. Nobody was. An array of men in black waistcoats and white shirts, all doffing their caps, stood before the shack that had been erected against an abandoned factory. And perched atop it, standing tall in his crimson greatcoat and golden lion's mask, was a ghost.

"Gentlemen," he said, voice echoing tinnily from the lion's mouth, "we stand on the precipice of a revolution. A step backward will send us plummeting into oblivion. A step forward will be our first on a grand march. Once begun, this march will not end. We will continue our journey, though our feet are weary and our hearts ache for home. We may die in the attempt, but we will have *made* the attempt.

"Our names, men, our names will not be remembered. History is not so kind to the common man. But our actions will be carved indelibly into the annals and histories of our grand country. For make no mistake: we—you—are the true servants of Licenia. More truly than its military; more truly than its government; and a damned sight more truly than *fucking* Candor Network!" He spat the last few words out as though poison, while the men set up a roar.

I stood there in the back, clutching the pamphlet my new

employer had given me. Emblazoned on the golden paper was a crimson "CN"; there could be no mistake as to the source of it. I made no sound. I made no movement. But I could feel the lion's dead eyes set on me, and slowly, the congregation turned. There were perhaps twenty men, Fergus among them, and they could all clearly see what I was holding, even in the dim half-light. The mark of their apparent adversary.

Before I could explain, before I could even think, a bruiser grabbed my hair and dragged me forward, nearly causing me to lose my footing in the process. He could have broken my neck easily, and as you can see, I am no pushover. Despite my instincts, I refrained from offering resistance; it would have been futile. My papers were torn from my hand, and I was shoved onto my knees. The sea of black rushed in around me, cutting off any escape route. I looked up, and saw the golden eyes and frozen snarl of the Licenian Lion.

"Are these your papers?" he asked, taking them from one of his followers.

I nodded, never taking my gaze from his. "Yes, sir."

"Would you like them back?"

It could easily have been a test, and perhaps I was foolish, but I nodded. "If it's not too much trouble."

He handed them to me, and motioned for me to stand. I did so.

"You must be Jackson." There was a hint of kindness in his voice, but I still wonder if it wasn't an act. "I've heard we have a new tenant in our midst: not from around here, I understand." Looking up, he turned his gaze to his small army. "This is no way to treat a new arrival to Priius, men; what of the unenlightened?"

As one, the men murmured, "The unenlightened are to be uplifted."

He nodded once. "Their ignorance is no fault of their own." Turning to me again, he extended his hand; I shook it. "Come with me, Jackson. I'm of a mind to meet you."

I agreed. What choice did I have? I would have known his voice anywhere. You would, too. Don't you recall the first color broadcast from Candor Network?

V.

I followed the man in the lion mask into his little shack. It was no larger than mine, nor much better-furnished: a tattered mattress set on food crates occupied one corner of the room, while most of the walls were covered in newspaper clippings and the torn pages of an atlas. World maps denoting natural resources and population density occupied the entire south wall, showing the rise of Licenia and the abrupt fall of Greenwood after the Grand War. Paperwork cluttered a small table set in the center of the room; chairs had been placed on either side. He sat, and motioned for me to do the same.

"I do apologize for that unpleasantness," he murmured, his voice still gravel and broken glass. "They're good men, really. Well-meaning. They just get excited, sometimes. I trust you've eaten." I nodded, and he did the same. "Cigar, then? Whiskey? We don't have much here in Old Hampton, but what we do have, we share. Not a man goes hungry. Not a crime goes unpunished. We have no room for cowards or knockabouts." I accepted the offer of whiskey, and he poured me a glass.

While I sipped, he reclined in his wooden chair, unbuttoning his coat. Beneath, he wore only what looked like a long, linen bandage, wrapped around his entire chest. Not an inch of skin was exposed, but his muscular frame was still apparent. He'd kept himself in shape, even after the war. Most of the soldiers were released from their contracts, after that one: they wouldn't be needed anymore. The war to end war had ended.

"So." He sat forward, leaning his elbows on the table. A steel trench knife stuck out of it; plucking it free, he began idly fingering the flat of the blade. The motion made me nervous; I watched him warily. "Tell me, Jackson: what brings you to Priius? You look like a strong fellow; you've clearly done honest work. Why come to a city of lies and facades?" No threat resided in his tone. He sounded almost fatherly.

Clearing my throat, and not taking my eyes off that knife, I replied, "I came to follow my dreams, sir. Grew up watching all the newscasts—I can tell you're none too fond of them, but... well, I was a child. Perhaps you can forgive me if I found them fascinating." He grunted, but said nothing. I continued, "I remember watching... watching you, actually. Watching the reporters as they hid from shells with the soldiers, eating MREs and interviewing folks. And I thought, 'Even if I can't be a soldier when I grow up, I want to be like them.'"

He chuckled. Not the most beautiful sound I'd ever heard. "I suppose it's not surprising. If there's one thing Candor Network's good at, it's rousing patriotism. We all watched it, even though they were reporting on us. Maybe because of it. But tell me, Jackson: what do you know about the Grand War?" I gave no answer, thinking it a rhetorical question. "Why'd we fight it?" he prompted.

Scratching the back of my head, I sipped the whiskey and carefully considered my answer. "Well... we were saving our skin, I suppose. Greenwood was an imperialist power; they had already marched into South Licenia, despite our warnings, and that made them a threat."

"Very good." He nodded. "The last part is the important one: they were a threat. I hate to be your history professor, but *why* were they a threat? What were they threatening? Why were we so afraid?" His fingers curled and uncurled around the knife's handle.

"They were a significant military power," I hedged, uncertain as to the direction of his inquiries. "I mean, we stopped them with no trouble, but even so, they were likely to try to take us on sooner or later." He tilted his head, and I realized I hadn't answered his question. "They were threatening... our establishment? Our way of life?"

"Oho. A smart one." There was no trace of sarcasm which I could detect in his tone. "Our... way of life. Quite. You were right the first time, though: they were threatening our establishment. You see," he said, knocking a stack of papers to the floor, to point at an old strategic map, "Greenwood's system of government wasn't much different from ours. Their ideals weren't much different from ours, and neither were their methods. You don't honestly believe we didn't take advantage of the countries Greenwood had conquered, during our 'liberation?' We were as imperialist as they were. Just..." He waved a hand in the air. "Subtle."

"If you don't mind," I interrupted, "I'd like to know the name of the man I'm talking to. You have me at a disadvantage, sir."

"We'll get to that soon enough." You could hear the smile in his voice. "I really don't mean to patronize, Jackson; I really don't. I just... I need to know what you know, so that I can tell you what you don't. There's much that the schools don't teach. No fault of yours, to be sure! Looking at you, I'd wager you're no older than twenty... five?" I told him I was twenty-one, and he nodded. "Too young to have known what was going on. It's not your fault. It's not your fault. You had to have my reasons to chart the happenings."

My whiskey was halfway depleted by now, and he refilled it without asking. "I hope you don't think I'm being opaque," he continued. "Forgive me, if I seem that way. I'm just not sure exactly where to begin. I've been a soldier all my life, and teaching is quite new to me. Where was I?" I reminded him. "Thank you. We were no different from Greenwood; few countries are. They have their own self-interest at heart, and as long as everybody knows it, that's more or less alright. We like to hide it, though, and that's... well, that's just no good. We hide too many things, in my opinion. Better to have it all out in the open," said the man in the golden lion's mask.

"When I went to war, Jackson, I went to war to fight for my country: North Licenia. You'll notice how we just call it 'Licenia,' now? South Licenia is a wraith. It exists, in the same way that a man exists on his deathbed. But I went to war to fight for our way of life. Our republic. Parliament—when was the last time we had an election?"

I couldn't answer him. I didn't know. I could vaguely recall that they had once had them every six years, but they were suspended in the war. It must have been over a decade.

"Mmhmm." He didn't need to read my thoughts: they were plain in my expression. "Almost as long as you've been alive, we haven't had a parliamentary election. Candor Network grew like Licenia: what it could take honestly, it did. The rest, it just blew away. And you'll notice that they don't do much reporting on the government, anymore. Now that we don't have a war to help people pay attention, they've stopped altogether. Everybody's got their eyes shut." He gave a long sigh, which whistled oddly through the mask.

"I'm not much of a philosopher, but I do have a few convictions to which I am deeply devoted." His speech was inevitable; there was no stopping him. He had a strange charisma, that one. "One of them is to freedom. Economic freedom. Political freedom. Freedom of thought. The liberty to know what's going on around you, and to fix it when it's broken. That's patriotism, there. Not what Candor Network does; not their fervent insistence on perpetuating the status quo. Patriotism is supporting your country when it's in the right, and denouncing it when it's in the wrong." I could hear the leather of his glove creaking as his grip tightened on the knife. "Licenia has been in the wrong for a very long time, Jackson.

"Do you know what it's like to go off to war? When you leave —well, it's like when you left your home, I'm sure. You leave a bright-eyed optimist, thinking, 'Yeah. I'm gonna go give 'em hell, and protect my country.' You think you're going to fight the good fight. Exorcise the demons that seek to undo everything you love. But... that's not how it is."

I remained in silence. What more could I have done? I doubt —and this is no judgment of your character—I doubt you would have acted differently. He had a gravity about him, that man. When he spoke, you listened, for here was a man who had one eye on Heaven.

I still respect him for that. Even after all of this.

"I was, as you can plainly tell, an officer. I made... decisions. And others were made for me." His throat must have been tightening, for his voice became quieter, rougher still. "I have committed atrocities which I hesitate to recount, for the simple reason that I don't have a mind to relive them. I wake up some nights in a cold sweat. Fireworks can set me into a blind, aggressive panic. Sometimes, I look around, and my friends are soldiers, my town a battlefield. And it's..." He drew a quivering breath. "It's hard to tell what isn't real."

It took him a moment to compose himself. Even under that mask, I could tell: the rapid movements of his chest gave it away, just like the pulsing vein on his neck and the way he clutched that knife. Eventually, calm again, he resumed his lecture. "I have burned down cities," he told me, as calmly as a Candor news anchor. "I have shot more men dead than I can even begin to count. I have ordered bombing runs on whole swaths of populated areas. I have shot up houses full of the sick and wounded. I have slaughtered men, women, and children who were just trying to hide from the war. I have made an ocean of blood, a mountain of patriot dead, and a nation of mourners.

"And I don't mind that." For just a heartbeat, we sat in silence. I stared into the lion's dead eyes, and he stared far past me, into places I dare not imagine.

"What fuels my rage is that none of it mattered." His gloved finger tapped the edge of his blade. "When I came home, a shaking and broken silhouette of what I once was, I got to see the grandest war on this planet. I got to watch as they raised up monuments to Our Boys, buried Our Boys, and then trampled on the memory of Our Boys by pretending that we were heroes," he spat. "I watched Candor Network, with a man named Beckstein at its head, as it turned our eyes away from war and politics, and onto the mindless, worthless fuckers we pay to play pretend for us." His unoccupied hand gripped the edge of the table, and I fancied he might break it off. "I watched as the parliament disappeared into the shadows. I watched as Anton Beckstein and Candor Network *destroyed* everything I'd fought for."

In a swift movement, he brought his knife down into the table. It went all the way through the thin wood. Thunk. Thunk. Thunk. Three swift holes in the table. His breath huffed tinnily through his helmet, and he leaned on the table, knuckles surely white beneath those gloves. He had bitten his tongue, for he turned to spit a glob of blood on the floor. "My vision for the world begins with Beckstein's blood painting the walls of Candor Tower, and his head swinging in Franklin Square," he murmured, so quietly that I had to lean in to make out his words. He terrified me. I had never seen a man like him: so... passionate. He was always passionate, unto the end.

"They made me into a monster," he whispered, tremulous and vulnerable. "And I forgave them. But now, I see that I have been deceived, and I will not stand for that." Leaving his knife in the table, he slowly rose, his chair falling over in the process. "I have raised a small army of men whose eyes have been opened to the crimes of Candor Network. Beckstein has dissolved our Parliament, replaced it with an enclave of men who dictate all policy from the shadows, hidden behind Candor Network's shield of lies. We have no freedom, for we have no voice. Our eyes are glued on the television, our mouths occupied by the words they have forced between our jaws.

"Their war may have ended, but mine rages on."

I believe I may have wept within myself, watching this ghost of a man slowly turn around, hands trembling as he moved to rest against the wall. His mask and greatcoat seemed more like a burial shroud to me; what remained of the man had been interred with his fallen comrades, back in the fields of South Licenia. They had broken him. The very company for which I now worked had deceived us all, and this soldier, old long before his time, was among the few who knew it. It was heartbreaking to watch him. Everything he knew and loved was gone. And I knew, I felt it deep in my heart: I had to help him win it back.

"Who are you?" I asked, almost afraid to hear the answer. I didn't know if he could speak, overcome with emotion as he was.

But he did. Clear and plain, I heard him slowly reply, "In war, a man is anonymous. There is only the truth of blood, pain, glory, and death. My name... I am forgotten."

It was a ghost.

It always was.

VI.

I don't really know how long he and I sat across from one another, both of us looking everywhere but at each other. It can't have been very long; perhaps just a few minutes. But I had to take the time to decide whether I really wanted to abandon what seemed the certainty of a comfortable life for the uncertainty of a meaningful one. He, I think, just used the time to calm himself down. I don't believe he was crying, but he sat as still as a corpse, contemplating the ceiling and letting his hands hang low by his sides, while I nursed my whiskey.

Make no mistake: I may not have excellent foresight, but neither am I a naïve farmboy. The decision to help him was not so quick as it may appear: certainly, I had that initial impulse, but I am not the sort to allow emotion to rule over my actions, no matter what you may think at the moment. I turned the idea over and over in my head during that vast silence, trying to think of how to offer my aid while not committing myself to what could easily be the fantasy of a madman. Eventually, I cleared my throat, causing him to loll his head back down.

"If what you say is true," I began, choosing my words and speaking slowly, "then I'll do what I can to help you. But I'll want to see some sort of proof. While I'll admit that most people don't strike me as particularly perceptive, you'll understand, sir, if I hesitate to accept your word on its face." I figured that was safe enough. The knife was still stuck in the table.

Contrary to my initial fears, he actually seemed rather pleased with my answer, insofar as I could judge by his voice. "Oh, but you are a smart lad," he murmured, mostly to himself. "You're right not to trust me. Really. If I'm to be entirely honest, there's a reason I settled down in Old Hampton, rather than using my pension to buy myself a nice little cottage on the fringes of society." Leaning in conspiratorially, and looking around as though there might be others in the claustrophobic shack, he admitted, "I tend to recruit those who're just a little bit desperate. The men who have nothing left to lose. There was a lady once, but after that bastard raped her—we executed him for that—I can't blame her for not wanting to participate further. It's not..." He paused, rubbing his exposed neck. "I have nothing against women joining our cause, but the type who are likely to join, like Fergus, are usually men."

My eyebrows furrowed. "How do you mean 'the type likely to join?'"

He shifted in his seat, perhaps uncomfortable. "Now, don't take this as an insult, for you seem an unusual sort for Old Hampton. But... we tend to attract a rather thuggish type. It's good, in a way; we need good, strong men like Fergus or Milcher. But—" And there he paused, probably eying me from behind that mask. "But forgive me. I don't mean to insult your intelligence by hiding things, but really, I have no more reason to trust you than you've to trust me. This is something to speak of when we know each other better. Yes?" He stuck out his gloved hand again. "Gentleman's agreement: if you join our struggle against tyranny, and prove your worth, there will be no secrets between us. Only honesty."

I shook his hand with a cautious smile. It sounded like a good deal to me: as I think I've said before, the only thing I've ever wanted was a bit of honesty. But it's hard to find unbiased opinion, isn't it? It's hard to find unbiased news.

Forgotten—for that's the closest thing he had to a name— clapped me on the shoulder, then led me back outside, where his followers were still gathered. Most looked "the thuggish type," as he had put it, but there were a few more like me, and even a couple smaller still. But they were all young men, all destitute and hopeless. Forgotten knew people, and he knew them well. Would that we all had such a blessing.

He gave me a slight jostle by my shoulder, then gestured broadly at me with his spare hand. Quietly, not like when he had given his speech earlier, he announced, "Gentlemen, meet our newest initiate. His name is Jackson; he comes from...?"

"Milton."

"He comes from Milton. Out in the farmlands, I believe? Yes. Do tell us about yourself, Jackson. I expect the men are of a mind to meet you, too." With that, he stepped back, leaving me to confront that gaggle.

Maybe you speak well when asked to introduce yourself, but in my experience, most people struggle with it, and I'm no different. I glanced around uncertainly for a few moments, then offered, "Well, I'm Jackson, like he said. From Milton. Grew up on a farm, working when I wasn't being schooled. Never went to university. I, uh..." I scratched the back of my head, while they milled about. "I came here looking for a job; hitchhiked my way up, worked for about a year in Barbier, and... that's about it. Got here yesterday. I look forward to working with you all." With that, I stepped back as well.

It didn't do me much good. For the next couple of minutes, I shook hands and exchanged quick pleasantries with each man in turn, looking up at a great many of them, and I'm not that short. Fergus, I already knew. Peters stuck out, him being a small, dark-skinned man. Indeed, he looked like he might have come from southern Greenwood, where the sun blasts your hide. I later discovered that was true, but the uncertainty at the time helped his name stick in my mind. Not a one gave me more than one name. Odd tradition, I thought, but I supposed they didn't need more than one.

I can't tell you how many of us there were, and I won't even be so honest as to say that the names I give are the names they gave me. The latter is for their own privacy; after this, I expect most of them that are left are going to want to slink back to the sidelines, and I don't intend to make it harder on them. As for the former, that's a genuine lack of knowledge: I never bothered to count. I'd reckon on around twenty, give or take, but that's none too important. What matters is that we were a few men, bound together by chance, circumstance, and the man who wore the face of Licenia.

Once the introductions were finished, Forgotten slipped back into his shack to "work on a few things." That left me a bit of time to talk with a couple of my new acquaintances, swapping interesting stories with them. Milcher referred to himself as a "myrmidon," like Fergus; apparently, they were the guards of the ramshackle neighborhood, named after some old legend. He told me about how Forgotten had personally broken him out of jail after he got caught nicking supplies from an "enemy shipping supply." Since then, he didn't leave Old Hampton much during the day, in case someone recognized him by chance. Peters didn't talk a whole lot, but he did mention that he'd served with Forgotten (they all called him that; apparently, that's just how he introduced himself) in the Grand War, as a spy and demolitions expert. With just a hint of an accent, Peters called him "a good man; a real man."

Fergus and Milcher were the two biggest men in the camp, but also among the more talkative: they soon convinced me to roll the bones with them for a few fractionals; none of us had enough money to wager anything over a single. We played a couple of friendly games, and a few of the other men donated some of the reclaimed furniture from a nearby scrapyard to my little shack. Our lives there were... uncomplicated. We lived on the edge between feral and civil, with neither the constraints nor the conveniences of modern society. I won't say it's a better life than most, but going back to it was always a refreshing change from Priius. But I'm getting ahead of myself.

After maybe an hour, half an hour, Forgotten called me back into his shack, and I went over to see what he wanted. He'd laid out old floor plans of what could only be Candor Tower, with its sixty floors and grand elevator, now heavily annotated. "Getting a job at Candor could be exactly what we need," he grinned. "I'd considered the prospect before, but a great many of our comrades have less-than-spotless records, as you may have gathered. Others, like Peters, might draw too much attention. But you're already in. Have you ever been a spy before?"

I shook my head, with a bit of a laugh. "Never. I've not concerned myself with anything greater than feeding hogs, I'm afraid."

He nodded amicably. "I wouldn't expect anything more of you. We're mostly ordinary men, around here. You might have a chat with Peters, though: he was a double-agent for us in the Grand War. Bright fellow, a touch reticent. Reminds me a bit of what you seem to be like," he added, off-hand. "But you're..." I noticed him trying to read the papers I still held, so I handed them over for his inspection. "Ah, a janitor. Perfect, perfect. I've thought up a way for us to perhaps earn each other's trust. Or at least work toward it.

"Beckstein is, above all, a businessman. I've not met him personally, but he's published a single autobiography, penned around the time Candor finished monopolizing the industry. Thin little thing, more a treatise on how to run a business than something to offer insight into himself. Background sort of guy. But, anyway. He strikes me as the type to keep records. Now, I don't expect you to get a hold of any mind-blowing, revelation-inducing type of thing, but I figure that sooner or later, somebody has to clean up the records room. Check your schedule, if they give you one. If not, find some excuse to get in there, or whatever it takes, and see if you can't find a record of Candor's campaign donations."

I held up my index finger, and he paused to hear my question. "What if they don't have records on that? And, no offense intended, but how do you know they even donated?"

He chuckled quietly. "If they don't have records, come back and tell me so, and I'll try to think up something else for you to do. But they donated; they made it very clear which candidates they supported, up until the Grand War wiped that away. Ostensibly, those who supported deregulation of the media, but I suspect they may have thrown their weight behind the big warhawks, too. I remember some of their names, but not which ones Candor specifically supported; I'm of a mind to find that out. It's nothing too important, but there may be other useful information in there, depending on how they keep it updated. But first, two things."

He held out his thumb. "Do it subtly. We don't want them to get suspicious." He held out his index finger. "Do it safely. Don't get yourself killed over this. On the other hand, don't be a coward. I'll expect daily reports on the situation; just a quick update on how you're progressing. You have a week, then I'll expect you to come up with a plan, if you haven't done it already."

I nodded to him. "I think I can do that. I'll at least do my best."

"That's all I expect of you men," he replied, with an unusual tone in his voice. "We have no room for cowards, but most of you aren't soldiers. Rest up, Jackson. You've got a big day ahead of you."

I left his shack and went to bed. I'd consult Peters tomorrow,

I said to myself; I wanted to try things out for myself, first. I've always been a little headstrong.

VII.

As I had promised the man at Candor, I rose with the dawn. The sun filtering in through the cracks in the shanty roused me; I stood tall in the crisp, morning air, and gathered the day's clothes up to make the walk to the shower-house. None of the others were awake at this time aside from Milcher—Fergus guarded the "neighborhood" from noon until midnight, and Milcher took the other shift. It struck me that I was the only one currently employed; I didn't pause to consider the ways the others provided for themselves.

After a reinvigorating shower, I dried myself off and dressed myself, conscious of every flaw and hole in my city clothes. The suits the others wore were hardly immaculate, and by no means tailored, but they were still neat: sewn of fine cloth, and each matching the others, like soldiers' uniforms. Indeed, they—well, no; I'll get to that later. Are you paying attention? I know I ramble, but I pray you indulge me. If you have something better to do, I'd be happy to hear it. But somehow, I suspect this is more important to you.

It's the pace of modern life, you know: the constant rush, rush, rush, the hurrying and bustling in your lonely home to get to the crowded streets to drive your lonely car to your crowded office, where you work in your lonely cubicle, only to join the crowded streets again. We live alone together, just like the people who scampered from crosswalk to crosswalk in the early-morning traffic. We work alone in our grand hives, just like those same people, who were all off to their workplaces. Each one walked the same route every day, probably, walking at the same time with the same people whose names they don't know.

We've been complaining about it for decades, if not centuries, I know, but it's always true. In all the rush, we don't think we have time for a quiet chat by the fireside, or to listen to a stranger's story. But calm, calm; we have all the time in the world. The car that nearly ran me over, that day, when I stumbled on an unfastened shoelace, thought that if it didn't make it to its destination in time, it would be a failure. But that's not the case; I know that's not the case; you know that's not the case. It's not. If we just slow down for a second, we get a better view of things: a more truthful view of things. Our foresight is much improved if we just take a single moment to consider the situation.

Too many people don't think they have that moment. Too many more don't take it when they do: I know that as I hurried along the morning streets to make it to Candor nearly an hour ahead of schedule, I wasn't taking time to think about my plans for the day. On my very first day working there, I was going to not only train into my new position, I'd also scope out the whole thing, and hell, maybe even steal the information while I was at it. Idiot. That's me, I mean, not you.

We rely a lot on hindsight: we dwell on our pasts far longer than we should, constantly psychoanalyzing, reflecting, paralyzing ourselves by failing to keep an eye on the present. We berate ourselves for our failures, we draw lessons from them, then we ignore them the moment we find ourselves in that same situation. But do you know the funny thing about all that?

It's not so much our mistakes we need to analyze. It's not our pasts we have to learn. We know those already. When you make a mistake, and your actions are thrown back in your face by everyone around you, by the universe itself, you know it. You know it, and there's nothing you can do about it except remember.

What we need to do, and what we seldom do, is look at

other people. That's the whole reason I'm here, isn't it? I want us to start looking at other people, so I'm opening up a great big, bleeding hole in myself and letting you see the filth, rot, and stench inside. Things look so nice from the outside: despite what Forgotten had told me about it, I still thought Candor must be the most gorgeous building I'd ever seen that next morning, standing outside it in the early-morning haze. My slacks were wet from where I had fallen, my sleeves scuffed and heart still pounding from when the car nearly hit me. In that moment, I had one eye on Heaven, but it saw nothing except a great big, bleeding hole in the sky. If you'll forgive a moment of cynicism from me, or at least pity it, I must say that I don't think anything stopped that car except the possibility of being stained.

Every so often, you should look at the filth, rot, and stench inside everybody else, and you'll know that deep down, deep in their very beings, they're no better than you. It's freeing, in a way: we're creatures of dirt, blood, and acid. And... that's okay. It's okay. All you have to do is look on the damned and tortured soul before you, and whisper to it, "I understand. I understand, and I'm sorry."

There is no forgiveness to be given, for to forgive requires that you be on some higher platform than the trespasser. We play at mercy, when we have none to spare, for there is none given us by the impersonal force of Nature. We are fragmented; we are shattered; we are the men of broken glass. But we can get better, if we can just understand. I really—deep down, I believe it with every synapse and sinew of my body. I'm no better than you, nor you than me: we simply *are*. We exist. And that's reason enough to offer what understanding we can to each other, even if we can't forgive, we can never forgive.

But I'm rambling again. Forgive me.

My fingers were trembling with excitement as I pulled open

the door to the lobby, stepping inside for the second time in my life—but this time, I was almost an insider. I gave a timid smile to the receptionist—not the same woman who had bade me farewell the night before—and quietly informed her that I was the new janitor. With a practiced smile, she directed me to the basement, where plant operations were headquartered. "Although," she added, looking over the papers I had brought with me, "you aren't due for training for another..." A quick glance at her watch. "...forty-three minutes. If you're hungry, there are bagels in the staff cafeteria, on the thirtieth floor; just show those papers, and you should get in with no trouble."

At the time, I wondered how she knew, but looking back, it's clear: I was drawn and small, then, smaller than I'd been in twenty-one years. My skin was sallow and unhealthy, marked and worn; the hunger showed in my eyes and posture. With a quick word of thanks, I hurried over to the elevator and took the first one to arrive. Unoccupied, it afforded me a moment's privacy to reflect; I sat down on the cool, marble floor, watched the brass doors slide shut, and let the rig carry me to the highest floor I'd ever visited in a building.

The thirtieth floor, far above where ordinary consumers and job-seekers would go, was where Candor kept its staff, of course. Hide them away from the public eye when they aren't working. The lounges, many of the lockers, and the staff cafeteria took up much of that space, along with a few meeting rooms. Higher still, the executives' lounges and boardrooms sat. The corporate world is always a caste system, isn't it? And there I stood, on the bottom of the pole, looking around and self-consciously straightening my ratty tie as I looked for the cafeteria.

It wasn't hard to find, once I stopped crawling at a snail's pace. There were quite a few employees already there, grabbing bagels and coffee from the bins and pots provided. None of them took any notice of me, nor did I have to show my papers; folding them again, I tucked them in my slacks, then fell into line. Other than a couple of polite nods from people who happened to make eye contact with me, neither I nor anyone else seemed to communicate with one another; most sat in the still-mostly-empty cafeteria, eating in silence. I grabbed my food, then slunk back to the elevator, opting instead to eat in the lobby.

When the time came for my training, I went down to the dark, cold, and unremarkable basement. I introduced myself to my new superior—I think his name was Steven?—as Jackson, and he delivered a perfectly polite and dispassionate description of my new duties. There's really no way to glorify the work of a janitor: you clean up the spills that other people make. It's a lot like what I'm doing now, really, except that I'm rather a clumsy one. He had me try on a red jumpsuit for size; I ended up with a large, which mostly fit, and he promised to have my name printed on it, just like his. All the employees had their names printed on their uniforms, in case they should forget.

He walked me all around the building, telling me the protocols for routine cleaning, cleaning up bodily fluids, reporting chemical spills and all the other kinds of hazards, and all the other work I'd have to do. In the back of my mind, I held on to the mission assigned to me: when he noted that the archives were always locked, but that I'd receive a key in a few days, I had to keep from smiling to myself. It would be so easy: I would just have to walk in, take them, and make sure I didn't spend too long. If, of course, the information was there. Nothing too important could be stored in such an insecure location, it seemed. But Candor Tower was a trusting place: who would hold a grudge? Crime was almost non-existent in Priius, and trust, if not sincerity, was in full bloom. If only the same could have been said for its leader.

I spent most of the rest of the day in training: Steven led me to every single room in that damned tower, and my feet ached by the time we were finished. Some rooms had to be cleaned in certain ways; he told me how to use the intercom to contact him, if need be, and gave me cheerful pamphlets on my new responsibilities and privileges as a member of the Candor Tower Maintenance Team. Even the lion's head printed on the back had been softened, made more palatable to the common eye. No snarl, no roar. They had declawed the Lion in many ways.

I think I may have eaten almost every dinner during my stay in Old Hampton in John's Kitchen. Already, the dangerous walk from Candor Tower to Franklin Square to the side-streets that led to Old Hampton was becoming routine to me. It was... I think it was a Friday night, and the tavern was a touch more lively than usual; I didn't have much time to chat with Mrs. Hughes, that day, and besides, my head was filled with my new duties. But not those given me by Steven.

Fergus greeted me with a friendly smile and a clap on the shoulder—he was always a friendly, loyal dog, Fergus—as I strode back into Old Hampton, ready to deliver my new intelligence to Forgotten. But just as my hand touched the door, I felt a firm grip on my elbow, and turned to see Peters' dark face giving me a warning look in the muted starlight. "He's eating," he grunted, in his unusual, though not unhandsome accent. "We don't go in when he's eating. He'll call you when he's ready; for now, you can report to me." Seeing my mild, unspoken confusion, he explained, "I'm one of his lieutenants. There's only two of us: me and Rothschild. We're right under him; if you need to talk to him, let us know. Alright?"

"Alright." I nodded, and he gave me a slight smile, beckoning me over to a barrel with a couple of logs set up on either side. We sat; he poured me a beer, and asked me to tell him how I was coming with the requested information. When I did, he snorted with amusement.

"Well, that makes your job easy," he muttered, in that quiet tenor of his. "That's good, though. Your first assignment should be an easy one. Mine wasn't." I waited patiently for him to elaborate, but he seemed content to sit there and drink his beer, watching the candle burn down, the wax dripping on the barrel. It took several minutes before I prompted, "Could you tell me about it? I'm interested in knowing about the war."

Peters sighed, and set down his mug, folding his hands in his lap. I feared I had offended him: he didn't move for what seemed far too long a time, thinking. Later, I came to recognize that as his way of speaking: he didn't converse, he lectured. Peters always took the time to consider his words carefully, to plan out a whole speech before delivering it in one fell swoop.

"My first assignment as a Licenian agent was to pose as an inspector, present forged credentials to the management of a factory, and use my architectural knowledge to establish the structural weaknesses in the building." He spoke like machine-gun fire, never lifting his eyes. "I was then to report these weaknesses and wait under guard while the engineers developed shaped charges to take unique advantage of them, and ruin the building. I was then to return, with a handful of native Licenian agents, and plant the bombs surreptitiously, where they wouldn't be noticed, under supervision and at gunpoint."

I nodded sympathetically. "That sounds like it must have been stressful."

He laughed at me. "It was. We detonated them the next morning, after the workers arrived. I lost my cousin and several of my childhood friends, without warning, for a country that hated me."

With a sad sort of smile, he left the last of his beer on the barrel, and walked away. I sat still and examined my hands.

VIII.

The following day was a Saturday—my one day off during the week, according to my schedule. I woke up at the same time every morning, anyway, but it was nice to have the entire day to myself, though I didn't know how I planned to use it. As ever, I took a shower; but this time, I wore blue jeans and a plaid shirt rather than my suit, afterward. None of the others were awake, and I had no idea what to do with myself, so I quietly slipped over to where Milcher stood, guarding the camp.

Both Fergus and Milcher were among the more talkative of our little club—did I mention that already?—but of the pair, Milcher was somewhat more reserved. He gave me an amiable smile as I walked up behind him, then moved to lean on the wall opposite where he rested. He'd strapped his cudgel to his right thigh, and a large hunting knife to his left, as if he needed help to strike an imposing figure. After offering me a cigarette, which I accepted, he gave me a light, and we smoked for a while, just thinking.

Eventually, I dusted my hands off on my jeans, and asked, "Say, Milcher: what's there to do around here? Anything good within walking distance, I mean? I've got a little spending money, and a day off: it seems like kind of a waste to just sit around all day."

He laughed for a short while. Poor Milcher was just a little simple. He had something of a stutter, and slurred his words from time to time. "Shit, I don't know. I j-just stay around th' camp. Help out. Forg-gotten says I'm real good at 'good, hard labor.'" He smiled. "Did I ever tell y-you 'bout how he broke me out of prison?"

I nodded, with a grin. "Yeah. It was quite a story. But, really, you don't just stay here all day, do you? I mean, you go out at night, when you're not guarding the place?"

He shook his head. "Priius is a bad place, Jackson. It's not made f-or poor folks li-like us, that's what Forgotten says. It's a rich man's town, and only Old Hampton's our poor man's town. That's wh-what Forgotten says."

With a slow nod, I replied, "Well, thanks for the advice. And the light, of course. I'm gonna head on out, though; you keep up the good work, alright?" Patting his arm, I crept away into the dawn sidestreets, toward the Humboldt Shopping Center and my usual haunt. A scrawny, sickly cat brushed up against my leg, mewling and begging; I knelt down to stroke it, and it fled before I could touch it, hurrying down into the alleys. I watched it go, frowning in confusion: I'd meant it no harm, but it knew hands as the bringers of pain. It'd probably been domesticated, once, but now wasn't sure just what to think of humans.

As I drew close to the shopping center, I saw what I had overlooked the previous morning, in my hurry: a few crumpled heaps of clothing sitting outside, crooked fingers and frail hands clutching tattered hats. The doors to the building were still locked; I waited outside with the beggars, shifting uncomfortably under the weight of my wallet. There were... three. Two remained still at my approach, but when the third saw me, he struggled to his feet. Naturally, I tensed, unsure of his intentions; he had a dark tan, perhaps South Licenian or even from northern Greenwood. Shuffling toward me slightly on his one good leg, he rasped, "Please, help me."

I don't know what it was about those words that wrenched my heart so, but I could hardly stand to look in his weary, bloodshot eyes. I imagine my mouth hung open slightly until I pursed my lips, staring into his creased and weathered face. He made no movement toward me, but neither did he move away: "Please, help me," he repeated, and all I could do was stand there like an idiot, stammering.

A few thoughts ran through my head simultaneously, and I'm not proud of any of them. "Addict," was the first; I fancied he might pull a knife on me if I got close. "Jobless," was the second; what good would a bit of cash do him? Another day of misery? "Wretched," was the third; and that one was true. "I'm sorry," I found myself blurting, shaking my head slightly. As if those two words would absolve me of my guilt. "I'm sorry." I didn't understand. Did anyone understand him? It's unlikely. Unless you've lived in a country that doesn't give a damn whether you live or die, begging for the money you can't earn thanks to the color of your skin, you can't understand him. I know I don't.

Before either of us could say more, I heard the sound of boots against the cobblestone street, and a guardsman in a bright, red jacket came clopping down the road. My wallet was already in my hand, half open, prepared to spare him a few singles; that's probably the only thing that spared me from the policeman's sudden shout.

"Clear out!" he cried, as the other beggars stood up, shaking out the night's unrest and gathering up their hats. "All of you, out! You know you're not supposed to be here." This was their daily ritual. "Come on, now. Hurry it up." They shambled off down the streets, and the policeman unlocked the door, then whistled once. A few shopkeepers, all dressed immaculately, crept cautiously around the corner, now that the coast was clear. Still dumbfounded, I looked around, while the policeman gave me a smile and offered to shake my hand. "I'm sorry about that, young man. I hope you're alright. They didn't give you any trouble?"

I shook my head. What else could I do? "No, sir. They gave me no trouble at all." I lied: my heart was troubled. Growing up in the country, I didn't see poverty; it was all around me. But we had hope, at least, and even that scant currency had long been stolen from those beggars' shabby hats. That kind of abject poverty was new to me, and it still pains me to look back on it. Please, help me. Please, help me. For the love of God, were those words all he could afford?

The procession wandered into Humboldt, and I followed behind them, after tucking my wallet back in my jeans, casting my gaze downward. Maybe I'd buy him some food, or something, I told myself, to assuage my aching conscience. Pretty words. Pretty, empty words. If I'm to be fair to myself, I can't say that I forgot him as I walked through the rich trappings of Humboldt. But if I'm to be truthful, neither did I have any intention of seeking him out, or ever seeing him again. I'm not sure I could have stood the pain.

Perhaps my words seem melodramatic to you. Perhaps you've seen a hundred beggars just like him, or maybe you haven't seen any. Maybe you don't know what it's like to stand there in the face of despair and know that you have no power to change that situation; to know that even if you did, there's a whole goddamned line of others waiting for that exact change to happen to them, too. But let me tell you: it fucking hurts. I have enough humanity left in me to remember that. Even now, I consider myself an idealist, but back then, there could be no questioning it. And I hated myself for having done nothing. I still do.

As I fell into a chair in John's Kitchen, which had just opened, I reflected that I hadn't sent my parents a letter in months, nor had they an address to reach me. They were probably worried; I resolved to send them a letter when I got back. The others moved toward the counter, but I wasn't ready to order just yet: I needed time to gather myself up again. I had to get out of Priius for a day. I had to do a lot of things.

I waited until the line had cleared before going back up to the counter myself, giving Mrs. Hughes as much of a smile as I could and ordering the usual greasy breakfast. She'd been in the middle of a conversation with another woman, probably around her age, which she paused just long enough to take my order. Though I honestly didn't mean to eavesdrop, I couldn't help but overhear their exchange. I kept my head turned away.

"How's your daughter, Sue?"

"Oh, she's alright. Getting teased in school; it's..." The drumming of fingers on the counter.

"Yeah. Yeah, I know what you mean." Was that sympathy in Mrs. Hughes' voice?

"You do?" came the embittered reply.

"No." A pause, then: "But I can imagine."

"Yeah."

And with that, she went back into the kitchen. I didn't dare turn to face the woman beside me, Sue, lest she think I'd been doing exactly what I'd been doing. Instead, I listened to the hiss and crackle of breakfast being made, while still wondering what it was to have her daughter getting teased in school. "Hard?" "Unbearable?" "Getting worse?" If I had one problem, back then, it's that I wanted to save...

No. If I had one problem, back then, it's that I didn't know how to save everyone.

I ate my breakfast in silence, though as I started work on the second biscuit, I became aware of Mrs. Hughes' gaze on me. Putting down my knife, I looked up at her, shoulders hunched like a delinquent schoolboy caught sleeping.

She tapped ashes from her cigarette, leaning against the wall and peering down at me through narrowed eyes. "So. When are you getting out of Old Hampton?"

My brows furrowed in confusion, and I gave her a guarded

look in response. "I have no intention of doing so in the near future, ma'am."

"Well, fuck. You're one of them, now, aren't you?" That, more than anything, took me aback. I had no response save the same idiotic stare I'd given the beggar outside, and she let out a humorless laugh. "Figures. They still come in here, sometimes, and order food from me. It's been five years, but most of them still remember."

If there's one thing I don't like, it's being left in the dark. Have I made that clear enough so far? I have a thirst, maybe even a lust for information: I want to know, to understand. My curiosity led me to regretted boldness last time, but I decided to pursue it once again. "Still remember what, ma'am?"

"Me." She took a long drag. "Look, kid. Old Hampton's not a place for you. You've got a job. You're not from around here. You're better than that, and you're better than him." Both of us knew exactly whom she meant. "Get out. Get out fast, and get far away. That's all I'll say, and I'll only say it once. Understand?"

I shook my head. "Ma'am, while I—"

She sighed. "Of course you don't. But, it's none of my business. Whatever." I was left to eat in peace, which I did, leaving my money on the counter. I didn't tip her, this time: I was getting tired of her references to something about Old Hampton she wasn't telling me, even after the short time I'd known her. That was the second time she'd warned me off of it, despite her promise of saying it only once, and I had the distinct impression that I was playing a game where everyone but me knew the rules.

It's hard to remember, sometimes, just what I thought. Maybe I thought I'd shape my own destiny, or perhaps I just wanted to defy what the universe had in store for me. Either way, I knew already that something was up, that I wouldn't like it, and that I'd end up hurt. But in my stubbornness, I paid that no heed. Making my way to Franklin Square, I caught the first bus out of Priius, and decided to see what the locals did when they weren't working.

IX.

With my life's savings still in my wallet, and nothing else save for the clothes on my back, I hopped aboard the nearest bus to the city's outer limits. In that moment, I desired nothing more than to escape from the crushing, choking atmosphere of Priius —the fabled city had already begun to lose its allure. In Priius, I saw the gilded plating chipping away, revealing all the rot and filth inside. It was just another city. But I clung firm to my illusions; I could not bear to believe that with all the technological advancements of the recent ages, we remained but mortals.

On that rattling, dirty bus, I sat among a few men and women, mostly from the southern cities. We were headed toward Tobit, where laid the casinos, bars, restaurants, and general tourist pits; Priius had been a stop along the way, so the visitors could see Candor Tower. Although I was part of Priius' small populace, I knew myself to be a tourist; it would have been a joke to pretend myself anything else. I crossed my legs at the knee in an imitation of how I imagined fine people must sit, and glared hungrily out of the window opposite me, watching the scenery roll by.

I couldn't help but overhear a couple of ladies talking beside me; hardly anyone else spoke. Most people had their heads buried in pamphlets or novels, for there were no televisions there on the bus. From their conversation, I judged they were part of some religious group which had cobbled together enough money to take their holiday in the big cities. They chatted about the museums and the galleries they had seen; how Candor Tower must be the most amazing building they'd ever seen in their lives; how Priius, and indeed, Licenia, was a gift from God.

The trip to Tobit wouldn't be a long one, but it gave me a chance to rest my eyes. Leaning back, I let my mind wander; it drifted to my childhood on the farm, and how I spent every Saturday morning readying myself to go to town. I'd put on my small, starched suit, and my mother would comb my hair; she'd spray on her perfume, and my father would splash on his cologne. Like some sort of painting of rural life, the three of us would pile in our grumbling old car, and drive to town, where the majority of that rural population would go every Saturday.

In a solemn procession, we'd park along with the trucks and station wagons, then march into the church and take a seat on the roughly-finished pews. With hymnbooks in our laps, we'd sing dispassionately along with the rest of the makeshift choir, while I examined my mother's rough hands and my father's tattered cuffs. Everyone sat, and the preacher would deliver a sermon I was too young to understand, and which usually neatly avoided theology, focusing instead on moral issues and emotional appeals. My gaze always drifted between the rafters and the floor; I flipped through the hymnbooks and the holy books, seeking something to entertain me.

As the years passed by, my attention moved from the rafters to the preacher, wherein I began to truly consider his words. He spoke of how we must give to the unfortunate when we have plenty, for we have been so commanded. We must give our souls, our hearts, our minds up to our creator, for we have been so commanded. We are nothing without our creator; he is everything, and we are to be grateful for the life he has given us. But never did he explain why the creator was worthy of this; nor did he ever make mention of any reason to give to the poor other than that we had been so commanded. I believe that's where my distaste for the whole business began; a country preacher is by no means a fair sample of the entire religion, but it remained my sole experience with the matter.

As the bus rolled past Tobit's city limits, I laughed to myself: it seemed so fitting that, on the holiday—the holy day—I should go to a place of indulgence with these ecclesiastics. I bore them, of course, no ill thoughts for the matter; we are all of us with our flaws, and none of us can afford to be religious all the time. Indeed, I have no doubt they had been more faithful servants than I had ever been, even as a child; though I'm hardly one to believe in moral accountancy, I suspect they may have earned a break.

I see you stirring, but I promise that I do not merely ramble— or perhaps I do, but my rambling is intentional. You see, my philosophies are what brought me to Priius. My sense of pride in humanity had always been wounded by the thought that we should obey any power blindly, even that of some grand Creator. As you may recall, I do believe in a sort of fate—but we need not rely on some supernatural power to achieve that fate. We are our own keepers, I believe; my attempt at keeping myself is what brought me here. Call me an anarchist, but I have faith in neither gods nor masters; I have faith only in humanity, and in the basic decency of people.

You'll understand, perhaps, if my faith has been strained in these last months.

The bus came to a jerking stop in the parking lot of a beautiful old building, with marble pillars and gorgeous stonemasonry. I recall being shaken and rattled as I had never experienced in a vehicle; the lady beside me grabbed my arm to keep me from falling to the floor, and I offered her a slight smile. She looked to be in her midlife; the hand that gripped my arm had thin, callused fingers and only light musculature. The faint scent of smoke clung to her, and her skin held an unhealthy pallor.

At the time, I didn't recognize it, but when I looked around, all the others on the bus had the same affliction. Their fine clothes hung well on their frames, the dresses and suits all with immaculate drape, but their flesh lacked something. She patted me on the arm and gestured up; I blushed, realizing I had been examining her overlong, and joined the exodus into the city proper.

Though I had no idea where we were, I found myself content simply to marvel at the building's architecture: it reminded me of the ancient temples whose monochrome images I had seen in my books. In a creaky, well-used voice, the woman who had caught me asked, "D'you know where we are, son?" When I confessed that I didn't, she informed me that we were visiting the Reynald Museum of Art, one of the oldest in the nation. I expressed an appropriate level of surprise and approval, and followed the churchgoers into the museum.

For the next hour or two, I spent my time pretending to be some bourgeois patron of the arts. Wearing my work clothes, stroking my rough beard, I examined every brush stroke and every statue, occasionally exchanging thoughts with Martha— the woman whom I have mentioned. Once more, I was terribly out-of-place among the silk hats and wool coats, but this time, I wasn't so much aware of it; the sculptures and paintings engrossed me, captivating my entire attention.

I have long enjoyed gazing upon fine works of ink, paint, stone, and music; however, this marked my first experience facing such things in person. Although some of the subjects eluded me—many depicted pagan gods or religious subjects, a fair deal of which had escaped my self-education—I could still appreciate them for the masterwork which had gone into their creation. For the first time in my life, I regretted not having learned a trade outside of farming: though I could care for livestock and crops better than most, the idea of putting brush to canvas and creating something so beautiful astounded me. Still, there remained a certain detachment, in which I remained merely an observer. Until, that is, I saw the mural.

I should think someone such as you has been to see the Reynald many times, and perhaps you recall the depiction of the Grand War. It consumed almost the entirety of a room; life-sized figures of Licenian soldiers, their faces illuminated by the sun, charged forth under the banner of the Lion, bearing their light machine guns and their rifles. And the snarling, fearful faces of the black-skinned Greens fell back in retreat, clutching to their comrades as painted bullets bit deep into their flesh. Somehow, it was depicted without gore, except a few corpses lying among Greenwood's ranks. But the subject! The glorious liberation of South Licenia from the savage Greens. The artist had depicted us as saviors, holy warriors who came on a godly mission.

And Peters' words came back to me, ringing heavy and solemn in my memory. A sickness gripped me as I turned to see the smiling, admiring faces of my fellow patrons. It wasn't their fault, and they weren't the cause of my sudden illness: it was the realization that I would have been among them. I would have smiled to myself, proud of Licenia's brave actions. But Peters— he now lived with the memory that he had damned his own family to die in an explosion of his own creation. The echo of that blast ripped through the fabric of time and space, blowing a giant, gaping hole in that mural and showing me all the rot and filth inside.

Shaking, I turned away from it, staggering out of the museum as a man stricken. Perhaps you think me melodramatic, but I promise, that is only because it is difficult to describe in words what that painting expressed. The golden head of the officer might well have borne a halo. Not a single Licenian had fallen.

And the savagery—the savagery—God, how he had painted the Greenwood soldiers. It was sickening, and I could look on it no longer. I knew that, just days before, I might have painted the same damned thing, and the very thought appalled me.

Leaving behind the church group, I walked back into the fresh air, shaking out my head. I knew that I didn't belong in such places; I belonged in the dark places, where no God shone his favor on conquering heroes, and no polemics tainted conversations. I spent much of the rest of the day exploring the side streets and alleys, ducking into curio shops and occult stores, where old foreigners told stories of how to ward off demons and win the favor of the spirits. I purchased a string of teeth from a bifocal-clad woman from the other continent, who fastened it behind my neck and chattered about how it would prevent the Raven Mother from touching my soul. Knowing in what condition I had left the thing, I figured it could use all the help it could get.

I wasted much of the rest of the day in different bars, either eating bland, greasy food or nursing scotch. Anticipating my first paycheck, I even bought a wooden box of cheap cigars, which I tucked under my arm and carried with me for the rest of the day. After my unfortunate experience at Reynald, I felt the need to bury my head in the consumption of useless wares and fleeting experiences. But I stuck to the darker areas, for my weak eyes could no longer bear that light which shone on the fine people.

As night crept in on Tobit, a young woman, undernourished and with the same affliction of the skin which marked all the others, approached me from the alleys. She bore a slight limp, walking uncertainly in her tall shoes, and inquired in a timid soprano as to whether I needed company. Once again, I encountered a situation unfamiliar to me, but her intentions were clear. Veiny legs and knobby knees were brought together beneath a skirt far too short for the chill night air of the northern country, and scraps of her small breasts were exposed by her thin blouse. I stared briefly at the slouching figure before me, and then wordlessly turned away, fleeing for the nearest bus back to Priius. The thought of purchasing the services of a girl who had barely bled roused a different sort of disgust in me.

But not at her. It wasn't her fault. She simply lived in the dark places, where no God smiled down.

X.

I spent much of the next week developing a daily routine: each morning, I would rise early, shower quickly, and eat breakfast in John's Kitchen. Mrs. Hughes and I continued to have brief chats with each other, usually nothing more than small talk. I would ask her about her business; she would inquire into my job. True to her word, she said no more of Old Hampton, nor did I inquire; I received the impression that she slept in the back room of the shop, rather than pay taxes for a house and a business. Considering the state of the place and of her clothes, I rather doubt she could have afforded a house save in the slums. Often, when I entered, I found her already occupied with someone else; she and the woman from before—Susan, was it?—seemed to enjoy trading books back and forth. Strange, that: almost everyone else watched television. But like me, Mrs. Hughes lacked one, for she couldn't afford it. Or so I supposed, at least. Rather than fall victim to an installment plan and run herself into debt, she went without. Such frugality is uncommon in Licenia. But then, such frugality is most common among the working class, and who looks at them?

Truth be told, though I hated the commute, I enjoyed my job at Candor. It was mindless work, to be sure, but it held a certain appeal for a young man such as myself. That bright red jumpsuit, that shiny, brass zipper. Why, after I returned from that first day off, they even gave me a patch with my name to sew on the left breast pocket. Despite knowing that I had sworn them my enemy, I couldn't contain a slight swelling of pride to know that I had really *made* it. I had a real job, beyond working on the farm, and I had the uniform to prove it. Not so different, perhaps, from the crimson uniforms of the soldiers who had gone off to war; the better to hide their wounds while they fought, and after they returned. The entire staff wore red clothing, if they had a uniform, from the janitors to the secretaries to the receptionists.

The receptionists. I saw two, while I worked there: one to cover the day, and one to cover the night. The latter, I liked a great deal. This is not to say that the former was by any means unpleasant to me; she smiled and nodded each day I entered, and we exchanged pleasantries. But the latter—Deirdre, if you know her—she was one of the most pleasant people whom I have ever met. Though not beautiful of face, she had an attraction; as an intelligent, kindly woman, she intrigued me. I had, even then, no heady thoughts of romance; I had no time for such things. And how might I court? Bring someone back to my hovel, and drink? But I once again digress. Forgive me.

Each day, in the cafeteria, I would meet with the other janitors, and we'd chat about whatever over our sandwiches. Television, mostly: I remember that Clifton was always fond of comedies, frequently reciting jokes that everyone but me recognized. Daisy tended to watch game shows, especially trivia; she had a memory for minutia to rival mine. And then there was John.

After Peters, John was the only Greenwood native I had ever met. I had seen them on television, certainly, but usually depicted by Licenians who had darkened their faces. He had been born in Greenwood, but lived there only a year before his parents decided to move to South Licenia. This was all before the war, of course; John was an older gentleman, his hair long turned grey. He spoke well, surprisingly well for someone who had never progressed menial labor in thirty years of work. The first day we met was my second day on the job; he shook my hand, introduced himself, and assured me that I need not worry, that he wasn't "some rebellious upstart." All he ever seemed to watch were documentaries: he wanted to know all there was to know about Greenwood and Licenia, and what made them different.

It was my fifth day on the job that I made my first mistake; I accidentally knocked over an ornamental vase, after slipping on a freshly-waxed floor. My head had struck its pedestal, and I fell, dazed, while the vase shattered across the floor. John had been working in the other room; he heard the crash, and came to investigate. By then, I had picked myself up, but I was bleeding slightly from the injury; he had me hold a paper towel to the wound, and cleaned up the vase's shards despite my protests. His insistence on ensuring my good health at first annoyed, and then amused me, in an odd sort of way: he refused to allow me to continue working until I stopped by the medical wing and ensured I hadn't a concussion from my fall. By the time I returned, he had already cleaned that floor, and told me that I was to take my lunch.

Shortly after that occasion, we had our first proper conversation. While I tried to find some way to thank him for his kindness, he just clapped me on the shoulder and told me, "My boy, we all make mistakes. You've been here, what, a few days? And you haven't set anything on fire? Well, that's an achievement, there!" We shared a laugh and ate our sandwiches, then got to talking about our lives before working at Licenia. I told him of life in the eastern farmlands; he had moved directly from South Licenia to the northern climes of greater Prius, and had never seen my corner of the world. Meanwhile, he told me about South Licenia, which turned out fairly similar: mostly farmland, though with larger, industrial hubs near rivers and lakes.

"So, how are you enjoying Prius?" he asked, with a smile. "I don't live here, exactly; I live in Decker, a little south of Tobit. It's not too bad a place, though I could do without the paper mill," he laughed, wrinkling his nose.

It took me a moment to gather up my opinions on the matter; I finally settled for, "It's nice. The air's not great, and the traffic's a pain to cross, but I think I like this city." His mention of Tobit brought to mind the museum I had visited, and I held back a shudder. "Lots of... of life, I suppose you could say. I haven't been around much, but I did visit Tobit; some neat shops up there."

"Oh, yes." He nodded to me. "I go there, from time to time. It's close by, after all, and you get a nice blend of cultures if you avoid the tourist areas. The rent's cheap enough that immigrants can afford it. Even those from Greenwood," he added. Though he smiled, I could detect a slight turn of his lip, perhaps a wrinkle below his eye, that suggested something more to me. Taking a bite of my sandwich to give me time to think, I mulled over a few different ways to ask the question I eventually blurted out: "What d'you mean, 'those from Greenwood?'"

He put down his sandwich, and frowned in thought for a time, most likely trying to find a way to say something without offending me. For he finally said, "It's hard to make a living when you're from Greenwood. It's why I'm still here." After a moment of silence, he resumed eating his sandwich, but I left mine on the table. My curiosity roused, I asked, "And why's that? The language barrier? I can't imagine you'd have much of a problem with it; you've lived here most of your life, right?"

Now, he put down his sandwich, giving me a smile that spoke of a deep weariness. I had seen it in Peters' face, and in Mrs. Hughes'. And when he spoke, it bore that same edge of longing that gave Forgotten such oratory power. "You're too young to remember the camps, aren't you, Jack?" Upon seeing my furrowed brow, he explained. "During the war, see, the government decided it had to guard against foreign spies. So, they gathered up anyone who looked like they might be from Greenwood. And believe me, this doesn't look like a tan." He tried to laugh, but didn't quite succeed. "They put us in camps. We weren't harmed—not usually—but we weren't allowed to leave. I'm a bachelor, and always have been, so it didn't bother me too terribly, but some of the families had troubles. It's hard enough to keep your child healthy under normal circumstances, but if someone caught a disease, we all caught it, and the children took it hard.

"We had doctors, mind you, and we had food and shelter. But we also had armed guards, and we had curfews, and we had nowhere to go." His voice nearly cracked that time, but he managed to keep up his smile. "And it lasted years. It lasted years. They sent a lot of us back to Greenwood, if we didn't speak the language or we didn't have work. If you were a vagrant, it was an automatic ship-out. But I don't think they... I don't think they realized," he murmured, "that just because we all looked alike, we weren't all *from* Greenwood. I considered myself South Licenian, despite having been born there. A lot of folks they sent back even lived around Priius. Their one kindness was in shipping whole families off together." He cut off there, staring into the distance slightly, grimacing.

"I'm sorry," I muttered. I couldn't think of anything else to say. "I... hadn't heard that before."

He laughed again, but it was forced. "Of course you haven't, my boy. How many Greens have you seen in your life?" He nodded at my flush of embarrassment. "Yeah, see? It's not your fault. A lot of us left on our own; I didn't have a job when I got back from the camp, and the only place that would hire me was Candor Tower. I've been a janitor ever since." He held out his arm, tapping it. "It's hard to get a job when you're as tanned as I am," he concluded, with another attempt at a smile.

For a while, I just sat there while he ate, trying to process this new information. "Why'd you stick around?" I asked, after a time. "Why didn't you leave? I mean, it sounds like you were unwan... it sounds like you..."

"Were unwanted." He nodded. "I was. Still am! I'm sorry I've made you uncomfortable, Jack; but you see, that's why they don't want me around." I looked up to see him doing his best to keep up that painted-on smile. "I make people uncomfortable, because that Grand War wasn't so very long ago. And on the television shows, all the Greens look alike."

"So why'd you stick around?" I repeated, feeling a touch ill again.

"Well, at first, out of hope." He continued to eat while he spoke, probably to give himself time to consider his answers. "I thought I could prove that I wasn't anything to be afraid of. I'm an educated man, Jack; I've probably forgotten most of it, by now, but I at least used to be. And I thought that, if I just worked hard and did my best to fit in, I'd change their minds. Well, long story short?" He shrugged. "I didn't. So I'm here. I haven't the money to go anywhere else, so I stick around here, and I hope for a change."

"You can't just hope," I mumbled, the words sounding as hollow then as they do now.

"No," he agreed, "you can't. But I fought it for years. I took other people's shifts, I volunteered around the community, and I wrote letters to Parliament. I shouted, pleaded, begged and demanded." His hand began to tremble slightly; in a voice barely above a murmur, he said, "But it's hard to hear a Green over the sound of his skin."

XI.

On that fifth day, I decided to finally steal the papers I had been requested to retrieve. Every night, I would return to our little camp at Old Hampton, and report on my progress toward that goal. It was on the third day that I received my key; they were always trusting people. They thought they'd cleansed the world of its corruption with their upbeat programming and their positive messages for humanity, and they let their guard down. I have only sympathy for them.

It was such a simple matter that I couldn't recall, after doing it, why I had delayed so long in taking action. The truth is simply that I was afraid. Forgotten could spin a sob story, certainly, but I had no reason aside from pity to believe or trust him. Some believe that young people think themselves invincible, but—at least in my meager experience—that isn't the case. At least not for me. I was all too aware of my mortality and my failings; they were easier to enumerate, then. I knew that in a moment, I could end up in prison, having lost my job and dashed all of my hopes and dreams. All it would take would be a single mistake: someone to look inside, or a security camera to catch me.

There were no security cameras in the record room. Who would steal the records, and for what purpose? Candor had no competition. It had no significant enemies, or so it thought. And what good were some old financial records? Everything they had done was perfectly legal. That's the one good thing I can say for them: they were lawful in their business practices. But it's easy to do that when you have the law on your side.

I can recall the way my heart leapt when I stepped into that room with my mop and bucket, cleaning off the tiles. Other than a dim, flickering light overhead, there was no illumination, and the hallway outside had grown dark. I'd insisted on covering the night shift for John, after his kindness, though I had to convince him that I wasn't hurt. At first, I mopped about half of the room, in case someone should happen to wander by and wonder why the door was ajar. Candor Tower was unique in many ways; that it remained the sole business open past nine at night was just one of them. After all of the cars had made their exodus from the city, there remained Candor Tower, as inscrutable and grandiose as ever. But that meant there were always people there.

The old filing cabinet creaked open with a metallic whine, and I stopped, turning around to ensure the noise hadn't roused anyone. But the floor was silent, save for the ever-present hum of the great engines down below. Their quiet reverberations echoed along the walls and hollow crawlspaces, bringing that soft rattle throughout the entirety of the tower. Such white noise was easily forgotten, but in the still nights, you could hear it as clearly as before. My heart thumped almost audibly as I turned back to the cabinet. The lock on the door was faulty, they had warned me, and it could lock you in if you weren't careful; maintenance intended to have a look at it. But until then, they recommended that I leave the door open. I'd left a broom handle in the way; I didn't want anyone to have more of a peek than that. My gloved hands flicked through dusty folders; I had to strain to read the labels by the dim half-light, especially since I was blocking it.

"I was straightening them," I thought I might say, if someone asked what I was doing. But that wouldn't convince anyone but an idiot. Perhaps I had knocked them over, or maybe... I didn't know what I'd say. I just hoped no-one would walk inside. I'd no idea how often they checked on the files, but given the thin layer of dust which had settled on them, even inside those cabinets, I suspected it wasn't often. At a guess, there might have been...

fifty? Some were locked, but not all of them. I looked first under "D," for donations, then "C," for campaign contributions. Both of those failed, though, and momentarily, I began to wonder if I'd have to search through every file. A few more wild guesses provided nothing; not "F" for financial, nor even "M" for money. I resumed mopping while I thought, lest I linger too long and raise suspicions.

It wasn't until I had nearly finished that I thought to check the numbered files: something periodic might be filed by year. If only I'd been hired on as a secretary instead of a janitor! But when I pulled at the handle for the last year before the war, the drawer stuck, locked. Cursing my luck, I fumbled in my toolbelt for a screwdriver, which I inserted into the lock, fiddling around with it to test the quality of the lock. A cheap one might come undone easily; I'd opened a few with scissors, in my youth. But never for any illegal activities; I had been a good kid, for the most part. Shame I ever went to Priius. I could practically feel the tumblers shifting, but they wouldn't turn quite the way I wanted. Grunting, I fiddled with the lock more, thumping the metal a few times.

Until I heard the clap of shoes on tile. I froze, pulling my screwdriver out of the lock and grabbing my mop up again. A sweat broke out along my neck, and I dropped my screwdriver, despite trying to hold it against the mop's handle. Just a moment later, the door creaked open, and a middle-aged man in a red coat pushed the door open with a smile. I did my best to return it, forcing myself to look calm as he stepped inside. My eyes narrowed when his flashlight shone in my eyes; he'd thick glasses, and likely couldn't see too well.

"Hello, young man!" he exclaimed, voice echoing off the walls. "Just security checking in—have to peek at open doors."

"Ah, yeah?" I asked, nodding amicably to him and wiping my

forehead. "I appreciate it. Haven't found any burglars, have you?"

He shook his head with a laugh. "Not in all my years on the job. I see you're hard at work, though, so I'll leave you be. Have a nice evening, there!"

I gave him a wave and another nod, then relaxed as he shut the door behind himself. Waiting until I could hear his footsteps fading away, I picked my screwdriver back up with trembling hands, and resumed fiddling with the lock. After perhaps half a minute, during which time I shook and rattled the drawer, it finally came free. I leafed with trembling hands through the drawer, eventually finding a list of donations and contributions made to various causes. I scanned down it until I located campaign contributions; then pulling the relevant sheets from the file, I folded them and tucked them into a pocket, closed the file, and went on about my cleaning, vastly relieved. Fortunately, the door hadn't locked behind the security officer.

That night, I returned late to Old Hampton; the traffic was practically non-existent, so I was able to rush all the way back without so much as stopping for dinner. Most of the men had gone to bed, but Fergus greeted me with a clap on the shoulder, and I stopped long enough to share a cigar with him, chatting about the latest events in the newspaper. We always found a copy or two, shared them about, and usually discussed them, though there wasn't often anything interesting to discuss. We mostly sat around taking potshots at humanity, sometimes laughing to ourselves about the kind of people who would read it, and always ignoring the irony in the latter. After the duration of a cigar, we'd managed to talk a lot about nothing, and I wandered over to rap on Rothschild's door, in case he was about.

I hadn't seen a lot of Rothschild since coming there; he was usually gone. When I did see him, it was most often briefly, just a hello before he slipped away into Forgotten's cabin, and usually either slept the night in his own shanty or left again. He preferred jumping the walls to walking in, for some reason I cannot fathom. Unlike the other men, in their white shirts and black waistcoats, he was dressed for hard labor. To my surprise, his bearded face appeared in the doorway, blonde eyebrows furrowed over his sharp, green eyes. I stepped back to give him space, glancing down at his untucked blue shirt and his stained, black jeans. His brawny arms had folded across a new gash on his chest, exposed by a tear in his shirt. For a moment, we stared at each other in silence; he was one of the few at the camp whom I could look square in the eye. Finally, I held up the folded records I had stolen, and he took them from me without a word.

He scanned down the pages with ferocious, almost ravenous intensity, and turned away from me, striding back into his cabin. As he'd left the door wide open, I leaned to the side to peek in: a gas lantern provided sufficient illumination that I could see him bent over a table much like Forgotten's; that and a cot were the only furnishings. He grabbed a fountain pen from the table, then began scratching and circling on the page, annotating and circling at lightning speed. Not knowing whether I was expected to wait or leave, enter or stand, I shoved my hands in my pockets and watched him, leaning on the doorframe. Just watching him work was impressive, even if I didn't know what he was doing. Eventually, he set the pen down and whirled on one heavy boot to stride over to me again, thrusting the papers back in my face.

I took them with one raised eyebrow, watching his eyes carefully. One regarded me with either curiosity or annoyance, while the other stared, blank. And slightly to the left. Once again, we stood across from one another, neither moving or speaking, until I again broke the silence.

"Do I take these over to Forgotten, then?" I asked, drawling somewhat in my mild exasperation.

He nodded, then grunted, "Yes." Even in that word, I could make out a foreign accent: he was from the other continent, though I wasn't sure where, exactly. Maybe he didn't know the language too well; that would explain his reticence. Still, he offered no attempt to so much as ask my name, and given the look he gave me, I suspected he would rather I were gone. Perhaps you can tell that I tend toward being a touch garrulous; I don't trust someone who keeps even their most public thoughts to themselves.

"Alright. Find everything you need in there?" I asked, glancing over his scribbles. Mostly, he had circled names of certain senators, but given the copious annotations, I seriously doubted there was a language barrier.

He scratched his chin, slicking his hair back. "Perhaps. We will see soon enough." After a moment longer, he blinked, adding, "And thank you for retrieving that information," almost as an afterthought. Probably as an afterthought, come to that; already, I could tell that pleasantries weren't his strength.

"You're welcome." I nodded to him, and stepped away, while he continued to stare. I turned back and examined him a while longer, in return; his left eye scanned me like an owl pondering a vole, but the right lacked that same luster. "Well," I shrugged, walking away, "I'll keep an eye out for you, I guess."

I could hear him laughing as I walked away, and paused. Turning back, he extended his middle finger to me, grinning broadly. "Bastard," he chortled, with a wink of his good eye. I hesitantly grinned back, returning the gesture, and he retired to his cabin, leaving me to bring the intelligence to Forgotten.

XII.

Although Peters had warned me not to approach Forgotten's cabin without alerting either Rothschild or Peters himself, I reflected that Rothschild had given me permission, in his taciturn way. At least, I supposed he had. The man had proven as inscrutable to me as Forgotten; perhaps more so. I walked across the camp and lingered at Forgotten's door, glancing down at the papers in my hand. I didn't dare unfold them to look at the annotations and notes, lest I break some unwritten code of conduct. After a moment, I rapped on the door three times, and waited.

After about a minute, I began to fear that he was away, busy, or asleep. Just before I turned away, however, he appeared in the doorway, clad in that same red coat and golden helmet. "Jackson!" he said, with a smile in his voice. "It's been a little while since we last spoke. I hope you're settling in well to the camp; you'll forgive me for my lack of... I'm not around very much," he revised, stepping back into the dim light of his cabin. "Do come in. Cigar, whiskey...?" He sounded almost chipper, despite that ever-present rasp in his throat, and when I sat, he hovered over me like a housewife with company. I declined both the cigar and the whiskey for the moment, and reached behind myself to wave the records at him.

That stopped his barrage of questions into my good health and spirits. Instantly, he transformed, solemnly accepting the papers and drifting over to his own seat, bringing them into the light. As I suspected, that helmet must have grown heavy on his head, for he supported his brow with one hand, bending over the table to read. I folded my hands in my lap, watching him in silence as he scanned each page, taking more time to look over them than Rothschild had taken to annotate them. When I grew restless, I poured myself a lowball glass of whiskey, to stave off my hunger, and lit one of his cigars. While I smoked, reclining as much as I dared in the wooden seat, he abruptly stood, and I feared another outburst from him. However, he merely began comparing the records to various newspaper clippings and other documents, all tacked up around the cabin. Every once in a while, he'd pause, leaning the paper against the wall and scribbling on it, sometimes adding to or redacting one of Rothschild's annotations.

By the time he sat down again, I was eying the last dregs of my whiskey, and I had already burnt down my cigar, lost in thought about nothing in particular. "Very good work, Jackson," he murmured; the sudden sound startled me. His gloved hand held out the papers, unfolded, and I accepted them, scanning down the first. It had been reduced to a list of names and figures, with a series of numbers denoting their place in the list. A few of them, I vaguely recognized as members of Parliament, whose names came up frequently during Candor's coverage of the war. Most were unknown to me. You'd probably know who they were, but I've largely forgotten, by now. Their names aren't so important, anyhow.

"You'll want to take that over to Peters, and from there, take it back to Rothschild. We can almost begin the real work." He quivered with that unique excitement of his; I still remembered it from our first meeting. From time to time, the man would nearly burst with energy, yet on such occasions, he nearly whispered. When he shouted, he usually said little. Forgotten's silence was the most dangerous. "Goddamn. Do you know how long I've waited for this?" he continued, rubbing his hands together. "You came up at a very opportune moment, Jackson: we were just finishing up our preparations to begin the first of our rounds of action. It's like... it's like setting up a house of cards. We spent a lot of time planning our method, and now you've brought us the cards. Soon, very soon, we can begin putting them in place."

I set down my empty glass, and leaned back to regard him. "Excuse me, sir," I said. "I don't mean to interrupt, but I've got a question for you." He nodded, and I fumbled over my words. "This is kind of a strange question, I suppose, but I'm curious. I mean, I only just met him, and maybe I should ask him myself, but..." I could think of no better way to phrase it. "Who is Rothschild?"

He chuckled, shaking his head. "No, Jackson, don't bother asking him. He won't tell you, as you guessed. I... you could say I worked with him during the war, I guess, but it's hard to exactly describe it. We were on the same side, as far as I know, but I didn't deal with him much, myself. Mostly, he was the name I heard whispered by my superiors whenever we dealt Greenwood a particularly crippling blow, or engaged in some act of cunning. He's from the other continent, as you can tell, but other than that—well, to be honest, I don't know much about him." He gave a helpless shrug, chuckling again. "He won't tell, and I don't ask. To be honest, I'm not sure I want to know. I've done some horrible things, Jackson." He leaned forward, until I could hear his breath whistling through the lion's nostrils. "But if I may share a word in private? Rothschild is the one man from whom I receive a dose of fear."

I laughed, as did he, though I don't think either of us knew why. "Well, in that case, I'll keep a careful watch on him," I grinned, drumming my fingers on the table. "Do you think he was... an assassin, maybe? Or a spy? Before he came over here, I mean, or at least before the war."

Forgotten pondered that, and decided, "I don't know. I've speculated on it, myself, but I suppose I might never discover that. I do know that, in the old wars, we did some fairly terrible things to the other continent, as did they to us. For someone like Rothschild, who must have grown up in Yrasmus, I doubt there's a word for 'normal.' They never quite recovered from the Fifty Months. It's rough." I nodded sympathetically, and he rolled his shoulders.

"The important things to know about Rothschild are these: he is, as far as I can tell, on our side as much as he's on anyone's. He doesn't take payment in the usual way; I think he's either a thrill-seeker or a death-seeker. He's your man if you ever want to find out anything about anything. And you don't fuck with him." He waved his finger at me warningly. "I first met him in person when we were mopping up the last of the Greens. My company discovered a camp in the woods that had probably been a Green base of operations. He was just... sitting there, eating." Behind his mask, he must have given me a meaningful look. "There weren't any Greens at that camp, and we hadn't found it until the war ended."

He clapped me on the shoulder and thanked me again for my work; I thanked him for the hospitality, and stepped back into the evening light, papers in hand. Light spilled out from beneath Peters' doorway; I knocked on his door, and soon sat down with Peters and, to my surprise, Rothschild. The two had been conferring, it seemed, while waiting on me to return from Forgotten's cabin. Before I could say anything, Peters took the papers from me, silently reading while Rothschild craned his neck to see what changes had been made.

Sitting with the two quietest men in Old Hampton wasn't my idea of a pleasant experience. They barely acknowledged that I existed, but on the other hand, I suspect they were fairly preoccupied with their work. For the most part, Peters nodded to himself as he checked over the list, but he occasionally scratched out one of the numbers on the left column and replaced it with a different one. When he reached the second page, I saw him truly frown for the first time in my life. Scowl, even. He circled one name in particular; reading upside-down, I could tell that it was one I'd heard, before. Forgotten had marked it with a "1." Rothschild had written notes beside it, and Peters' hand nearly trembled as he stared at that name.

"Jackson," he said, in his quiet voice, "do you know who George Lampton is?" I admitted that I knew only that he was a member of Parliament, or at least had been, and Peters nodded. "He led the charge against the Dignity in Warfare bill, which would have outlawed... how did they word it? 'Acts of interrogation, in times of war or peace, which undermine basic human dignity.' Or, in other words, torture." He looked up at me, more serious than I had ever seen him. "It would have spared a lot of good men. He stood up against it. Said that it would destroy all our progress toward ending the war. The others believed him." For a moment, he closed his eyes; Rothschild and I watched him, impassive, until he spoke again. "It would have spared a lot of good men," he repeated. "Rothschild..."

"I will be on it tomorrow," said the same, with a nod. With that, he stood up and walked away. Peters sat there for a while, reading the list and resuming his work. In the company of those three—Forgotten, Peters, and Rothschild—I never knew when to leave or stay. Usually, I found that the latter was expected of me, so I remained sitting, looking around the shack. Little adorned its walls, unlike Forgotten's, but it bore similarities in its sparse decor and furniture. A gas lamp on the wall, a table, a cot, and some chairs, all made out of old, worn wood.

When Peters finished looking over the documents, he set them aside, and looked up at me once again. "I never told you why I came here with Forgotten," he noted. Making out his words always challenged me: he spoke so rapidly and quietly that I had to listen closely to understand. "I served with him in the war. I think you know that. It's hard to remember what I've told people. He got his pension, but he didn't want to move to the countryside; he wanted to remain in the heart of the city, and dirty Old Hampton was the only place he could do it." I felt a shiver run down my spine: any time Peters took me into his confidence, I felt vaguely honored; he was so... private. "As an officer, he got a hefty amount of money. It's one of the ways we keep ourselves fed. As an agent, I should have received even more. But I'm not a citizen. Worse, I'm a Greenwood citizen." He favored me with an unsettling smile. "I received no pension, but I wasn't deported."

My jaw went slack. He nodded once. "They never gave me a uniform. They never gave me their trust. They never gave me my pension. I have scars, Jackson. So do a lot of those men who went off to that war. So do a lot of the women and children who had to stay behind. But many of us aren't allowed to show our scars, because in the eyes of Licenia, we don't exist. The bastard child, the shell-shocked soldier, the hungry child, the raped..." He paused there, and blinked once, then finished his thought a moment later. "We don't exist in the eyes of Licenia.

"I didn't receive my pension, and I had nowhere to go, because they wouldn't deport me. So I stayed with Forgotten, with whom I had worked in the war. He shared his cabin with me during the war, and he shared his pension with me, afterward. And I stayed with him. But not like a child, Jackson." He clenched the edge of the table in his grip. "I don't need him, you see. I'm not relying on him for support. I never did. I stick with him not like a hungry dog or a frightened child, but because in this whole goddamn country, he's the only person who ever treated me with even a modicum of respect." Years of silent rage boiled up from his throat. "They fucked me over, Jackson. They fucked me over again, and again, and again, because the Licenian parliament doesn't give a shit about anyone. I'm not here because I share Forgotten's dream for the world." He stood up, breathing shallowly, trembling in anger as he stared down at me. "I'm here because I cannot rest—I will not rest—until my scars, and the scars of everyone who suffered at the hands of a few arrogant men have been repaid in blood."

He sat. I resumed breathing. He smiled. I quaked.

"Jackson," he said, "you seem like a capable man. I'm glad you came to Priius."

Until that moment, I had never wished so fervently that I had stayed away.

XIII.

In the week or two that followed my theft of the papers, my life resumed some semblance of normality. I went to work each day except Sunday, though I took fewer meals at John's Kitchen. Much of my former strength had returned, and I looked healthy again, healthier than I do now. Still tanned from my years on the farm, I stood out from the pale denizens of Priius: most were middle-class office workers, with slender arms and tender hands, their skin smooth and pale. You know them: the kind who commute in their cars from the suburbs, where they separate themselves from their neighbors with picket fences, and separate themselves from outsiders with golden gates. In turn, those who lived in the urban centers just outside of Priius— towns like Cavallo, or Veraart, where the factories and mills lie— provided gruesome contrast to the suburbanites. Since Tobit, I noticed it: the rougher folk who lived in such towns bore the sallow skin and sunken eyes of the church-goers I'd met. Many of them gathered in John's Kitchen in the mornings and evenings, resting before and after work.

Mrs. Hughes grew more distant yet; we were reduced to brief exchanges of greetings, outside of ordering food. I suspected it had to do with our last notable exchange; she knew something of Old Hampton which escaped my notice. But I didn't dare ask: I've learned that cities like Priius aren't like Milton. People value their privacy more, or maybe they simply come by it more easily. For the first twenty years of my life, I had known everything about everyone. My world remained small, close-knit, and safe. But in a place like Priius, the community sprawls like the buildings of Tobit, and we crowd close in our solitude. In the shadow of the skyscrapers, we can't make out the blurred lines of faces.

While I drifted away from Mrs. Hughes, I drew closer to Deirdre. The receptionist, you recall. Each night, when my shift ended, I would linger near her desk, sometimes striking up a conversation with her. Other times, I simply rested my weary legs in the padded chairs of the lobby, my back turned to the television. We spoke, fleetingly, of our lives before Candor; I told of life on the farms, and she listened with bright eyes, eventually sharing her own story. Being a few years my senior, she had been of an age to work in the factories of Cavallo in the latter years of the war.

"They had me making bullets," she laughed, resting her elbow on the desk and her chin in her hand. "It was awful! I spent every day doing the same thing, over and over again. All I did was pull a lever to dump some hot lead into a mold." Her nose wrinkled, and she glanced over at the door, expecting someone to walk in at any moment. "A few of the girls got hurt; that lead was as hot as anything, and if you touched it..." There, she trailed off, with a shudder. "By God's grace, I kept free of it." Though I lent her my ear quite willingly, my thoughts always wandered somewhat, as they ever do. I found myself pondering her voice—that being the prettiest thing about her. She'd nice eyes, and a lovely voice, but as I believe I've mentioned, she was otherwise quite plain. A mite heavy. Still, I couldn't keep from her desk for long; I genuinely enjoyed her company, and she was one of the few who had offered me genuine kindness.

I came to ask questions of her, later on: why she had left the factory, what she had done in the interim. With a shrug, she explained that after the war ended and the men came home, they wanted their jobs back, and the women were pushed out. She'd tried the university, but hadn't been able to afford it with the scant pay she'd been given during the war, so she came here. In a rare moment of charm, I told her I was glad she had; she blushed, told me I was very kind, and I drifted back home soon after.

Perhaps you question why I bring up people such as John and Deirdre, Mrs. Hughes and the homeless man. They are surely unknown to you; perhaps you fail to understand their significance to my story. There are many others whom I have glossed over, certainly; I have kept you too long already, I know, so I have left out some of the more mundane details. Still, I feel compelled to give you the honesty I have promised. Honesty, however, takes time to deliver, and in this case, it is a many-faceted thing. If you are to understand what I have done, I need you to understand me on a visceral level. I have opened a hole in myself, to show you the rot inside. You see, despite the time I've spent here, I don't consider myself a citizen of Priius; I remain detached, maintaining the abstinence of the observer. I have changed the city, and God knows it has changed me, but I am not a part of it.

The truth, as far as I can see it, is that you and I dwell within Priius, but we do not comprise it. Nor do the suburbanites who walk in and out for their jobs, nor even the menial laborers who work in the basements and the hallways. Priius, Licenia, our very civilization—it's made of the people who are forced to keep one eye on Heaven. John's calluses form the walls that keep us safe and separate. Mrs. Hughes' sweat and blood form the rivers which cut through soil, sand, and stone. The bones of a thousand nameless wanderers pave our streets, and Deirdre's wistful sighs echo through them. We claim that great men have shaped our history, but this is nothing more than a dark sarcasm. The immigrants, the women, the vagrants, the forgotten—they waste their lives away to provide for us, and we visit only scorn upon them.

Forgive me—did I frighten you? It wasn't my intent. Get

yourself a drink; I need a moment to gather my thoughts. And thank you: I've seldom had such a captive audience.

My job continued in its bland way: it kept me occupied for hours a day, though, and kept me in enough money to live fairly comfortably, by my definition of the word. Even though I didn't watch the shows, I was able to glean enough about their content to have polite, sometimes even lively discussions with the other janitors. Clifton would entertain us by reenacting scenes from his comedies; Daisy filled our heads with interesting facts about everything under the sun; and sometimes, when we were alone, John would teach me some of the history of Greenwood and South Licenia. You don't get much of it in the history books; they focus on them only so much as they concern North Licenia. In other words, they mostly focus on our wars with them. Sometimes, he just told me stories from his younger days. I think he was searching for a satisfying explanation for what happened to him; maybe someday, he'll find it.

The next Sunday, I arose as early as ever, and cooked up some salt pork on the tiny gas stove I'd picked up the other day. After breakfast, I put on my town clothes; fortunately, I hadn't had occasion to wear them throughout the week, and they were no more worn than they'd always been. I'd received my first paycheck the previous day, and with it and a great many notes in my wallet, I half-walked, half-jogged out to Licenia's grand streets. Saturdays were the least busy, since many business closed early that day; not for the first time, I wished my day off were one day earlier. Still, I walked along with the morning crowds—not to Candor Tower, for once, but to a bank I'd found one evening.

I pushed open the steel doors, and walked onto the marble tiles, again bewildered by the grand trappings of Priius' buildings. The scents of expensive perfumes and colognes mingled in the air, and each footfall echoed mightily in the vast lobby. I waited in line for a few minutes, eventually to be directed to sit and wait for a representative. Eventually, a short, thin man in a suit walked over and shook my hand, leading me into his office; soon after, I was in possession of my first-ever bank account, and even a booklet of blank checks. I wrote my account number down on a slip of paper, and wandered out feeling like a true professional. My theft still gnawed at the back of my mind, but such a small thing could hardly be missed: I had made it. I was in.

Not wanting to waste my Sunday, I decided to use my new found riches to engage in some travel. I'd seen Priius and Tobit, but there were so many other towns nearby, just waiting to be explored. Deirdre's tale of her work in Cavallo came to mind; although I had heard about the enormous factories, I hadn't ever seen one in person. Supposedly, Cavallo sat on the river, as well; I thought that might make a nice trip, so I caught the last morning bus over to it.

Other than the driver and myself, the morning route to Cavallo had no passengers. It had been packed to the brim, not long before, with workers from the city making their way to work. I sat near the front, and kept the driver company; I could only imagine what it must be like to spend all day navigating the busy streets around Priius. Even though the city's own tended to clear between morning and evening, the streets outside remained heavily clogged with traffic. None of the other towns held to the same clockwork schedule; many of the factories operated all day, all week, to provide for the limitless demands of the growing market. At least, that's what the educational film the town theater once played for my class had said.

That old machine rattled along the pavement, the wheels rumbling and air rushing by as we sped along the early-morning highway. With the sun low on the horizon, its rays shone through the vapors in the air, producing a spectacular display of orange and pink. The fiery glow filtered in past the grimy window to my right, and lent some warmth to the stark wasteland of highway before us. Traffic picked up a few minutes into the drive; my temporary chauffeur grumbled under his breath, and I let my mind drift. It tried to roam toward the sun, far across the planet's curves, back to my home. But as with all things, the reality of the blazing pavement bound my thoughts close to Priius.

The closer we got to Cavallo's heart, the more I found myself sniffing at the air. Reminded of an experience from my youth, I laughed. "Did someone burst a sewage pipe, d'you think?" The driver chuckled, shaking his head. "Nah. You really haven't been up this way, have you? That's the pulp mill. Smell of progress, that." I murmured some sort of assent, and before long, we rolled up to the bus stop. I thanked him for the ride and hopped out, to consult the town directory; he lingered a few minutes for passengers, found none, and began his return to the fiery wasteland.

I regret to say that I have little to say of Cavallo; the only remarkable aspect of that whole vast city is how unremarkable it is. For the better part of three hours, I wandered around its rambling sidewalks, to find only half-deserted slums, intermingled with ancient storefronts and modern buildings. They had made a mosaic of architecture, and a portrait of Licenia: wherever a building had collapsed or fallen into disrepair, they simply removed the remains and put something new atop it. Nothing restored, nothing repaired; always a hurried attempt to flush out the old and replace it with something prettier.

The longer I walked, the more I found my nose filling and throat growing scratchy; the scents of the belching factories irritated my sinuses, setting me to coughing. Certain that I would find something of interest in that vast town, I wandered further and further downtown, until the houses gave way entirely to more and more factories. My feet ached and my throat burned by the time I reached the town square, dominated by a tremendous industrial park. The blackened air singed my eyes and clogged my lungs; I had just enough time to survey the stark walls of the four giant manufacturing plants before giving up and turning back. I never even saw the river; I had to flee back to cleaner air, hacking and coughing all the way.

In Priius, you can't see the stars for the light.

In Cavallo, you can't smell the air for the stench.

XIV.

When Rothschild returned, I don't think any of the men were prepared. I know I wasn't. After my pitiful visit to Cavallo, I'd returned to my ordinary life again; the routine had grown familiar to me. I can understand why the people of Priius are so content: when you have just enough money to afford a few simple luxuries, and no pressing bills, it's easy to fall into the comfort of routine. Going to work in the morning, coming home in the evening, and relaxing in between.

He didn't come back until several days after that Sunday. In that time, I had almost forgotten my theft, even living among and fraternizing with that rough horde. Though this may sound strange, you have to understand: we didn't speak of revolution on the quiet days. These were not men who held lofty ideals; they simply owed Forgotten some sort of loyalty. Most had crawled from the rainways and slums, creeping out of the shade to lurk in Forgotten's shadow. Several actually fervently agreed with what Forgotten said, but most were dazzled by his prestige and his skill. Here was their savior, whose crimson hand reached through the darkness to lift them up.

The real exceptions were, of course, Peters and Rothschild. Peters had his own vengeance in mind, as he had outlined to me. As for Rothschild, I suspect that he took some perverse pleasure in his occupation. What of me? I was hardly an exception. Though I had more of an education than, say, Fergus, he and I were no different in our incentives: the urge to be part of something drastic and dangerous; to change the world, and to be like the great men we had grown up hearing about on the television.

It's easy to forget that each of those men had families. Mothers, fathers, siblings, someone who cared about them. In that regard, I was by no means unique. We tend to forget that the Greens have artisans and intellectuals like we do, even after we bombed their land beyond recognition. We tend to forget that women have desires and lives outside of our inflated sense of influence and importance. We tend to forget that the poor could have been the rich, had they been born to a different family. So, too, do we forget the humanity and dignity of our adversaries.

When Forgotten walked into the camp, out of his cabin, every man stood, as though at attention. But whenever Rothschild hopped the fence, not a one cared to meet his eye. The man commanded a terrible admiration, even when you didn't know just who he was. That evening, he looked almost dignified: his thick beard had been trimmed neatly, and he wore a fine suit—a far cry from the tattered rags in which I had seen him last. I looked up, then looked back down to my hand of cards, expecting him to either retire to his cabin or visit Forgotten's. Instead, he strode over to me and grunted, "You."

Suppressing the urge to give some irreverent reply, I turned to face him, putting on my usual facade of indifferent amusement. Without a word, he turned and walked off; I took this to mean I was to follow him, and did so. Fergus received the same treatment, but he followed without hesitation. We were marched over to Forgotten's cabin, and without so much as knocking, Rothschild opened the door. A quick glance to my right showed me Fergus' nervous twitch. My beating heart, though more subtle, expressed that same trepidation.

Peters and Forgotten waited inside for us, seated next to one another. Forgotten leaned forward with his elbows on the table, while Peters reclined in his chair, studying our faces. It's how I remember them, to this day. "So," said Forgotten, when the rest of us showed no sign of speech. "Are these your men for tonight?"

Rothschild nodded, and my brow knit. "I have his number," he muttered, producing a scrap of paper. "He should be alone in one of the penthouses. Owns a car. He can be back before sunrise." Both quite aware we were under scrutiny, Fergus and I did our best to remain calm and professional, not daring to so much as exchange glances. Forgotten nodded a few times, and Peters remained silent, apparently thinking. "I think you made a good choice," said Forgotten, tracing a design in the table with his ever-present knife. "Fergus is a good, strong one. One our best." The pride in his voice sounded almost paternal. "And Jackson, he's efficient. Did us proud with his last job; I think he can handle this one." Turning to me, he asked, "Do you think you can?"

After waiting a few seconds for more information, I confessed that I didn't know what this new job entailed. Forgotten made a sound as though to answer, but Peters cut him off with a motion. "You'll find out once you're there," he said, with an easy smile. "Forgive the clandestine nature of our work, but it's... sensitive. You understand." I didn't, but lied and said I did.

Fergus, who had until this point remained silent, raised his hand. Upon being given leave to speak, he asked, "Personnel or materiel?"

"Personnel," replied Rothschild, and Fergus smiled. While I scratched at my arm and tried to determine their meaning, Fergus and I were led back outside, to Rothschild's shack. He told us to wait, then hopped the fence again, returning with a hefty pack slung over his shoulder. This, he set in the doorway, and opened. Fergus was handed a fairly ornate wolf mask, of some light material (not at all like Forgotten's heavy helmet). I received a similar one, though mine was a crow. For himself,

Rothschild took a fox's likeness. "Wear something worth soiling," he instructed us, and the three of us hurried away to change.

Returning in a set of work clothes, I met Fergus doing the same. Rothschild had already changed out of his suit, his mask gripped in one hand. "Empty your pockets," he grunted; I produced my wallet, and he stuffed it in his pack, then shoved the whole thing into his cabin. Before I could even protest, he assured me, "You'll get it back. I'm in a hurry. Knife?" I showed him my pocket knife; he and Fergus shared a laugh, and he rifled in his pack for a trench knife, which he handed to me. "Souvenir." Becoming less and less certain of my involvement in this "job," I belted on the sheath. Not a moment later, I was following Fergus and Rothschild over the wall.

Perhaps it should be to my shame that I admit I hadn't explored Old Hampton much. The truth is, I desired to get away from it every Sunday. Though the company bore me no ill, the very atmosphere reeked of age and decay. I'd still take it over Priius' empty, clinical air, but I longed for a livelier place. Somehow, though, the back of Old Hampton proved less lively than the fore: we landed in an abandoned lot, where I suspect a gang would have taken up shop, had there been a gang in Priius outside of our little organization. None of us wore our masks, yet, so as not to limit our peripheral vision. Priius' side-streets weren't so tidy as its highways.

Rothschild led us with expert precision through a series of dark old alleys, where creatures rustled among long-forgotten trashbags full of rot and stink. This part of the city, John later told me, had been largely condemned thanks to a chemical spill during the war, and progress had overlooked it in the same way it had overlooked Old Hampton. Pausing at a half-shattered wooden door, Rothschild listened, his breathing still. His fingers gripped his knife all the more tightly, drawing it from its sheath by a few inches—and then he relaxed, pushed the door open, and crept inside.

The place had clearly been a meat factory, at one time: hooks and chains hung everywhere from the metal rafters, and the vast floor had once supported a maze of conveyor belts. Grimy windows allowed a scant trickle of the city's lights to shine through, illuminating enough of the floor to let us find our way to the far wall. Either by memory or touch, Rothschild knew to vault himself onto a creaking metal staircase there; I followed him, with the heavy Fergus taking up the rear. It held, though it groaned incessantly, and we made our way up the building.

A ladder took us to the roof access; it left grimy marks on my hands, which I wiped on my jeans. We had to carry our masks in our teeth, or at least I did. Once atop the flattened roof, Rothschild eyed Fergus, and then looked over at the next rooftop. Apparently satisfied, he sprinted to the end of the roof, then leapt over the slightly-raised edge, to land on the next roof over. The distance proved none too great: I leapt it easily, and Fergus followed behind. Before our silent tour guide could lead us further, though, I hissed, "Why not take the streets?"

Rothschild favored me with a particularly exasperated look, and muttered, "Because nobody else does at this time of night." Taking that to be the most I'd get from him, I silently leapt from rooftop to nearly-adjacent rooftop, until we stood at the edge of the last one in the row. From there, Rothschild gripped the drainpipe and carefully clambered down; it had been built of sturdy stuff, and supported our weights, one at a time. We landed in a recession cut for a rainway; thankfully, Rothschild climbed out of it. I wouldn't have put it past him to try to squeeze into that tiny space.

Rather than the dirt and sparse grass that covered the

ground around Old Hampton, we were once more on concrete, standing behind a strip mall. Rothschild opened a door for us, holding it and gesturing us inside with a smirk and a sweep of his arm. Once inside, the concrete and tile of the narrow hallway echoed mightily; we crept forward at a slow pace, lest some city guard or cleaning crew should have been wandering the buildings. The maintenance hallway did, however, prevent us from any eyes on the street: people were always driving to and from Candor Tower, as well as making trips through the city.

A brief snag caught us by surprise: Rothschild had intended to lead us to the stairwell up to the higher levels of the mall, but it had been locked. "Fergus?" he whispered, and the large man prepared himself to charge it. But it was a steel door, strong and secure; he could have easily hurt or even broken his shoulder. Fortunately, I'd neglected to empty my breast pocket: I had a cheap pen on hand. Catching Fergus' arm, I had him break the thing, and I knelt down to use the slender remnants to pick the lock. When I took too long, Rothschild took over for me; still, as I walked past him, he whispered, "Good job, that." I will confess that I had... some small swelling of pride.

The rest of the trip consisted entirely of creeping through maintenance areas and fire escapes, until we stood high up on the side of the penthouses, the chill night air brushing about our arms. One by one, Rothschild checked the windows, though I couldn't divine what he saw through the darkened glass. Up two flights, he finally stopped, pointing at a chalk mark on a sill. After trying the window, and finding it locked, he stepped aside. "Fergus," he said, again.

Fergus, that bear of a man, kicked the damn thing in. It shattered with more noise than I would have thought wise, given our earlier caution, and Rothschild urgently hissed for us to put on our masks, while he did the same. One by one, we leapt in past the shattered window; the smaller shards stuck in the soles of my boots, harmlessly. Still, I found my breathing and pulse both quickening at an alarming rate: what *were* we doing? I had expected another theft, or perhaps meeting some contact, but with Rothschild and Fergus having both drawn their knives, I began to fear we had some other purpose entirely.

Once inside, I could hear the thud of someone's feet on the floor. No lights were on inside, but those from outside gave off just enough of a glow that I could make out dim outlines of expensive furniture. Rothschild pointed a finger at Fergus, then at one side of a doorway; he took up a position there, back to the wall, knife raised. Increasingly nervous, I almost failed to respond to Rothschild's urgent motion for me to stand behind the bookshelf. He had already positioned himself on the other side of the door, which was now slightly ajar; through the fox's eye sockets, Rothschild watched the slit between the hinges.

I trembled, fingers flexing along the shaft of my knife. There came the click of a gun being loaded, despite firearms not being sold anywhere near Priius. The floor creaked slowly, and my heart threatened to burst. Creak. Beat. Creak. Beat. Creak. Leaning just far enough around the bookcase to see around its corner, I could make out a hazy silhouette in the doorway, making a cautious approach, barely nudging the door open further. The figure trembled slightly, walking forward with a gun raised. And Rothschild slammed the door with violence force against it. At the same time, Fergus grabbed it from behind; the figure cried out in pain as the huge man broke its little finger, prying the gun from its grasp. It had been on safety, anyhow, but we couldn't know that. A moment later, acting on nothing more than a barked order from Rothschild, my foot crashed solidly down on the man's gut, making him double over in pain.

Rothschild flipped on the lights, showing our victim to be a middle-aged man of no great charisma, with a bald patch marring his head of chocolate hair. "You speak, you die," Rothschild growled; the man was crying quietly thanks to his broken finger, but offered no resistance. He knew himself beaten. Rothschild was quick to gag him with a sock from his drawer, binding him with a dampened undershirt. A burlap sack from the kitchen over his head, a bit of twine to secure it, and the car keys from the dresser, and we were making our way back down the fire escape.

At the time, I dared not say anything, but even then I knew that I had now involved myself in something much more sinister than I had realized.

XV.

Once we had made our slow, silent journey back down the fire escape, Rothschild led us through the parking lot to our captive's car. Though the man's arms remained bound, Rothschild refused to lower the gun we had taken from him until he was seated in the back, with Fergus and I to either side of him. With Rothschild driving, we pulled out into the streets, one hand on each of the bound man's arms.

He cried for the first minute or so; then, to his credit, he remained silent, possibly trying to remember the course we were taking. For now, we removed our masks, and quietly enjoyed that small relief. Slowly, carefully, attracting no attention from the other drivers, the luxurious vehicle rolled along the darkened streets. The trip took only a few minutes; we parked in the abandoned lot behind the meat factory, then led our hostage through the doors, under the cover of night.

Once inside, Rothschild made a gesture to Fergus, who easily upended the man while our spymaster tied a chain around his legs. From there, he was suspended upside-down from one of the low-hanging meathooks; we replaced our masks, and removed the bag over his head. "Mr. Lampton," said Rothschild, gathering up a chain in his hands, "welcome to Hell. Mr. Crow, if you would be so kind, please show our distinguished guest all the hospitality he deserves, while I fetch a few things." With that, he walked away with deliberate speed, leaving Lampton there to dangle.

I recognized the name, in a vague way: it had been among those on the records. A member of Parliament, then, or at least a former one. His unique importance eluded me, then, but a chill ran through me as I realized the heat of the flames with which we played. Face reddened with anger, humiliation, and blood, our "guest" angrily sputtered, "Who in the goddamned hell are you people?"

"I'm Mr. Wolf," chuckled Fergus. "This is Mr. Crow, and Mr. Fox just left. We're your hosts for th' evening."

The man struggled against his restraints, uselessly, and did his best to sit up. "I'm a member of the Licenian Parliament!" he snapped, as if that would make us let him go. "You'll be fucking shot for this. You think you can kill me? You think you can get away with..." He trailed off, staring into our masks. "What do you want?" he then asked, more calmly. "You want money? You've got it. Thousands of dollars, all yours; I'll pay in cash, if you take me back. My wife will be back next week, with my children." My stomach clenched. "Let me go, and we can forget this insanity."

I knew better than to answer him. So, too, did Fergus. Whatever I had involved myself in, betraying them now would only get me killed. Besides, I didn't know what this man had done, nor even if he was telling the truth. Forgotten and Peters had to have some reason for what they were doing, and until I found out, I would take no further action, I reasoned. He continued to plead and beg for perhaps a minute longer, before falling silent. At that point, Fergus held him upright for a while, so as not to render him unconscious.

Eventually, the sound of heavy boots on the hard floor made me look over; as they marched through the pale lights that shone through the windows, I could make out Rothschild, Peters (sporting a viper's head), and Forgotten. His crimson and gold were unmistakable in even that dim light. The trio stopped a few feet away from Lampton, and Fergus let him drop. The chains rattled and the man grunted, while Peters slowly tilted his head. For once, he was the first to speak.

"The Honorable George Lampton," murmured Peters, who

made no attempt to disguise his accent. He had taken the chains from Rothschild, and I could make out the silhouette of his hand gripping them tightly. "You must forgive me, sir; I am not one accustomed to speeches. I don't like them. I know you do, but this time, you're going to be listening. It's a rare enough experience for you, sir."

When Lampton tried to reply, Peters wasted no time in flogging him with a length of the chain, just once. Lampton let out a strangled cry; Peters continued speaking in his quiet, passionless way. "Shut up. I know who you are, but you don't know who I am. Let's fix that, shall we?" Fergus dragged over a stool, on which Peters sat, leaning down to stare into Lampton's narrowed, tear-filled eyes. "I'm one of the men you decided deserved to be tortured for being born in the wrong place."

Once more, he swung the chain up over his head, before bringing it down with a sickening smack over Lampton's gut. I winced at the sound, while Peters continued speaking. "I came over to your country because I felt mine was in the wrong, sir. It made me sick at heart to do it, but I had to take a stand for what I believed in. Your response was to have me interrogated for three long weeks." Rothschild sat down and opened up a small case, and handed Peters a scalpel from it; using it, he cut the buttons from Lampton's shirt, pulling it open over his chest. "In spite of scientific evidence and humanitarian pleas, you and certain other members of Parliament decided that torture is a perfectly acceptable tool in war." He paused, bringing the scalpel down to rest between Lampton's eyes. I dared not stir, but to my relief, he didn't cut. "Sir," he whispered, "we are at war."

In the pause that followed, Lampton took a shuddering breath. "Listen to me for a second," he urged, trembling uncontrollably. "That was years ago! The war is over; let it stay that way. Look. We've all done things we aren't proud of," he said, with a desperate quaver in his voice. "I was trying to do what I thought was right for the country. Let's talk this out, okay? I'm willing to make amends."

Throughout this process, Forgotten remained still, off to the side. He had his own battles to fight, but he knew that this one was Peters'. I sweated in my mask while that small, quiet man stared down into Lampton's eyes, silently allowing him to speak. His response came almost silently; I had to strain to make it out.

"'The defeat of the Dignity in Warfare bill is a great triumph for North Licenia,'" he recited, sliding off of his stool to kneel by Lampton's head. "'It will provide us with the necessary tools to defeat the Greenwood oppressors, who have offered their victims no such dignity. At times, good people must do terrible things to protect their loved ones.' Remarks by Mr. George Lampton, as recorded by the Candor News Network." Standing again, he drew a single thin line, a few inches long, down Lampton's chest. It barely broke the skin, but it drew droplets of blood that beaded up along the wound. "Sir, you have before you three veterans of your Grand War. One of Licenia, one of Greenwood, and one from overseas. We three bear scars which you cannot see, and which you cannot begin to imagine. And we intend to exact those 'amends' you promise in such a way that you will never forget your words." Another line, perpendicular to the first, a few inches long. "T." Lampton whimpered, squirming.

"'Pain is finite. It ends. But our dead soldiers won't come back to life; we have to protect those who still live by whatever means necessary,' grated Peters, spitting out each syllable like so much venom. "'The harm we cause is far less than the harm we would cause by inaction.' Do you believe your words now, sir? Did you ever believe them? Or are you just a spiteful, hate-filled

man who thought he could play war?" Another line down, a
little deeper, to the right of the first. "We have come for you, sir.
And we will come for the others, as well, unless our demands are
met." A quick curve, then a sharp hook that brought more tears
to Lampton's eyes. "R."

Pausing a moment, Peters stepped back, hoisting Lampton
halfway upright. "I could show you my scars, sir, but I doubt they
would move you. Still, I am not an unreasonable person, no
matter what you might think. No matter how you portray my
people. Tell us: does Parliament still hold meetings?" He waited,
but Lampton remained obstinately silent. Letting him sway
again, Peters walked over to Rothschild, who handed him a salt
shaker. Pouring a bit onto his hand, he returned to Lampton,
and smeared those crystals into the still-fresh wounds he had
caused. With a hiss of anguish, the captive man began to swear
and sputter. "Yes! God! Yes, damn it!" he growled, and Peters
relented.

To watch him work was a terrifying thing. Some part of me
knew that it would be right to stop this horrible process, but the
rest bound me where I stood, staring on in shocked silence. The
most frightening of all, to me, was Peters' dispassionate manner:
his fury was cold and tempered, not the heat of passionate
vengeance. "Thank you," he murmured, making the bloody edge
of the scalpel visible to Lampton. "Where do you meet?"

Once again met by silence, Peters shrugged, and cut another
line in the man's chest, a diagonal slash. "Go to Hell," cried
Lampton, and Peters let out a mirthless laugh. "I have been
there ever since your Grand War ended. Insofar as it did end. If I
walk out in the streets, I am not met with smiles, nor do I expect
to be. Nor am I met with scowls and words of hatred; at least
that would be bearable. You can meet hatred with pride,
knowing yourself a martyr." He made another slash in the other

direction, meeting the first at its apex. "No, I get averted eyes. Fear. People refuse to meet my gaze, because I'm a member of those savage Greens. Those savage, godless greens." A shorter mark connected the two. "A."

"It's one thing to be hated," he continued, eying the salt shaker. "But it's quite another to be ignored. The fear is one thing, but it's not even that that's the worst. The worst," he breathed, "is when people try their best to pretend that I don't exist." A slash directly down. "It's like being cut. But those cuts don't heal, because a knife only rends flesh. I gave up everything I had to save your worthless country, and I am offered neither pension, nor thanks, nor even acknowledgment." Two marks, this time: a short, horizontal line on either end of the first. "I."

"All of that, though—all of that, I could stand. The cruelest indignity of it all is one that my associate, here, and I share." Another downward slash. Blood had begun to run down Lampton's chest in hazy dribbles. "The knowledge that we fought, we watched our friends die, and we committed and suffered atrocity after atrocity to support a government that then went into hiding." The same perpendicular line. "T."

"I'm not here for myself, sir. I'm here for everyone else in this shithole." The scalpel pressed into Lampton's skin, slowly dragging itself down in a lazy arc. "I'm here for everyone who died to protect it. I'm here for everyone who died fighting against it. I'm here," he said, raising his voice to a conversational tone for the first time, "because I once believed in Licenia." The knife repeated the motion, cutting a deep circle in the whimpering, shaking Lampton's chest. "O."

"Now, you see, you are given two choices. You can end this torture, which is more than was ever offered me. All you have to do is let us know where and when we can find the rest of Parliament, and you can be the war hero you never got to be.

You can end it all—save lives. You can stop this madness."
Slash. This one was clumsy and deep, cutting a gash in him. "We just want to be afforded the simple dignity of having some say in what our government does. We want you to be... accountable, when you have been unaccountable for so many sins, so many years." Another curve and hook. "R."

"What's it to be, then?"

Dangling there from his chains, sobbing uncontrollably, with "TRAITOR" carved into his very flesh, Lampton made for a pathetic sight. Peters put the scalpel down, and sat once more, folding his hands under his chin and waiting patiently for an answer from Lampton. It might have been a full minute or two before he stopped crying; I forced myself to breathe, for I had been neglecting that necessity. "Kill me, you fucking animal," groaned Lampton.

Peters shook his head sadly, and slid off of his stool. He didn't even deign to respond to that, but I could see in his face a certain disappointment. Sorrow, even. Forgotten stepped slowly into his place, unscrewing the top of the salt shaker. "Mr. Snake and I had a bet," he said, pouring out a palmful of the stuff and then smearing it liberally over Lampton's chest. The man screamed in pain, sobbing again, chest heaving; Forgotten waited for him to finish. "He thought that if we could just teach you some empathy—make you understand what you had done, on even a small scale—that you would repent. He's a very nice man, that Mr. Snake." Into Lampton's open mouth, he poured the rest of the salt, causing him to gag and sputter. "How unfortunate for you, then, that I am, under this mask, the most human of any of us."

Forgotten stepped back, then took up the forgotten length of chain, bringing it down hard across Lampton's back. "Animals have some decency. Cats may toy with their prey, but they kill it eventually. Humans, though... Humans are vicious bastards." The chain rattled and clinked, then struck him again, leaving a red mark across his spine. "Fox, Wolf, Crow, Snake—all fine, respectable animals. But me? I'm a human. An animal would have the decency to kill you. I'm afraid that decency is among the many things I've forgotten." He unhooked Lampton from the post, then wrapped the chain loosely around his neck, suspending him by it. Those bloodshot eyes were wide with terror, staring at the golden snarl of Forgotten's face.

Forgotten took his right hand, and made a horizontal slash across the wrist. Then, to staunch the blood, he wrapped a cloth tightly around it. But that hand shriveled up into a claw; at this point, I stumbled away, pulling off my mask to be sick in a corner. I couldn't bear to watch any longer; I walked out of the factory, into the open air. But even so, I could hear Forgotten's voice echoing through the factory: "You can tell your friends in Parliament that the Forgotten will come for them. They will pay for their sins in blood, pain, and terror."

It wasn't until after Rothschild and Fergus had departed with Lampton that I stalked back over, to where Forgotten and Peters were walking away. I grabbed the former by his coat, and forced him to turn and face me, to see the horrified rage in my face. I called him a monster. I cursed them both. I told them that I would have no part of this, invited them to kill me. They remained silent until I had finished, shoving Forgotten back and staring between the two, prepared to defend myself.

Peters simply unbuttoned his shirt, removing it and standing still. There, in the dim predawn light, I could make out an endless pattern of scars, some long and narrow, others short and deep. Some bore discolorations, others looked as though they had been the victim of infections. Panting, I surveyed him. There were easily a hundred marks there.

"Jackson," he said, as quiet as ever, "you're a good person. I respect that, Jackson; I really do. But there is nothing you can say, nothing you can think or feel, that I haven't already. They drilled holes in my skin; they cut me, they beat me, they starved me. I don't care that they did that; not anymore." He stared deep into my eyes, which I have no doubt were wide with fear and confusion. "But I do not intend to allow it to happen to anyone else. Go, if you want; I won't hunt you. But I want you to understand why I'm doing this."

They walked away. I saw before me a fork in an endless stretch of road, with the fiery glow of the Licenian sunrise illuminating both paths. Wordless and numb, following a feeling, an instinct that I could not explain, I followed them back to Old Hampton.

XVI.

I had not much calmed down by the time we were back in Old Hampton. To be sure, I no longer felt the urge to savage the three ringmasters, but I still seethed at them. I managed to hold it back until Forgotten and Peters retired to the former's cabin; without receiving an invitation, I followed them in.

Peters looked mildly surprised to turn and see me, and I think Forgotten might have, as well, but I doubt it came as a total surprise to either. Closing the door behind me, I stood across from them, staring from one to the other for a long moment. I could feel my pulse starting to quicken, and my throat was still raw from my earlier sickness. Folding my arms across my chest, I finally said, "So. This is the glorious revolution?"

Peters put his head on his hand, and Forgotten slumped down into a chair, head tilted as he regarded me. For perhaps the first time since meeting the two of them, I found myself not intimidated, nor awed; merely disgusted, and with a strange sense of pity, particularly for Peters. I cannot pretend that his scars didn't move me. But so, too, did those I had seen inflicted today. I offered no further query until my initial question was answered; Forgotten finally replied, setting his knife down on the table. "Jackson," he said, in that same half-cheerful, half-patronizing tone as ever, "you came into this late. You didn't know our methods, and you don't really understand our goal. For that, I apologize, but there are some things that we just can't tell—"

With a sudden movement, I stepped forward and slammed my fist down on the table, knuckles rapping sharply on the surface. "You'd damn well better!" I remember yelling, gripped with a frustration more intense than I had ever felt when speaking to Mrs. Hughes. It wasn't often I interrupted

Forgotten, Peters, or Rothschild, but I was hot. "Ever since I came here, I've been playing blindfolded, guessing at information and doing as you bade me for a shady explanation of a shadowy cause. All I get are hints and suggestions of connections, but nobody ever tells me anything; I'm left in the dark. At best, I get sob stories about how badly you were treated in or after the war. I've served you faithfully," I snapped, "without so much as knowing what I went to do. I think I deserve a minute's honesty."

While I stood there bellowing, Peters looked as though he might have fallen asleep: he sat with his chin on his chest, eyes closed. Only when I finished speaking did he look up, fixing me with a weary, jaundiced gaze. "Are you finished?" he asked. We stared at one another for a moment, before I gave a short nod. "For now, yes."

Without moving, he closed his eyes again. "Then allow me to remind you that you've been here all of a month, and in that time, you've successfully carried out a total of two missions for us. You did them well, but you've only done two things. You're a relative unknown, with connections, however tenuous, to our enemy. You came out of nowhere at an opportune moment. I don't dislike you, Jackson, but you're unpredictable as yet."

Forgotten stirred at this point, picking up where Peters left off. He spoke softly and earnestly; I took a seat, if just so that I could lean in to hear his words. "I had been going to say that there are some things we can't tell the... uninitiated. Those we don't know would give their lives to the cause. Because we stand, Jackson, on the precipice of great change. This is, as you put it, the glorious revolution, but I regret to say that you came in on the tail end of it. You've been useful, so far, and may prove more useful in the future, if you can just stick with us. But you're right." He sighed, leaning back again. "You deserve a minute's honesty. So ask what you want to know, and I'll..." He paused to resume sawing his knife against the table's edge. "I'll see if I can answer."

I sat across from him, listening to the hiss of the lamp and considering what I really wanted to ask. I had many questions, but didn't know how many he'd answer then, so I decided to go for the big one, first. "You keep talking about the wrongs that Beckstein committed, but you just crippled a man who, for all I know, is innocent of everything but holding a belief you think is incorrect. What makes you anything but a terrorist?"

He let out a short, sharp bark of laughter, and responded much sooner than I'd expected. Much more frankly, too: "Nothing. We are terrorists, as surely as we're revolutionaries." I opened my mouth, but he allowed me no time to speak. "As trite an observation as it may be, the truth remains that history is the polemics of the victor. The Greens are portrayed as bloodthirsty mongrels because they lost. An unsuccessful revolutionary is called a radical, or a madman. And 'freedom fighter' is just a nice way to describe someone willing to kill and die for an idea. In this case, we're literal freedom fighters; we're fighting to wrest back the freedom—the right—to an accountable government. But make no mistake: we are most definitely terrorists."

While he paused to grab up a bottle of beer, I gave him a disgusted look. "What happened to activist campaigns and appeals to the public?"

As soon as his swig was complete, he shrugged. "Hard to make appeals and campaigns when there's exactly one media outlet, and it owns the government. It's lulled the people to sleep; we intend to wake them up. Here; give me a second." Standing, he searched the walls for a while, before plucking down an aerial photograph of the city, laying it before me. "The thing you'll notice about Priius is that it's the showiest city in the whole damn world. Look at all those skyscrapers. Giant pricks thrust up into the air. They're a symbol, but they're practically empty at night; there's not a lot of people left to hurt. But if one were to be taken to its knees..." He spread a hand. "That doesn't happen by accident. People wouldn't just forget it. They'd start to wonder who did it, and if it might happen again."

Here, I frowned, looking up into his mask. "So, you're trying to be noticed. Get everyone up in arms against you, to 'wake them up.' Not much into winning hearts and minds, huh?" He chuckled, but let me speak. Peters remained where he was, as still and silent as could be. "I guess you want people to start asking why the government doesn't pull its head out of its ass and do something?"

He nodded, pointing at me. "That's right. Smart man. The government's goal is to make sure people forget it exists; it's a short leap from 'What are they doing?' to 'Who's in charge?' to 'When was the last time we voted?' And so, our goal is to make sure they never forget again." The intensity in his voice seemed edged; I could hear his excitement growing as he spoke. "We'll remain shadows in the mist; a threat so uncertain and yet so real that paranoia and fear take deep root. This won't be our revolution; it will be the people's revolution. But we'll guide them all along the way; we'll help them unravel the truth, until they clamor for Anton Beckstein's blood to paint Candor Tower, and his head to swing in Franklin Square." Hearing him was like hearing a man describe a church revival. His words were tinged with agitation, full of a bloodthirsty sort of spirit.

"Fine," I said, a little unnerved by this show of fervor. "I have other questions, though. For one, what evidence do you have that Beckstein was behind any of this?"

Forgotten and Peters exchanged a look. They turned back to

me, slowly, and Forgotten picked his words carefully. "Forgive me," he began, "because that's a difficult question to answer. The problem, here, is that we're dealing with a conspiracy—and that makes us conspiracy theorists. And conspiracy theories are based more on the lack of evidence than on the presence of it." I knit my brow, unimpressed, but he held up a hand. "However, we've received enough evidence to rouse suspicions. After Peters and I found Rothschild again, we... contracted him to hunt out the cause of the lack of media coverage. He hit dead ends in every investigation, but Beckstein was a commonality among almost all of them, if just as a name mentioned casually. It didn't take much research to peg him as the head of Candor Network; that's a suspiciously advantageous post. Considering their monopoly, which nobody's dared to oppose, it seemed..."

He waved a hand. "It was a good lead. And those papers you brought confirmed our suspicions: Candor donated heavily to the war-mongers. The war brought Candor ratings, and gave the government an excuse to suspend elections. Today, it's never mentioned in the media that elections were never resumed. Nor is anything else related to the government. They've gone silent, and the only channels belong to Candor." Pausing there to take a breath, he looked up at me. "It doesn't strike me as coincidence. What about you, Jackson?"

I couldn't answer him. Not immediately. I wanted to believe him—to believe that I had sided with the right people, joined the right cause. But I couldn't quell my deep misgivings from the scene I had witnessed earlier. Disregarding his question, I asked one in return: "So, what's your plan? Torture people until you find out what you want to know? Why not just find Beckstein and shoot him in the head?" I'll confess that, in a moment of sarcasm, I added, "Or would that be too 'decent?'"

If my barb caught him, he made no indication. Instead, he

shook his head. "That's just the thing, Jackson: I don't want Beckstein dead. Far from it: I want him alive and questioned. Tortured if we have to, but I want to make him so afraid that we don't even have to touch him. Just find him, render him helpless, and make him talk. But before he'd be truly helpless, we have to tear his empire out from under him: weaken his supports. And those supports, as far as we can tell, are Parliament. It's just a theory, I'll admit," he cautioned, "but even if he's not the ringleader, we'll find out who is. Ideally, though, the people will take care of this before we do. If we have to blow up a few buildings to wake them up, so be it. I just want to revive democracy."

I turned now to Peters, who had huddled back down into himself, apparently lost in thought. "But not you, huh? You want vengeance. What happens if we succeed, if we find Beckstein or whoever and end this thing? Do you just keep kidnapping and torturing members of Parliament until you're satisfied?"

The look of disgust with which I was met silenced me. Peters regarded me with narrowed eyes, much the same way he had sneered at Lampton just earlier. Without his characteristic reserve, he snapped, "Goddamn it, Jackson, give me some credit. I'm not some petty child; I'm not taking an eye for an eye. And I'm not a sadist, either: I didn't enjoy what I did, and I'm not proud of doing it." He leaned forward, resting his hands on his knees and glaring at me. "Lampton was right about one thing: sometimes, good people have to do terrible things. If you're looking to keep your hands clean, you're in the wrong damn place. This is filthy, dirty work; this is war, Jackson." I sensed a weariness even in his anger. He sounded tired and sore as he spoke. "What we're doing isn't moral. People are going to get hurt. But it's necessary to achieve our goals, and our goals are worthy. Life isn't black and white; what's good isn't always what's merciful. If your only concern is in throwing moral trappings on your actions, then get out now."

I realize, now, that I had mistaken his expressions: I thought he was lost in contemplation, utterly calm after the gruesome punishments he had inflicted. It wouldn't be until later, in the quiet contemplation of my own actions, that I'd suddenly understand his silence. Peters spent almost all of his life in remorse. And at times, it would grow so thick that it consumed him. If you've never felt that, then take my word when I tell you that it will eat at your very being until you're too weary even to stand.

Silence hung over all of us in the ensuing minute. Chastised but still petulant, I stared at my hands, while Peters leaned back in his chair again, regarding the ceiling. Eventually, Forgotten asked, "Do you have any more questions, Jackson?"

"No," I grunted. "I think I've heard enough."

"That's fine." He nodded, as calm as I've ever seen him. "Then it's time you make your choice. Think on it. Think on it hard and well. I know we've given you little enough reason to trust us, but I think you'd be an asset to our cause, should you have the stomach for it." He paused for a moment, then faltered uncomfortably over his next words. "I've learned better than to force someone's hand in matters of trust, so I'm leaving it open: there will be no repercussions, should you want to leave. But let me say this, Jackson."

His hands moved briefly to his helmet, and for a moment, I thought he'd remove it. Perhaps the thought crossed his mind, but in the end, he left it on. Leaning toward me, he said, "Whatever you do, wherever you go, just remember that we aren't villains. We're trying to do what's right, Jackson; I promise you, that's all we've ever wanted. You're a good man, Jackson.

But so am I."

To this day, it remains one of the most difficult decisions I've ever made. And I've made more than a few in these last months. Perhaps you can't imagine how I felt to hear all that I'd heard and think that I might be forsaking my one chance to really make a difference in the world. You've had dreams, though. Haven't you? Didn't you grow up and say to yourself that one day, you'd fix everything? It made me sick at heart to say it, and don't think I don't still wonder if I did the right thing by it. But I stared him right in that golden mask, and said:

"Where do we go from here?"

XVII.

Returning to civilian life for the next days proved a difficult change for me. I do not recall when I next enjoyed restful sleep: Lampton's crippled hand haunted my dreams, alongside the bloodied words Peters had carved into my mind. "We're still considering our next move," Peters had told me. "At any rate, you deserve a bit of a break; your first real mission is never easy. You'll be back in the action soon enough, though." I remember wondering, even then, how he must view me: the man who had retched and rebelled against a single act of interrogation, while Peters had been forced to endure the blood forced upon his own hands in silence.

Work offered some solace, in routine and in the company of people who approached that asymptotic standard of normality. At that time, I needed some normality in my life; I am yet young, and the world in which I had grown shifted rapidly around me. I had expected changes, moving to the city, but I could never have anticipated the people I would meet or the things I would do. Life had become a blur around me, events swirling too rapidly for me to comprehend them. Perhaps that explains the decisions I made at that time. Even if it does, it hardly excuses them. But, forgive me: you aren't here to listen to me beat myself over past mistakes. Though... I suppose that's the entire point of this exercise, isn't it?

John remained my favorite of my fellow janitors; I found myself increasingly taking shifts to complement his, at times covering for him, should he have some other obligation to which he needed to attend. I couldn't guess at what these might be, for by his own account, the university at which he had once lectured had never contacted him since the war. But then, getting him to talk about himself proved somewhat difficult. I could tell he had a story—a long and melancholy story, at that. He had made that clear enough when he had once opened up to me. But no matter how I tried to peek into the private world of his memories, he politely and kindly shut me out.

"I'm tired, Jackson," he remarked, one day. "I'm getting old; I know it, and there's no use denying it. Now isn't the time to dwell on the past and relive old battles." He had fought his fair share of them, I knew. He had worked as a janitor for years, acquiring calluses and a bad back, and yet had been offered neither thanks nor reward—the most educated man I personally know. He had fought and lost his battles so far, and saw no point in perpetuating them. And I, in my selfish shortsightedness, saw no need to offer him either encouragement nor assistance. Instead, I clung to him like a child, using him as a surrogate father while my own laid far across the country. How could I expect mail when I had no address, a call from no phone?

I suspect that I tethered myself around his ankles, forcing him into a servitude no less demeaning than his servitude to Candor. I suspect also that he was too good-hearted to tell me that. I... consider myself honored to call myself his friend, though perhaps that would be presumptuous. I considered him my friend, at least, and hope the feeling was reciprocated. At the time, I considered myself an independent person. Indeed, I wonder if I didn't take some pride in my selfless befriending of this "friendless" man. Those days seem to drift further from me as I speak of them, and it's a welcome sensation. My arrogance then disgusts me now. I suppose I'm hardly endearing myself to you with this constant self-abuse, but my words are heartfelt. This testimony I offer is as much a chronicling of my flaws as it is the tale of my eventual transformation into the man you now see.

Perhaps I repeat myself. It's not easy to recall what I have and haven't said, for my thoughts are scattered and restless. I find that a few faces return constantly to my memory: John's, certainly, but also faces painted in blood and pain. Deirdre keeps creeping back to mind. I loved her, you know. Not in the way you might expect—at least, not to my knowledge. But I loved her as a friend, in a way that I haven't enjoyed since I was a boy. She and John were the two true comforts of my work.

Saturday evening, I worked late, lazily mopping the cafeteria's tiles in a distracted, hazy motion. I finished my assigned tasks, simply in more time than normal; I received no overtime pay, and so long as the work was complete, being a little late was no concern. Even the bureaucracy had more pressing matters than the punctuality of a janitor. When my work was complete, I crept downstairs, delaying the inevitable meeting by not using the elevator. I am not typically one to shirk from company or interaction, nor have I ever been. And yet, for one of the first times in my life, I now knew what it felt like to be shy.

I stood in the lobby, acutely aware of even the most miniscule flaws and specks on my jumpsuit. Wondering if I stank, and only failed to notice it by being continually subjected to it, I discreetly pressed my tongue to the back of my hand, let it dry, then sniffed the result. Shrinking internally, I shifted from foot to foot, pondering my likelihood of making it past the couple who stood before the counter without attracting attention before making it to the door. In a moment of weakness, I started in that direction, my confused feet stumbling awkwardly across one another. But the couple moved away before I could even reach them, and I heard my name being called cheerfully from the counter. I would like to believe I offered nothing but a smile and a greeting in kind, but I fear that I may have squawked.

"Hey, Jackson!" she said again, smiling to me as I sheepishly slunk to her counter. "Heading out for the night?" I nodded with a timid grin, and we made small talk for a while. She spoke to me of her parents—they were doing well; she'd just received a nice letter from them, and planned to call them in the morning. I mumbled something about my own being well, though I had no more reason to believe that than to believe they were both dead; internally, I resolved to send them a letter with Candor Tower as the return address, and ask the postal department to hold any response for me.

Somewhere amongst the easy laughter and polite remarks, I was gripped with an urge to do something that a normal person would do in my situation. It's something of a blur, but I think I cut her off in the middle of a sentence, blurting out, "Tomorrow's my day off—would you like to get something to eat?"

I immediately regretted it: she looked uncomfortable, glancing down with a nervous chuckle. At that point, I knew I had become attracted to her, and in more than a purely intellectual way. Still, that remained secondary to my tentative friendship with her; desperate to not alienate one of the few people whose company I really enjoyed, I gave a self-conscious grin and added, as if I had meant it all along, "Just... as friends, of course." Whether or not she believed that was my initial intent, she at least gave me a more assured smile, nodding. "That sounds nice," she said. We worked out a time, and I promised to meet her at Candor. Soon afterward, I hurried out the door, more excited than I had any reason to be.

I stopped by John's Kitchen, on a sudden whim. Mrs. Hughes was there, and she looked me up and down once, her brow knitted when she saw my tremendous grin. "Rob a bank?" she asked, lighting up a cigarette. With a laugh, I sat down, and told her the good news—that I was going to have dinner with a very nice young lady. As friends. She just chuckled, shook her head, and took my order. "Well, don't bring her here," she eventually said, before disappearing into the kitchen. I ate, and while I ate, Mrs. Hughes studied me. She didn't say much, the entire evening, but I couldn't shake the feeling that she was taking my measure.

My sleep that night was as restless as ever, and I woke before sunrise, unable to fall back asleep. With precious little else to do, I walked to the shower-house, to wash up for the day's events. But before I could get to it, Milcher rushed over to grab my wrist, tugging me away. "Forgotten's in there," he warned me, with wide eyes. I nodded slowly, curious as to the urgency of his warning; ordinarily, if the door was closed, you just knocked. But Milcher offered no explanation, aside from, "You d-don't go in there when Forgotten's in there." I assured him that I wouldn't, and he relaxed, nodding cheerfully. Placing his huge arm around my shoulders, he led me to his post, and we played cards by candlelight. A few minutes later, the sound of the shower door closing made me turn around, in time to see a silhouette trudging back toward Forgotten's cabin, clutching its side.

"You don't go in there wh-when Forgotten's in there," Milcher repeated, following my gaze.

After showering and changing into my nicer clothes, I played a few more hands with Milcher, and we kept each other company. The more we spoke, the more I became certain that the poor man wasn't entirely... there. A bit slow, if you follow my meaning. Still, he had a good heart; I admired Milcher for that. When I mentioned that I had a dinner date, he congratulated me several times, laughing and smiling pleasantly. I regret that I didn't get to know him better, now that I think about it. I think I was too busy pitying him.

My thoughts are as scattered as the day that happened. Let me try to focus.

I met Deirdre for dinner and immediately decided that I needed to buy a new suit. In truth, her clothes were no nicer than mine, but I was wracked with an odd anxiety. She seemed as relaxed as ever, and I reminded myself that I ought to be, as well: it wasn't a date; we were just enjoying an evening out as friends during a time when neither of us happened to be working. Neither of us owned a car, so we walked along the evening streets, keeping one eye on each other and one eye on the passing cars.

It would be difficult to recount what we discussed that day, for we discussed anything that came to mind. I think both of us were so relieved to find someone else as uncomfortable as we were that we just rambled at each other about everything, desperately hopping from subject to subject so as not to let the thread of conversation die. Neither one of us wanted to allow a pause to enter, lest it grow awkward. More than it already was, that is.

We crept into the first restaurant we saw, and ended up slightly overdressed for the occasion: the place was more like a cafe than a proper restaurant, and fairly empty save for some younger folks. Much like ourselves, in fact: they had likely come from their low-paying jobs, to relax for an evening before returning to life's little worries. A hyperactive waitress took our orders, and we enjoyed more nervous, raucous laughter at unamusing jokes in the meantime. And yet, for all the strangeness of the meeting, I think we became more calm in each other's presence. We were both afraid of one another, you see; we just had very different reasons for it.

The evening wore on, and we ate a moderately-palatable

meal, while we calmed down a bit. We were able to have real conversations—we spoke of our favorite books, comparing motifs and characters and plots. She talked about the live theatre show she had once seen as a girl, and I told her anecdotes from the farm. The more she spoke, the more I liked her, and as I grew more comfortable, I grew more bold. I tend to be fairly direct, in conversation—had you guessed?—but I was in rare form that night, or so I believed in the giddy rush of the moment.

"So," I grinned, twirling my fork in my spaghetti, "I hope your boyfriend doesn't mind you having dinner with a strange fellow from work."

She laughed, shaking her head. "I haven't got a boyfriend, Jack. What made you think that?"

With a shrug, I turned my head away. "Well, you know. You just... seem like the type who'd be in a relationship. I imagine you've got a whole crowd trailing after you."

That remark made her glance aside, drumming her fingers on the table; I'd screwed up again. "No," she eventually said, forcing a smile. "No, I can't say that I've got much of a crowd. I've never had a boyfriend."

My eyebrows raised in genuine surprise. "You haven't? I'm shocked. You're doing at least one man a grave disservice, Deirdre."

She made no response, just gave me an odd smile and resumed eating. From then on, I kept my remarks purely aromantic, and away from flirting. Certainly, she wasn't pretty in the conventional way, but I saw no reason she should react so strongly. Perhaps, I decided, she simply didn't have interest in me. That was acceptable, of course; what made her attractive was her mind, and I could share that without any sort of romance. Still, as I escorted her to the bus stop later that evening, I couldn't help but feel that I had said something I shouldn't have.

XVIII.

I saw Deirdre to the bus stop and waited for her to board it, for I knew better than most that the streets of Priius are not so clean at night. Crime rates remained nonexistent, of course, for those who would be missed had already cleared the streets by then. Only those few who scrabbled in the city's filth for the leftovers they could not scavenge elsewhere fell prey to each other, and no reports were ever filed. But I had been largely insulated from them, as they knew not to enter Old Hampton. Indeed, it seemed to me that I was the only person who didn't know any better.

Walking back along the deserted streets took longer than usual: I seldom traveled far past Candor Tower's flashing lights, and my steps were slow and meandering, that night. In my discussions with the men at Old Hampton, I had learned to avoid the darkened places and sidestreets, for there laid the beggars and ruffians whom the city guard swept away with the dawn. Instead, I walked along avenues of unbroken light, where the beautiful, painted faces of Licenia's favored people smiled on me. At times, I smiled back, but I grew increasingly inclined to a melancholy pondering as the minutes wore by.

Upon my arrival in the city, I had thought Priius to be a collection of individuals who concealed themselves from one another, interacting like the teeth of a gear: a brief contact to keep the machine moving, but no more. But now, I felt the beginnings of a new theory creeping in. The city's inhabitants formed a web of interconnected threads and points, just like the towns I knew while growing up. The difference came in the size: in a rural town, you could see the entire web, if you just asked the right questions and knew the right people. But in a place like Priius, only a few threads were visible. To me, at least;

Rothschild surely saw many, many more. For that matter, so did Peters and the Forgotten. Perhaps Mrs. Hughes. Those closest to me remained the greatest enigmas, for they offered me just enough of a glimpse into themselves to let me see the complexity, but not so much to make sense of it.

I continued thinking, trying in vain to expand the mental web of connections which slowly took shape in my mind. But gradually, the grasping at straws began to overtax my weary mind, and I turned instead to distracting mundanities. I stared at the sidewalk's cracks and grooves, watching the grass which still clung to life among the concrete gardens. I looked straight ahead, at the endless array of streetlights, stretching out into infinity and across the slopes and curves of Licenia's northern hills. And I looked from there to the sky, but only briefly—it held nothing but a yawning void, and that blank immensity confused and unsettled me.

From streetlight to streetlight I crept, following the lines and pathways which had grown along the tangled wilderness of Priius' streets. But as I stepped into Franklin Square, the very heart of the city itself, I saw a silhouette standing in the darkness of a broken streetlight. A red-orange ember still glowed in the filament, and that light proved enough to show me the drawn and worried face of Fergus. At my approach, he had silently drawn his knife, and when I drew close enough to see him, he raised it. But on seeing my face, he relaxed, though he didn't smile.

"Fuck, Jackson, you scared me," he breathed, shifting from foot to foot. He wouldn't stop glancing around, anxiously passing his knife from one hand to the other. "Look, I'm in a bad way. The boss sent me here to meet two guys, but they didn't show. You've gotta help me, Jackson; I don't think I can do this alone." I had never seen him frightened before. He spoke barely above a whisper, just loudly enough that I could hear him. There were no others visible on the streets, but he seemed paranoid, uncertain.

"Fine," I said, after just a moment's pause. "What do you need?"

Fergus took a deep breath, swallowed once, then stared straight into my eyes. Speaking slowly and carefully, he told me," I need you to go into that building, find the supports for the television, and help me blow them up."

I glanced up to see that yes, this skyscraper had a television mounted on it. But the supports for such a screen had to be immense, or at least immensely powerful. "How?" I finally asked, straining to make out his face in the dark.

He shifted his weight, very slowly, and showed me the backpack he was carrying. The thing was tremendous, with an external frame. And when I flipped open the top, using the dim light to see inside, I recoiled as though struck. "Holy shit, Fergus! You've been carrying—" He clamped his hand over my mouth for a moment, then withdrew it apologetically. "Yeah," he hissed. "And I don't fancy carrying them any longer. You with me, Jackson? Because if you're not, I'm going back to Old Hampton." He shivered. "I don't much like the idea of disappointing him."

For a moment, I held my face in my hands, shaking my head. Less than an hour before, I had been eating dinner with Deirdre. I was still wearing my town clothes, though he, too, wore his waistcoat and slacks. "Oh, my God, this is insane," I groaned, mind reeling. "We could level the whole damn building with that much ordnance. Where did we even get...?"

"Rothschild," he shrugged. "He knows things I don't want to know. But come on, Jack, I need you with me on this. Are we doing it? Or do we go back and tell Forgotten that we..." He stopped there, and frowned down at me thoughtfully. "That I couldn't handle it," he amended. "I'm sorry, Jack. I don't need to pressure you: this isn't your assignment. Two of the other guys were supposed to do it, and I guess they got cold feet. I guess I'm getting them, too," he laughed, before sighing. "Fine. Fine. I'll head on back."

"No." I had to force the word out, but I did manage to say it. "Hang on, Fergus. I might help, but... this is crazy. How many people are in there?"

He shook his head, staring at me as if to assure me of his sincerity. "Nobody's there. Forgotten said so. He said he checked it out, and everybody's gone, this time of night. We won't hurt anybody, as long as we do it now. He just wants to blow the TV up, not a bunch of people; he said it's because that Lampton asshole didn't get the results he wanted. Didn't get Parliament to come clean."

Already, I could feel my pulse racing, and hear the dull thud of my heart in my ears. "So now we blow up part of a goddamn building," I snapped, pacing agitatedly. "I swear to God, if I get out of this alive, I'm getting *out*. This is... fuck, Fergus, this is nuts. But I'm with you." He stared at me, and I reached out to grasp his meaty hand, giving it a shake and meeting his gaze. "I'm with you, because I don't want you getting yourself killed. But you owe me one for this."

He shook his head out, then nodded. "Yeah, yeah, whatever you want. Can we get moving, though? You ain't got a backpack full of..." He glanced from side to side once more, then muttered, "...stuff."

My hands trembling with uncertainty, I knelt down to examine the door to the building. My hand touched the smooth glass of the door: easily broken, but what alarms might that sound? Clumsily, I felt around my pockets for something that might help me with the lock, wishing I had the tool belt I used for my job. "Hey," I hissed to Fergus, "do you have a screwdriver, or scissors, or anything?"

Fergus, in his typical manner, lifted his foot and kicked the door, shattering it. He leapt in over the shards, and took off running down the hallway; I swore under my breath, following him into the marble floors of another skyscraper. But over the sound of our feet on the tiles came the shrill ringing of an alarm.

"Shit!" I hissed, ducking down beneath the counter of a cash register. "We've got to get out. Why'd you have to kick the door in?"

Fergus impatiently waved for me to be quiet. Leaning toward my ear, he whispered, "Calm down and follow me." I glared at him, but he took no notice: instead, he listened for a few moments. Nothing could be heard, save for the ringing alarm and my heart in my ears. Without a sound, Fergus slipped out from around the counter, and positioned himself behind a display table. I took a moment to calm down and listen for myself, while peeking up over the lip of the counter.

The dim light from outside helped to confirm what my nose had already suspected: we were inside an upper-class clothing store, with the acrid scent of mixed perfumes and scented candles. Distantly, I heard Fergus sniffle: it irritated his nose more than mine. Clothing racks and displays littered the immaculate floors. There were plenty of places to hide, at least, and the dim lighting assisted with that. But my dress shoes were noisy: I yanked them off and grabbed them by the shoelaces, then hurried over to hide between a rack of dresses; their length would help to hide my feet. After waiting until I could hear Fergus' feet pattering on the tile, I checked for a way up. Other than the exit signs, little enough in the store was illuminated. Nonetheless, the brass rails of a spiral staircase gleamed in the light through the windows. I crept out to see Fergus already poised beside it, waiting for me.

"If there's security, it's probably waiting by the elevators," he muttered, a knife clenched in his fist. "We go up the stairs. You can get back down those, but in an elevator, you're stuck in a box." He could likely see the way I shook, for he took hold of my shoulders. "I need you to stick with me, man. We're gonna get through this. Forgotten wouldn't have sent us if it were too dangerous." I kept my opinion to myself, and just gave him a sullen nod.

With that, we crept up the stairs, walking on the balls of our feet and fearing every tap of our feet on the tiles. The alarm had been shut off, so that every breath I took rattled heavy in my lungs. From time to time, I had to force myself to resume breathing, for I had bated my breath in my anxiety. Fergus, I must admit, proved a much more stolid companion: he resembled a lion in pursuit of prey. For my part, I felt more the antelope.

The higher we ascended through the flights of expensive clothing and gaudy accessories, the more I allowed myself to relax. I could not even begin to avail myself of any perception of time, and I assumed the alarm had shut off automatically after it had run its course. Priius was, after all, a safe city. The rabble knew to keep to their holes. The friendly security guards you saw in the corners of stores, there to help you with directions or questions you might have, also bore cudgels. Pistols, now, I take it. But at the time, they had nothing to fear. Aside from us, that is—but we were ghosts and feral dogs, then, and nothing to be concerned about.

You must pardon me if my account of that night is hazy: my memory of it is marred and fogged, and I had to get much of it second-hand. Adrenaline surged through my body at a rate I had never before experienced, and it stilled my thoughts, in a way.

Even as we neared the floor of our destination, high above the streets, my pulse refused to return to normal. All the same, it nearly stopped when we heard the distant sound of conversation from above. I almost froze in place, but Fergus jerked on my arm and hurried me up the stairs. From there, we huddled together under the nearest display, burrowing away from the streetlights seeping in through the windows. The conversation drew nearer, along with the sound of footsteps: two men chatting, relaxed.

"...you, it was probably nothing," insisted the first voice. My eyes had somewhat adjusted to the light, and I thought I could make out the outline of a foot as it fell on the tiled floor. I began alternately holding my breath and then breathing slowly and deeply, occasionally grimacing at the stench of the thousand-or-so mingling perfumes.

The other man, who sounded as though he were walking slightly before his comrade, spoke with a breezy indifference. "You're probably right," he said, as he approached our hiding-place. "Still, might as well earn our keep, eh? I'm guessing it's a couple of kids out past bedtime who were playing ball. Little urchins don't know better'n to stay out of the streets."

The first gave a slight chuckle. My blood ran cold: they continued to approach us. "Can you blame 'em, though? I'd hate growing up in one of them penthouses. No space to yourself. No yard for a dog. Every boy needs a dog, don't you think?"

They stopped, so close that I could have touched one leather shoe. For a desperate moment, I contemplated it: reaching out and grabbing his ankle, flipping the display on the pair so that Fergus could incapacitate them. But how many more might come? What if I failed? Failure has always been one of my biggest fears, you know. I didn't want to let Fergus down. And I certainly didn't want to be killed in a daring, foolish escape.

Pressed in close against Fergus' hot, sweating bulk, I became aware of every itch, every tingle in my body all at once. The men continued to talk, and naturally, they lingered near the display where we hid. It took all of my willpower not to move, not to breathe, not to make a sound.

It's a crazy sort of relief to me that Fergus was the one who sneezed.

XIX.

The next few minutes, like the rest of that night, are little more than a distant dream to me, but I shall relate them as honestly as I may. Insofar as Fergus can be believed—and I have faith in him, of all people—I can vouch for the truth of it. There came first a deathly pause, with both the guards and the two of us trying to make sense of what had just happened. And then, or so I am told, I snapped.

With my hands above my head, planted on the underside of the display, I rose with a terrible cry. The products, mostly fragile bottles of cologne, toppled onto poor bastards who lingered too long near us. Hardly a second later, Fergus fell upon the one to the left, while I gave the other a punch to the jaw. I remember the blood on my knuckles, at least. Taken by surprise as they were, the two had little chance to draw their clubs; we fell together, grappling on the floor, rolling back and forth in the jagged shards. Fergus being who he was, he quickly had his adversary's head locked in his arm, choking the man to unconsciousness. He said, later, that he was afraid to get between the other man and myself, which I take with a grain of salt.

After a flailing display of teeth, fists, and nails, I managed to sit astride the man's chest—he was older than I, and had not worked long hours in the fields. From there, I punched him and throttled him, beating his head into the floor for a good few minutes after he lost consciousness. Once it dawned on me that there was no need to continue savaging the wretch—I can only assume, and hope, that he survived the ordeal—I stood shakily, turning to Fergus with a silent stare. Without a word to me, he gestured onward, and I followed.

Any attempts at stealth had been abandoned. We fled like

beasts up the stairs, making a mad dash away from the scene of our crime. I had left my shoes somewhere in the meantime, and my socks occasionally slid on the waxed floors as we scrambled across them. I suppose it was a few minutes later that we finally reached the door to the maintenance area. For a moment, I began to panic again: the metal door couldn't easily be broken down, and I had nothing with which to pick the lock. But Fergus produced the ring of keys he had taken from one of the guards, and soon, we were inside.

Even as fractured as my memories of that evening are, I can't forget the view from that room. There was only one window, the rest of the wall being dedicated to the supports of the television screen, but the vantage point it offered—I doubt I can put it into words. It looked like a painting: the streets below forming a crisscrossing circuit, with the streetlamps and neon signs giving the whole scene an ethereal glow. And there we stood, panting and bloodied, ready to blow shards and wires across the whole damned thing.

My hands shook as I helped Fergus get the pack off his back. We fumbled for a light switch, and were soon illuminated in a dim, dingy light from overhead. Nobody really needs to do much with the televisions: they're never turned off, and the channel never changes. You know that, of course, but my point is that the maintenance area hadn't seen much use, if any, in the last few weeks. Perhaps longer. It gave us time to work, in case more unpleasant surprises were in store. And so, we knelt beside the supports, and unpacked our bombs.

"These are pretty small," noted Fergus. "We don't want to take the whole building down, or anything. Just the TV." He handed one to me, and I held it gingerly, not daring even to turn the thing over in my hands. It bore a small dial, not unlike an egg-timer, and had clearly been handmade. I still don't know just where Forgotten obtained his materials, but I assure you, not all of Licenia is so sleepy and content as Priius is. Or was.

There were a handful, and they all adhered easily to the surfaces of the television supports. "You're sure this isn't going to kill us?" I asked, as the last of the adhesive took hold. He nodded, standing back. Not without my doubts, I moved to set the first timer—but it had only numbers, not units. "Are these seconds or minutes?" I asked, glancing over my shoulder.

I received only a blank stare from Fergus. "They didn't tell you?" I demanded, my face flushing. He began explaining that he wasn't the one who was going to set them; that was the job of the men who hadn't showed up. I cut him off with a tirade of profanity; in a fit of angered imprudence, I set the first timer to "30," and flipped the switch to activate the bomb.

The dial shifted after five seconds. "25," it read.

With another oath, I tried to deactivate the thing, or to adjust the timer, but could do neither. 20. These had been constructed hastily, and hardly with the safety of the operator in mind. Though not powerful enough to destroy much of the building, if Fergus could be believed, I had no doubt they could deal more than enough damage to destroy much of me. 15. I shouted to Fergus, and we fled from the room, not waiting to close the door behind us. We ran as far from that little room as we could, diving for shelter under a table. But we were met with silence.

I expect you understand that I hadn't been counting, but I felt sure, after a time, that more than fifteen seconds had passed. We slowly raised our heads, looking to one another in confusion, then slowly rising to our feet. Under my breath, I counted to thirty, but still there came no explosion. After a few moments, we laughed the nervous laughter of relief, and walked back into the room. "Dud," remarked Fergus, nodding at the timer. It had counted down to zero, but without triggering anything. Shaking my head in disgust, I told Fergus I'd try again. He left the room for safety's sake, and I set the next timer to a full sixty seconds, activated the bomb, and turned to walk out of the room.

I recall an intense, blinding pain, and nothing more.

What were the odds of two faulty explosives? Fairly high, in hindsight, considering their rough-shod construction. But such a cruel irony, finding the dud and then the short fuse. Fergus says I had actually walked out of the room, even closed the door, when the explosion erupted; the relative weakness of the blast saved my life, but the door splintered into pieces, and lodged itself deep into my leg. My sides were peppered with wood, my clothes ruined; something struck my head, and I crumpled.

Fergus ran over to grab me, and without so much as checking for a pulse, he scooped me up as though I were a child, and fled down the stairs with my broken and bleeding frame. He had been far enough back that he remained unharmed, for which I remain grateful: I wouldn't have been able to carry him, he had fallen. But he carried me, all down those flights of stairs and through the glass-strewn streets of Franklin Square. I expect you remember the sight of the wreckage: all those bombs went off, sure enough, after the first one exploded. That huge television screen dropped like a rock, sending glass, wires, chips, and twisted metal for hundreds of feet. We got lucky: no cars happened to be passing there at that late hour. Think what you will, but even now, I don't want to hurt anyone if I can help it.

I woke, to some degree, as we neared Old Hampton. I remember screaming out in the night, trying to move the legs I could barely feel. The coppery scent and taste of blood mingled in my throat, and my hands grasped handfuls of Fergus' shirt, leaving bloody prints on the fine cloth. From there, I faded in and out of consciousness, while he cradled me to his chest. We arrived in the camp in the dead of night, when most of the men were asleep, but Fergus woke them with a bellow. I was laid across a few barrels, and Forgotten himself came out to see the source of the noise. They say he had thrown on his helmet, but not his greatcoat, and watched over me for minutes in silence.

They had neither the time nor the money to take me to the hospital, and that trip would have incriminated us all. Instead, Peters became my nurse, applying bandages and tourniquets, prying chunks of wood from my mangled flesh. I fought, when I was conscious, writhing in pain and loosing inhuman howls. All I can remember are the nightmares and hallucinations I experienced. Apparently, it took Fergus himself to restrain me, at one point: I was beating at Peters with my fists while he was trying to extract a particularly large piece from my side. I suppose I wasn't thinking, delirious from blood loss, pain, and whatever struck my head. But then Milcher brought something of his own over. He stuck me in the arm with it, and I stopped struggling. I laid still, and slipped into a euphoric oblivion.

In those fleeting moments of consciousness, I saw God.

He walked with a limp, clutching to his side. His body bore innumerable scars, and discolorations from what might have been past infections. My body felt weak in his presence, my skin warm and prickling. As he moved away, I saw the weight of a million sins weighing heavy on him. My dry tongue ran along my dry lips. Darkness claimed me, but I swam back to the surface long enough to watch his lion's head disappear into the distance.

When I woke the next morning, I had been stripped bare, covered in bandages. My muscles ached, and my head swirled uncertainly. The entirety of the previous night seemed nothing more than a nightmare, save for those last moments in Heaven. A single crutch, looking as though it had been repaired many times over the years, laid within reach. The sun already filtered in through the cracks in my cabin; I hurried to put on my jumpsuit, for I was already late for work. Propping myself up on the crutch after dressing, I limped slowly across the camp. No matter how bruised and battered I may have been, I had to go to work. I needed that normality in my life. I needed to distance myself from the night before.

It took nearly an hour just to get from Old Hampton to Candor Tower. The traffic actually stopped for me as I made my slow way across the crosswalks, even after the lights had changed. Every step was a challenge. Breathing didn't come easily. But when I stood at the rope boundary keeping pedestrians out of Franklin Square, where the ruins of that vast screen were strewn across the street, along with much of the window, I smiled quietly to myself.

I felt powerful, despite being faced with the undeniable weakness of flesh. And my thoughts turned once more to the euphoria of the previous night—I wanted more. But that would wait. I had earthly duties to mind before trying for Heaven again, but never doubt that I didn't keep one eye on it.

XX.

Until that day, I had never properly appreciated the difficulty with which a crippled man must surely make his way. The simple act of pushing past the double-doors into Candor Tower proved difficult: I had to shoulder them open, using all of my body's weight to find passage. I nearly fell, on the second set, but managed to catch my balance with the frantic flailing of my crutch. As I stepped into the lobby, my bad leg alternately tapping and dragging along the tiled floor, I heard a woman gasp to my right. Turning to face her, I saw the day receptionist staring at me, eyes wide with concern.

"Oh, my God, Jackson!" she cried, hand clasped over her mouth. "What happened? Are you okay? You can't work today!" she rattled off. I waved my free hand, shaking my head, but she hurried around the desk to inspect me. The jumpsuit covered the majority of the bandages, but she could see the way I kept my leg hovering off the floor, wary of placing any weight on it. "You can't work today," she repeated, more firmly. "I'll tell Vance. You go home. Do you need help?" Sad that after all her caring that day, I still don't remember her name.

Fixing her with as kind a smile as I could manage under the circumstances, I grated out, "I'm fine, but thanks," through my pain. She began to protest again, but I placed my hand on her shoulder. "I have to work," I told her. "I need the money." The woman sighed, shaking her head and taking a step back. "Fine," she muttered, "but you'll still have to see Vance, to let him know what you're late. Don't clock in today. Just go upstairs." She proceeded to give me the directions I needed, and I began my weary ascent up the elevator, to the office of human resources.

It occurs to me, now, that I may have been unkind in my earlier assessment of the people of Licenia. They weren't blind to suffering, merely myopic. They had to be faced with it to understand its enormity—but so did I, you know. As I walked along the carpeted halls, people moved out of the way, giving me a clear path as I limped along. It was the visibility that got to them: they couldn't ignore the man slowly limping his way across the hall. Perhaps if my skin had been a shade more tanned, but perhaps not, even then. The poor among them, the sick and weary among them, all they lacked was the obvious disability to receive the respect they deserved. Without that, it's too easy to make the assumption that they're just faking it. Another drain on the system. Whatever system that is.

Vance was an older man, perched in an office of glass doors and the midmorning sun that came shining in. He huddled in a small pile of paperwork, and looked up as I walked in—first with a smile, then with a concerned knitting of his brows. "Oh, dear," he muttered, peering through a pair of thick-rimmed spectacles and running a hand through his thin, sandy hair. "I hope you're not feeling too awful, sir?"

With a slight chuckle, I shook my head. "I'm fine, really," I told him, telling the same sort of lie so many of us do. "Just hurt my leg. It's why I came in late today. I was directed to talk with you, sir."

He nodded, pulling out a form, which he handed to me. I filled it out with my name, address, and the like; it was an excuse for tardiness. I hesitated briefly over the checklist for "Reason For Tardiness," but eventually decided on "Injury Outside Workplace." That seemed appropriately vague. Nonetheless, as I handed it back and he stamped it to file it away, he looked up with a cheerful smile. "Might I ask what happened, there? Looks nasty, that. Nothing's broken, I hope?"

I returned his smile, but remained silent for a few heartbeats as I tried to think up a good excuse. But the best lies are simply the truth, with a strand or two broken, as you know. "I went out for dinner last night, and stepped in the gutter on my way home. Took a nasty fall; banged up my shin pretty badly. The doctors said nothing was broken, but it hours to walk."

He tutted sympathetically, and put away the paper. "Sorry to hear that, Mr. Jackson. Feel better soon! And don't worry: it won't count against you in the slightest." He winked, I smiled, and I stood to leave. As I did, however, he stopped me with a sound. "Before you go! You'll be on a light duty, today," he said, rummaging for another piece of paper from his stacks. "We don't need you hurting yourself, eh? Just... ah, here we go." He handed me a piece of paper with the "light" custodial duties: dusting, replacing misplaced items, and other such things. "Just do what you can. We understand if you can't do everything while balanced on one leg," he laughed.

And so did I wind away the rest of the day. My duties seemed to take twice as long as normal, despite being half as difficult: the chore was moving from place to place. My armpit grew sore and tender from the rough, unpadded cradle of the crutch, and my fingers began to ache for holding it so long. Not to mention the number of times I put my leg down too firmly, or twisted my foot the wrong way, and had pain shooting up along the muscle. All I could do was bear through it, and hope it would end soon.

The most curious thing which occurred that day was a simple one, easily overlooked, at the time. I was on the fifteenth floor of Candor Tower, just cleaning the windows in the doors with a spray-bottle and a rag. I didn't frequent that floor; I tended to mop and wax, after all, and the carpets hardly needed that. Like many of the executive-office levels, it was comprised of office upon office, all stacked up against one another. But there was a small hallway, unlit and with just enough space to admit one person moving through at a time, placed between a cluster of them. Curious, I followed along it, to find an unmarked wooden door, with no window or sign. Whatever was inside, it had to be a small room, for it was sandwiched between the eight adjacent offices. But when I tried the handle, it wouldn't budge.

I spoke of it to John, over lunch, in passing. He just shrugged, and gave me a smile. "We don't clean that room," he told me. "Don't worry about it." When I asked why not, he looked momentarily confused. "It's not on our list of duties, and it's always locked. It's probably just storage." It seemed fair enough to me: many of the storage rooms weren't accessible, save to those who had reason to get inside. Some were even dangerous, like the electrical storage room on the twentieth level. I put it out of my mind soon enough, but for a few fleeting moments, I felt something familiar about it.

Ah, but the television. I remember this scene, above others, with distinct clarity. The noon sun had risen above, and I was halfway through my chicken and rice. One of the omnipresent televisions had been situated in my peripheral vision, and I could just catch the flash of color on it. With idle curiosity, I looked over—and I saw the Candor News Network showing the wreckage I had created the previous night.

It seemed almost a glorious thing to me, then: beautiful in its perfect destruction. I suppose I assumed that would be the end of it: we blow up a television, the people become afraid, and they look for a government nowhere to be found. Naive. Stupid, even. But I suppose it's what I had thought until that day. I hid my smile behind another bite of chicken, and watched as the camera scanned across the scene, from the shattered fragments of the window which still clung, tenacious, to the frame, to the twisted metal and scorched grass below. Some of it had still been hot on impact, evidently. But that which most caught my eye was the graffiti scrawled on one of the larger pieces of metal.

"THE FORGOTTEN DWELLS HERE."

One of our men had clearly done it while I was unconscious; it was a clever move. Even if the people didn't recognize its significance, I knew at least one member of Parliament who had to have been shivering. We were serious: we didn't just beat people up, we also made things explode. Terrifying. I looked on my work, and felt a strange sort of pride swelling in my chest again: that was my contribution to the liberation of Priius: an altar of twisted metal.

The day dragged slowly by. I saw Deirdre, briefly, and she expressed the concern I had expected. She just had so much love in her. I hope she still does, after all this is over. I'd hate to have torn that from her. But she gave me a careful hug, told me she was sorry, and promised that if we ever had dinner together again, she'd be sure to stand on the side of me nearest the gutter. I laughed, and hoped we'd have dinner again soon. For a few hours, life was good. I was in pain, but soon, things had to be back to normal. Or even better.

And then, a few hours before my workday ended, I saw a face on the television in the lobby. It looked oddly familiar to me; a hazy vision, perhaps seen in a dream. It took a minute to realize that he was the other guard in the tower Fergus and I had invaded: the one Fergus choked out. He was being interviewed by Candor, with his friend conspicuously absent.

"It's all kind of a blur," he muttered, clearly uncomfortable in front of the microphone and camera. I winced slightly as I realized his age more clearly; we had assaulted a man whose hair was starting to thin. "I was patrolling the floor below, when suddenly, I just heard a bang." He looked off to one side, cheeks slightly reddened. My own were flushing, too, for I knew the truth of his tale. "There was, like... a creaking, and then a crash, and I ran upstairs to find that whole darn thing just... gone. Shorn clear off. Must've been some sort of metal fatigue, I wager."

I was furious. It's stupid, perhaps, but I couldn't believe that he could stand before the entire nation and lie. Who had gotten to him? What had they said—what had they offered? That wasn't the truth of the tale; there was no way he couldn't have known. He wouldn't have been unconscious more than a few minutes, and it surely took us that long to rig the explosives. Nor did he make any mention of his coworker, which still worries me, for I'd like to think I didn't somehow kill him.

But that wasn't the worst of it. After I left the tower, as I was walking through the night streets, I saw an electric screen suddenly light up like a message from God. It interrupted whatever programming had been playing with a picture of the wreckage, then zoomed in on the graffiti. "THE FORGOTTEN DWELLS HERE."

And on a stark, blood-red background, with letters as golden as the gaudy decorations of Candor Tower, it read, "The Candor News Network would like to apologize for any inconvenience or fear caused by the recent explosion. Please do not worry: no-one was harmed in this controlled detonation. Please be on the lookout for more Enhanced Reality(TM) marketing as we gear up for our new drama, 'The Forgotten,' beginning next year."

My heart stopped.

XXI.

When I stalked back into Old Hampton, the others were all gathered in the center of the camp. It rather reminded me of my second visit, when I had first met Forgotten—for indeed, he was once more standing atop his own cabin, facing the twenty or so there assembled. Fergus and Milcher were poised in the center; when I drew closer, I could see that there were two men, bound and kneeling, in front of them. Their faces were vaguely familiar to me; I remembered having seen them around the camp. As I moved to lean my good side against a shack, Forgotten looked up and pointed at me.

"Jackson!" he cried. "Good of you to join us! I trust the pain of walking hasn't been too much for you." I watched in silence; he spoke with a bitter edge to his tongue, and that worried me. It wasn't frequent that he spoke harshly to his men. Looking back down, he spat, "Jackson, there, has suffered for your cowardice. He chanced upon Fergus, who stood faithfully by the door, waiting for you long after he had any reason to expect your arrival. And without being charged with the task, merely for the protection of his comrade, he joined Fergus on a mission meant for three men. One of whom, I might add, was the only one with the knowledge to correctly plant the charges!"

He leapt down, and moved toward the two kneeling men. All who stood in the way quickly backed out of it, leaving him a clear passage. He clutched his knife so tightly that, in the sudden silence, I fancied I could hear the creaking of his leather gloves. As he approached, Fergus and Milcher both stepped back. My eyes widened, and I took hold of my crutch, moving forward as quickly as I could manage.

"We will not abide by cowardice here," he grated, lifting high his blade. The two men made no protest, despite not being gagged. They simply hung their heads in shame. I believe I made some wordless sound to try to stop him from slaying them, as the light from a far-off sign glanced off the metal of the knife. Then, with a spurt of blood and a pained cry, one of the men fell over, clutching at his left ear. The other soon did the same; both fell on the ground, screaming and writhing. I stopped, shocked, but relieved to see they weren't dead. Fergus and Milcher grabbed their wards at Forgotten's command, and dragged them off to have the bleeding staunched.

The other men shuddered, then dispersed, going back to their cards and drinking. I stood in the middle of the camp, bewildered and terrified, while the old soldier approached me. "Well, then, Jackson!" he said, as cheerfully as might a man at a party. "How are you feeling? You looked in a bad way when Fergus brought you in; he told us the whole thing. But you're a strong man; you'll only be the stronger for it." He clapped me on the shoulder, while I stared at him, open-mouthed. "You mutilated those men," I eventually sputtered.

He shrugged, and nodded to me. "They knew the price of cowardice. This is not a pleasant business, Jackson, and I am neither a schoolteacher nor a father. Their fear prevented them from carrying out the task before them. They're children no longer—only barely, but all the same, they are men. I cannot coddle them. It's the same punishment anyone would face who failed in his duty only for want of courage. But, there's no use dealing with that unpleasant business. You succeeded in your mission, and we're one step closer to waking up a sleeping country."

I hesitated, then followed him into his cabin. I didn't want to break the news to him in front of the entire camp, and at that very moment, I needed a moment to recover from the gruesome sight. Think of me what you will, but after his explanation, I was not so bothered by it; I had, indeed, suffered for their cowardice, and they hadn't been killed. A harsh punishment, surely, but not death. We sat, and he said, "You look pale, Jackson. Are you well?"

Slowly, and coldly at first, I began to recite the words I had seen on the television screen. The words which claimed that what we had done was nothing more than an advertisement for a television show. And as I spoke, the anger that had coursed through me then at seeing blatant lies broadcast to the whole nation rose again. It rose to a fever-pitch as I recited the last few words, spitting them out like poison. He sat motionless for a few moments. And then he kicked the table over, nearly hitting me in the process.

"Damn them!" he roared, loudly enough that I'm sure those in the camp without could hear him distinctly. "Does Beckstein think he can make a joke of me again? Does he think he can profit off of *my* works again? Does he think he can use me again?" Whirling, he stabbed his knife a solid inch into the wood of the cabin, repeating the motion twice more. "God! fucking! damn the man!" he howled, each syllable punctuated by another violent outburst. And then, as suddenly as it had come on, he calmed. Slumped, even: he looked exhausted, and fell into his chair. It rocked, and nearly tipped before stabilizing. I calmed my heart, and slowly climbed back into the chair, having leapt from it onto my bad foot during his rage.

His chest heaved as we sat across from one another, staring in shared outrage—though I'd wager his was a bit more intense than mine. "What more do we have to do?" he asked, barely more than a whisper. He clutched his helmet in both hands, and addressed his lap. "They don't react to a member of Parliament savaged. They don't react to a building partly demolished. But, by God, they *will* react," he hissed. Standing again, he threw open the door to his cabin, marching outside and howling for Rothschild and Peters. I followed, in a state of utter bewilderment.

The other two were soon gathered, though Rothschild had to be stirred from his irregular sleep. He walked blearily along with them, stripped to the waist. As I gazed on his striations, I began to wonder if a single member of the Licenian military walked unscarred. Forgotten's lieutenants entered the cabin, and I almost did the same, but Forgotten stopped me with a hand on my shoulder. I looked up into his mask, and for the first time, saw the dim image of his dark eyes. "No, Jackson. You've done enough for now. Rest. Recover. We'll have need of you later." And with that, he closed the door.

I moved back to seat myself at one of the makeshift tables, not far from where the two deserters were being restrained on two other tables. Their heads were wrapped in bloodied bandages, and they blubbered and whimpered incessantly. Not that I can exactly blame them: I never saw their faces clearly, but I doubt they were much older than I. Perhaps younger; I was certainly not the youngest of Forgotten's crew. But then, we were all young, save perhaps for his lieutenants. Young men, hard up, with nowhere to go. As I sat there, propping my injured leg up on a barrel, they were released from the table. Without hesitation, they bolted, fleeing the camp, shouldering Fergus out of the way, and running off into the night.

That was the first time, since I had arrived, that our little company shrank.

I napped fitfully, my head cradled in my arms on the table, while I waited for the others to exit the cabin. I awoke at one point in time to see Rothschild get dressed and leap the wall, off on another of his missions without nearly enough sleep. Peters gave me a pat on the shoulder as he passed, and left a small bottle of whiskey in front of me. Forgotten never left his cabin again that night. He had other matters on his mind.

It wasn't for three days that I would see their mission come to fruition. My injuries had healed somewhat by then, and though the soreness had increased, I could see the skin healing each time I redressed the wounds. None of the nerves had been deadened, thankfully, and my injuries were nothing that couldn't be mended with time. I counted myself lucky for that. Still, I walked with my crutch, though now more for certainty than as a necessity.

It was the second rain I saw in Priius, that morning: it spattered heavy on the grass of Old Hampton and on the sidewalk without Humboldt, mixing with the oils of the road and running off in shimmering rainbows into the rainways. I had no umbrella, so I wore my old cap; my jumpsuit, at least, served to keep the wet from seeping into my bones. Every once in a while, a thunderclap shook the city, but it could barely be heard over the din of traffic all around me. There seemed to be more cars on the road, at first; but I soon realized they were merely stuck, creeping along at perhaps ten miles per hour. As busy as the streets could be, they seldom jammed like that; Priius was, if anything, optimized for motor traffic. But as I stepped into Franklin Square, I saw the source of it.

Perhaps a hundred cars were spread in wide array around the spectacle, with a line of the city guard blocking civilians from crossing the line they had set up. Most of them were portly men, or even older men; others were young and drawn, veterans of the Grand War who saw few other opportunities open to them when they tried to readjust to civilian life. A photographer was trying to snap a picture, and the sidewalks were crowded with people sneaking out of their offices to see what the dim midmorning light could barely illuminate through the storm.

His clothes clung close to him, sodden with the rain. It gave him a long and gangly look, almost unnaturally so. One of his fine leather shoes had come off, leaving his expensive, silken sock showing through. Blood covered his once-grand waistcoat and shirt, though it could hardly be distinguished from the crimson-dyed wool. Still, it had been spattered along the golden tie around his neck. And his neck! It had been split from ear to ear by a knife, drawn wide in a disgusting grin and left to spew its contents over his front. His eyes stared glassily forward, mouth hanging slack, with stains of blood-trails leaking down from the corners of his mouth. And he swung from a long rope, slung across one of the twisted metal supports that had lately held the screen Fergus and I had blasted off.

It was a member of Parliament, someone behind me said. No-one knew what had happened, exactly: he had been discovered early that morning, with the first of the traffic. There were mutterings of how the guard should be increased, and how they thought some people watched too much television—a remark I didn't understand until I heard about the paper that had been driven into the man's chest with a nail. "THE FORGOTTEN IS NOT A JOKE. WHERE IS YOUR GOVERNMENT?"

I felt sick, neither for the first time nor the last. Although I knew I would have to go back once more, confront that strange, sick man once more, I nonetheless trudged on toward work. The rain continued to fall heavy around me, mixing with the pool on the ground and running into the cracks and crevices of the sidewalk. Down it went into the soil, where that man's blood, like the blood of so many others, mixed with the soil of Licenia.

XXII.

For the first time I had ever seen, the flags flying outside Candor Tower had been lowered to half-mast. They were always displayed, come rain or darkness. But that day was the first they weren't proudly hoisted. The whole city seemed somber: they'd had their first taste of murder. They couldn't ignore it, couldn't shrug it off: it stared them in the eye, as brutal and visceral as anything. It wouldn't be the last, I knew. As I walked through the double-doors yet again, I couldn't shake the awful feeling I had. Once again, I came to the conclusion that I had gotten in over my head. I had chosen the wrong side. How could murderers be in the right?

I stumbled through my duties half-dead, somberly dusting the wooden end tables in the lobby and polishing the doorknobs. Everyone but me seemed eager to chat about the killing; I remained silent on the matter, especially when they inevitably began to speculate on the identity of the "Forgotten." I couldn't stomach the thought of talking about a matter with which I was so intimately involved. Though at the same time, I was thankful —thankful that I hadn't been forced to dirty my own hands in that sordid affair.

I think John might have noticed it. The pall over me, I mean. He was a perceptive man. Intelligent, to boot. Perhaps it's retrospective paranoia, but I seem to recall him looking over me frequently that day. But then, I'm sure I looked as depressed as I felt, for I made no effort to hide it. I was listless and unhappy, reevaluating every decision I had made since arriving in Priius. Would I even be able to remain? Would they let me go so easily, when I knew so much? They claimed not to hunt down their former members, but at that moment, I had no trust in their word. At the time, I could hardly stand the shame of returning to my little farm, trying to go back to the so-called simple life of old.

Several times that day, I almost left early. I hadn't been late again, after the first day; I forced myself to walk more briskly, despite the pain. Pain, after all, is... finite. I felt roughly the same sharp stab each time I took a step, and it became no worse. There's a certain strength in that knowledge. When nothing you do can make anything worse, there's nothing to hold you back anymore. It works the same way with desperation, you know. When they've stripped you down to nothing, taken away everything you care about, you're as vicious and as cunning as a wild dog. Or maybe a lion. You'd do well to remember that.

As evening set in, darkening the windows and causing the neon lights to silently flicker on outside, I sat in the breakroom, watching the television. A group of men in suits were discussing the murder, identifying themselves as members of Parliament. My mind's eye could already see X's drawn over each one. They'd given away their names, and with that, they'd given away everything Rothschild needed to track them down. Briefly, I entertained a wild notion of killing him, to prevent the madness from continuing. But that wouldn't end it. Blood begets blood. As ironic as it may be for me to say that now.

Like a good little worker, I finished out my shift before leaving Candor Tower. I trudged back along my familiar path, not even bothering to avoid Franklin Square. The crowd had dispersed by that time of night, and I couldn't see the bloodstains where the man had hung. I was angry. Angry at being deceived, used, part of something I had thought was noble. Angry at myself for my naivete, and angry at the whole damn world for not being simpler.

Much of my life in Priius has been defined by rage. I suppose it's the natural reaction to discovering that the world is not so much a photograph in black and white, but a mosaic in varying shades of grey. Or maybe it's just my own instability. Who can know for sure?

I strode past the marble floors of Humboldt; past the sad and faded population of John's Kitchen; past the alley where the homeless man had begged; past the smiling face of Fergus; and past the gathered ruffians of Old Hampton. I wrenched open the door to Forgotten's cabin, finding him studying a map of the city. He looked up sharply at my arrival, and started to speak. I threw down my crutch, and spoke in his place.

"I'm leaving," I stated, drowning out whatever he was about to say. "I've had my goddamn fill of Priius. Of your good intentions. Of your violence, and your hate. I know you claim to fight for the people, but I've yet to see your enemy—no, not "our" enemy—do anything so cruel, or so vicious, as what you've done. I have committed theft for you. I have borne witness to torture. And now, I've got blood on my hands. No end justifies every means, Forgotten, and I'm damn well sick of it."

He sat quietly all the while. When he stirred, I expected him to explode. I was prepared for him to yell at me, berate me, attack me. I could have dealt with it if he had condescended, reminded me of the last time I almost left. But his silence disarmed me, and so, too, did his reply.

"I'm sorry to hear that, Jackson, and I understand." He sounded sad, if anything. I could detect no hint of anger, bitterness, even disappointment. Just a sort of melancholy. "It's a wretched, hateful business, and I have no right to force you into it. You've lived a happy life, Jackson. You really have. You've been blessed. I suppose I should have known you couldn't fit in—it's no fault of yours!" he quickly added, when I started to stir. "It's a good thing, really. You're innocent, Jackson. And you should hold onto that. I wish I could." His hands moved to the bottom of his helmet, and I think he considered taking it off. But in the end, his hands moved back down to the table, folded before him.

"I recruit thugs, for the most part," he told me. "Young men. Young, violent men who've never known anything but hardship, bitterness, and misery. Because... well, because they have nothing else for them. You have opportunities, Jackson, and maybe you should take them. You could do something great. Invent a new medicine, write a symphony, sculpt a masterpiece. But the rest of us... we're broken. I've probably said it before, but it remains the truth. We're broken, Jackson."

I took a seat, watching him warily, but saying nothing. Although part of my mind knew that this was a man who had ordered another's throat slit, the rest couldn't help but pity him. Damn his charisma. "I understand if you want to leave, and I'll bear you no ill-will if you do. I can throw sob stories or angry rants at you all I want, and it won't change your morality. If you believe that our end doesn't justify the taking of another's life, so be it. I do, though, and that will never change." He looked up at me, head slightly canting to one side. "I believe that we, too, are doing something great, Jackson. I'm giving these men something to work toward. Something to improve the station of their fellow men. An opportunity to make a difference—they've never had that, before.

"But to do that, some others will have to die." He sat up, resting his elbows on his knees and still coolly regarding me. "The man we slew was a vocal proponent of the wholesale slaughter of the people of Greenwood. He pushed to make our invasion of South Licenia not a liberation, but a genocide: to make an example of them. He unleashed an ocean of bullets and blood. And like all of us, his sins came back to haunt him. We gave him a choice. Either he could make his crimes public, or we could do it for him." He leaned back again, chair creaking. "He told us he'd never admit to anything at the hands of terrorists. And so, we took his life, in the hopes that it will prevent the taking of more."

I pondered his words for a long while, but I couldn't wash the image of that dead man from my mind. "Those are pretty words, and sincerely meant, I'm sure," I murmured. "But you're right: it doesn't change what I believe. Killing won't end this. Violence won't end this. I was willing to put up with inflicting wounds, even grievous ones. But I simply cannot tolerate outright murder." I stood to leave, but he shook his head.

"Please, Jackson: grant me just one request. Stay here for... three days. Talk with the men. Talk with Peters, especially. It may not change your mind as to what we have done, but perhaps you'll understand what we shall do. I am a monster— we are monsters—yes. But so are our adversaries. They have led to more deaths than you can possibly begin to comprehend. And they will again, sooner or later, if they aren't held accountable."

I gave him a long and searching look, then slowly nodded. "Alright," I sighed, "three days. I'll give you that much. But this changes nothing. Having monsters for your enemy doesn't justify being one yourself." And with those words, I turned and left, closing the door behind myself. I left my crutch behind, wincing as I walked on my still-tender leg toward my cabin. Across the camp I strode, before collapsing on my bed and closing my eyes. I had nearly fallen asleep in my clothes when there came a knock on the door. At my invitation, Fergus entered, carrying with him a small pouch.

He had been concerned after me. In all this time, I had seen him as a bruiser of a man, or a loyal dog, but never quite as a person with genuine emotion. At the same time, he'd never given me much reason to do so. But as he sat to the other side of my bed, regarding me with something approaching tender concern, I couldn't help but feel as though he were my friend. He asked into my health, complimented my performance during our horrid escapade into that skyscraper, and apologized more than once for not setting the bombs himself. I was hardly in a jovial mood, but nonetheless, I was willing to talk with him. When he relaxed, he had an easy manner about him.

"So, then," he grunted, unfastening the top button of his shirt (for his waistcoat had been discarded before he arrived), "what had you all up in a hurry, today?" I spoke to him of what I had seen, and of my intention of leaving. That seemed to dishearten him, much as it had done Forgotten. I suspect that they thought more highly of me than I of them, and I feel I did Fergus some disservice, for that. He was one of the few who really believed in what he was doing.

Eventually, he revealed the contents of his pouch: more of the drug they had used to calm me down during my surgery. "This shit's expensive," he warned me, "so I ain't got much, mind. But... hell, Jackson, you've been through a lot, and you just got here. The rest of us haven't done much more than you; you arrived just as our plan was coming into place. Good timing, I'd be inclined to say, if it hadn't been so much, so soon." He sighed, and shook his head. "So, I just figured I'd come and help calm your nerves some."

I hesitated, then accepted. Within a few minutes, he had inserted the needle into my vein, and soon enough, the euphoria spread across me again. I remember little of that night, save for the few moments of euphoria which came on fast, and faded far too soon, before I slipped into sleep. It seemed wondrous, then. The closest to a religious experience I'd ever come. But there was no God in that place, for there is no God in Priius, nor even Licenia. Neither God nor devils; only truth and Candor.

XXIII.

I awoke the next morning, groggy and disoriented, with Fergus still lying in my bed, one brawny arm loosely draped over me. Sometime during the blur of the night, we had both stripped to the waist, perhaps due to the body heat of having two figures in a small cot. He was still asleep, and had evidently not been awake to guard the camp by night. I sat up, resting my back against the wooden wall and watching him. He slept with one arm extended, the other tucked beneath his head for want of a pillow. His left leg lacked enough room, so it had fallen to the floor, twisted at an awkward angle, foot resting by the kit he had brought to administer his drugs. As he slept, he twitched every so often, fingers clenching and unclenching into a fist. I brushed hair from my face, and carefully stepped over him, covering him with the blanket that had been thrown aside in the night.

It was a rare moment of tenderness, one of the few since I arrived in Priius. While I gathered my clothes and prepared to shower, I made as little noise as possible, so as not to wake him. For I had never seen him sleeping and vulnerable, and even now, I never saw him at peace. I wanted somewhat to reach out and stroke his stubbled cheek, to calm him from whatever had seized upon his unconsciousness, but I refrained, for fear of waking him.

At the time, I was certain I would leave Priius in three days' time. My dreams of becoming a reporter for Candor Tower seemed far away, now; I knew the truth of their broadcasts. There were no heroes nor villains there, only a band of twenty outcasts who were no better than the faceless government they fought. I no longer knew what to believe, for I had seen the lies of Candor with my own eyes, but had no more reason to trust Forgotten. And meanwhile, I had worked hard each day, in a position lower than any I had held—and, it occurred to me, with pay that would have been insufficient, if I had to pay for my residency.

As I showered, I turned over in my head the possibility of avoiding work. On one hand, I needed the money; on the other, I felt fatigued and unhappy. Had I not served them faithfully in my time in Priius? I had come in with a bruised, mangled, and wretched leg. For my own gain, of course, but that wasn't how I saw it. Every day offered the same monotony, comforting in its familiarity but crushing in its boredom. Although I had no formal higher education, I am hardly an uneducated man—are there not examples of other great men with such a background? I realized that I had little chance to progress, in my current station: being a fine janitor made you exactly that. For the first time in my life, I knew true alienation. Or at least a hint of it. It seems petty, now, when I consider those who had labored far longer and harder than I, and who had actively striven for advancement, but had been denied it.

In the end, I went to my work anyhow, to serve my time and collect my pay. But my actions were filled with bitterness, now, which only grew as the day passed by. I had a set of chores to do, and I knew there would be consequences if I failed to complete them in time. But I was paid by the hour, and if I finished early and clocked out, I would receive less pay for the same labor. If I finished my tasks and was discovered sitting around the rest of the time, I would be fired. And when I finished my tasks early and asked for more work, more work was the only thing I received. More work, and a pat on the back. No extra pay. No raise. No promotion. It was a hateful system, and already I had resolved to attack it.

I caught John before he left for the day, and led him over to the custodial closet. There, I closed the door, and began my diatribe against the unfair conditions I had faced. All the while, he watched in silence, his face betraying no emotion. By the time I had finished, with a curse on the name of Candor, he laughed mirthlessly.

"Jack," he sighed, putting a hand on my shoulder, "you're preaching to the choir. I know how you feel, and I'm sorry. But welcome to Priius. I've thought the same things; I've felt the same way. I do, every day. I've told you before, and I'm sure you remember, but I fought against it for years. I worked hard, just like you did, and I begged, cajoled, and even threatened to try to get recognition for it. But it just doesn't work that way."

I tried to begin to argue with him, to claim that we could make it work that way, if we just tried. But how could I argue with this aging man? I could see it in every callus and wrinkle; his pain and loss had been branded into his very flesh. He knew a bitterness far deeper and darker than I could imagine, even now. I had lost nothing besides my innocence and ignorance. He had lost everything. Once more, I felt the cold truth of Licenia's wealth settling around my shoulders, and the weight of my fortunes. The state had paid for me to be educated until I was a young man, paid for the roads I walked and the grain we grew on our farm. We grew crops when there was no market, for the government to purchase so that we didn't starve. I had only known the kind and gentle hand of the government. And with the knowledge of all that, I felt as though I were being drowned in the money they had spent, all gained by the labor of men like John and spent on the likes of me.

"Then fuck it," I finally said, resting my head in my hands. "Fuck all of it. If things aren't going to change, why bother with it? Why play along with any of it? Why work, when your incentive is to do the bare minimum necessary? Life has to be more than this," I said, more of a question than a statement.

"God, John. If we can't make a difference, what's the damn point of living?"

He considered that for a while, leaning on the doorjamb. "I don't think there's some mystical Purpose for which we've been set forth," he mused. "Life's what you make it, Jack. And if you've decided to make your purpose the assistance of others—well, that's a noble goal. But don't look to today for change. You have to learn to be satisfied with knowing that you tried, even if you fail. Maybe you make things easier for those who come after you, or maybe you make things a little better now, or perhaps you don't see anything for your work. But mostly, I think you should just try to be happy," he smiled. "I'm not saying you should give up on your dreams, though. Don't ever do that."

His answer, though said and meant well, offered me no comfort. It was cruel of me, I know, but I remember an odd feeling coming over me as I narrowed my eyes at him. "That's insufficient, John," I told him. "But, all the same... it's interesting for you to be the one to say that," I slowly murmured. He didn't deserve my scorn. But I gave it nonetheless, and I strode out past him to make my way downstairs. This time, I didn't take the elevators, with their grand, brass doors and fine trappings. I walked through the hallway to the often-forgotten stairs, descending them with an unhappy stomp. I had been denied what I wanted, and now I stormed off like a tantruming child.

I saw Deirdre at the counter, and impetuously strode over to her, grabbing her by the hand. "I'm leaving, Deirdre," I told her, like some hero in a drama. "I'm leaving this wretched city, and I'm never going to return again. You should come with me!" She regarded me with wide, confused eyes, while I continued: "There's nothing but hatred and misery in this city. I've seen both sides of it, and neither's in the right. But we can find something better. I know we can." I must have sounded like a lunatic.

She gently patted my hand, and withdrew. "Jackson," she said, slowly and carefully, "I'm not sure what you're talking about. Are you feeling alright?" I assured her I was, and she gave a doubtful nod. "Well, I'm sorry to hear you're going to go," she said, with a sad sort of smile. "You've been a good friend while you were here. It's too bad we couldn't have dinner together again. That was fun." Her expression became uncomfortable, and she paused for a time, looking aside. "But I... hope you don't have... feelings for me, Jackson? I don't want to think I led you on."

I was stopped short by that question, because I did. An infatuation with the first woman I had known in the city, simply because she had offered me the same kindness that she did anyone. In my arrogance and narcissism, I took it to mean something more. "I see," I said, looking down. Recalling her earlier discomfort on the topic of a man back home, I ventured so far as to say: "Well, if there's a man in your life—or if there ever is—I hope you two are very happy together." I meant it sincerely; I never wished her ill.

She sighed, and looked away. "Since you're leaving, Jackson, I suppose there's no harm in telling you. But I... hope you won't think ill of me for it. And you must keep it a secret." Turning to face me again, she locked eyes with me. I gave a terse nod, fearing that I had made things uncomfortable by trying to force my attentions on her with dinner and nightly chats.

"I don't... like men," she breathed, so quietly I could barely hear it. As she spoke, she fidgeted in place, a blush rising in her cheeks. It took me a moment to understand what she was saying, for I had never personally met someone of that particular persuasion; I had read about it in my books on psychology, of course, but that's very different from finding that someone you know is like that. But that's the funny thing about getting to know someone: they're not like the case studies in books, or the cold assessment of an expert. They're warm and alive, full of the wonder and mystery of every individual. If I had not seen her kindness, if I were not indebted to her for the job I was now leaving, and I knew only that one statement, I suspect I would have viewed her with the same suspicion and fear that the unknown brings. Instead, I saw only Deirdre, the same kind and loving woman she had always been.

"Oh," I said, with a faint and confused smile. "Well, that's alright, too." There are very few cases where I can look back on my actions with any degree of pride, but that is one of them. So much of my time in Priius was a blur of action and reaction, and I acted so foolishly and childishly, that I cannot help but continually self-deprecate. Perhaps you grow tired of it, but you're the closest thing I have to a confessional, right now. I don't pretend that by announcing and repenting of my vast multitude of sins, I can hope to undo the damage I have caused. But maybe I can make you understand why I have done what I have, and why I will do what I will.

I'm not sure that anyone does, least of all myself.

XXIV.

True to my word, I remained in Priius for three days after the time I claimed I would leave. However, I didn't speak to Peters, as Forgotten had suggested, nor did I speak to many of the other men. I lived as a simple beast does: I ate, slept, and passed the time in my dwelling. More than once, I almost wrote a letter to my parents, to let them know that I was going to be returning in a few days' time, in hopes it would reach them before I did. But I could never find the words to explain what had happened; they died on my fingertips.

I became morose in the next two days, and spent a great deal of time lying in bed and thinking. In my head, I turned over a thousand plans for overthrowing Beckstein and this wretched government, and a thousand more for preventing Forgotten from hurting anyone else with his noble intentions. Neither proved fruitful: my mind was restless and clouded. It's difficult to plan an attack when you're angry, and I found myself flooded with anger, regret, and depression.

Fergus took care of me in those two days: if not for him, I doubt I would have had food, drink, or company. He went with little sleep, to bring me meals and talk of whatever came to mind. We spoke largely of our lives before joining that ill-fated band: I told him about the farming life, and he gave harrowing accounts of his life as a common thug, turned out on the back alleys of Tobit with neither an education nor prospects. The truth is that I was lonely, he was lonely, and we both knew it. In our brief and crazy escapade together, as I laid bleeding and unconscious in his arms, he had formed something of an attachment to me. And while he laid on my cot, eyes focused on the ceiling, I believe I formed an attachment to him.

Despite what he'd said about the expense of the heroin he

always brought with him, he was liberal in sharing it with me. I appreciated that perhaps more than anything else: though conversation helped, that euphoria, however short-lived, was the only thing capable of drawing me fully out of my depression, however briefly. I sank right back in each time the high had passed, of course, but that only left me keening all the more for the familiar pierce of the needle. It was the closest I came to sex, in those days: animals eat, sleep, and fuck, and I am no different.

I understand what you're implying, and I cannot deny that I felt a certain attraction to Fergus, and not a natural one. You might think it a product of my depravity, and that is possible. Maybe I'm just romantic, or I become attached too much, too soon. It would hardly be an understatement to call me "passionate." But in those last days, he showed me kindness, just as Deirdre had done. That matters to me much more than the size of a woman's bust or the beauty of her eyes. Someone with integrity, kindness, and love is...

Forgive me. I'm rambling about inconsequential things again.

It was the third day after I made my promise, and the sixth following our discovery of Candor's reaction to our pitiful attempt to terrify the populace. Only a week had passed since my injury, but you'll find that I'm quick to overcome wounds of the flesh. I had packed my scant belongings, dressed in the same rough clothes I had worn on my entrance to the city, and exited my cabin for the first time in over forty-eight hours. My beard was growing unkempt, and I stank of sweat; my hands trembled and my eyes had grown sunken and weary. For all my rest, I'd not slept well for the past few nights.

I recall that the nearest neon lights had been extinguished: that stood out, for it so seldom happened. The sudden darkness gave a better view of the hunter's moon which shone down on

Old Hampton's tired shacks. As always, the men lounged around. It is my understanding that a few of them had been sent out on various assignments, Rothschild among them. Pulling my cap down over my eyes as if to ward off the sun, I regarded the ground so as not to meet the gazes of those who looked up as I passed. My feet moved slowly, boots dragging along the ground. The weight of my pack seemed multiplied tenfold, and I walked with a stoop to my shoulders. I had no intention of lingering to say my goodbyes, but I lingered all the same.

Milcher nearly bowled me over as he rushed past; had I not looked up at the sound of his feet thudding along the ground, I would have been trampled. He carried a man in his arms, and for once, he didn't stutter as he cried, "Make way! Injured!" That caught my interest: like a carrion crow, I turned to follow, curiosity quickening my pace. Fergus wasn't far ahead of me; he had fallen in behind the other guard as Milcher ran by him.

Several of the men gathered around as Milcher laid the stranger down on the same makeshift table where my own wounds had been tended, and where the two deserters' ears had been removed. The bloodstains had soaked into the grain of the wood, giving it the distinct impression of a butcher's block. This stranger took little enough notice of that, however. He was glancing around wildly at all of our faces, his hand clutching at his chest beneath his suit jacket. "Thank you, sir," he breathed, in an accent I recognized as that of the moneyed natives of Priius. "I don't expect it's anything too bad, probably just a sprain, but I want to be sure that it's not broken."

The left leg of his trousers had been torn and bloodied, but the cuts were superficial. He likely could have walked all the way, but we declined to remark on that fact. After all, the wealthy classes aren't quite so weathered as we were. "I f-found him in th' st-streets," explained Milcher, with a smile. "Poor fellow looked in a bad way, a-and I thought I'd bring him in. For doct'rin'." The stranger's fair-haired head bobbed in agreement. "And I'm much obliged. I think I'm a bit turned around. This is... Old Hampton, is it?" His gaze lingered on the black waistcoats all around him. Mine rested on his face, my brows slightly furrowed.

Fergus had been tending to him, using what first-aid he knew. He used a bit of cloth to bind the bloodied leg, but announced, "I can't find nothing amiss. Think you've likely just sprained it. But stick around a while, and we'll see about getting someone to take a look at it. Peters, maybe, or Rothschild."

The stranger sat up, shaking his head. I thought I saw a flash of fear in his eyes, but he seemed calm enough. "Oh, no; that's quite alright, sir. Thank you, though. Let me just see if..." Placing his foot down, he nodded to himself. "Ah, yes! I think I can walk just fine, now. But if you're ever around, ...Milcher, was it? If you're ever around, just let me know if there's anything I can—"

He stopped short in the middle of his offer. Rothschild had clambered over the wall, scuffed and dirty. After dusting himself off a bit, he'd wandered casually over to the gathering, and frozen, himself, upon coming in view of the stranger. His jaw hung somewhat slack, and he narrowed his eyes. "Hendrick?" he breathed, suspicion and aggression mixed in his tone. "What the hell are you doing here?"

The stranger had slid his hand back into his coat, and before I could turn back to him, there came a deafening crack. My ears rang horribly, and I saw Rothschild fall over, clutching at his shoulder. A blur of motion beside me, and Fergus was leaping toward Hendrick, who clutched a pistol and fired again. Fergus' trajectory shifted in midair, and he fell on the half-standing Hendrick, knocking him back. I could see a hole in the back of

Fergus' shirt, where blood was bubbling up. All of this had occurred in the span of a few seconds; there was no time for me to take stock of the situation. I merely acted on instinct.

In a moment, my hands were on the pinned Hendrick's head, fingers pushing into his eyes and palms gripping his cheeks. I'm told he howled horribly as I gouged out his eye, but I was too deaf to hear it. Around me, men scattered in all directions, but I wasn't aware of their presence. My hands jerked, Hendrick's neck gave a sickening snap, and he went limp, dropping his gun. Fergus' heavy form, gasping for air and twitching atop his assailant, was pulled over by Forgotten, who had run out of his cabin at the first gunshot. I stood with blood and fluids on my hand, my nails having dug into his flesh and eye, still gripping the intruder's head.

My gaze turned to Fergus' prone form. He laid gasping and heaving, blood pouring from a gaping bullet wound in his gut. His eyes were wide, blank, both focused firmly on Heaven. More blood poured up over his lips and chin; he was rolled over so that he didn't choke on it. There was... so much. I dropped Hendrick, and stared at Fergus, unable to move, act, or think. My ears still rang with the two gunshots. I watched as Fergus clutched at his stomach, writhing and moaning in silence. And slowly, he grew still.

Not long before, I had vomited at the sight of a man tortured. Now, two had died before my very eyes, one by my own hand. But I felt nothing, save for an electric prickling in my hands. They were half-numb. I couldn't feel the smallest finger of my right hand. Rothschild had risen, clutching at his shoulder, and he made his way over to start digging in the wound with a pair of tweezers, eventually extracting the bullet which had struck the bone. Only a handful of us remained, the rest having fled in the confusion for fear of death.

Forgotten. Peters. Rothschild. Milcher. Jackson. Fergus. Forgotten. Peters. Rothschild. Milcher. Jackson.

I stood in a pool of his blood, gaping at his corpse. He still had the rosiness of life: his eyes were wide with pain, and his mouth hung open in a silent cry, blood drenching his beard and his clothes. Fergus, that great loyal dog, had been killed. It didn't seem quite real to me; it was like entering a wax museum. While Rothschild doctored himself, Forgotten wordlessly began to drag Fergus' lifeless form away, smearing a trail of blood and a few scraps of innards in the grass.

I can still remember his face, you know. It was outlined in the hunter's moon, blurred and uncertain from the dark. It was the last thing I saw before I closed my eyes, shivering, clutching at my face with my soiled hands. Though I wanted to scream, no words came. Though I wanted to cry, neither were there tears. Only the great, gaping hole Hendrick had blown through me.

"We have to move," Rothschild rasped, as he finished the sling around his arm. "We're safe here no longer. Hendrick's a Licenian agent." Peters stopped to pick up the pistol, putting on the safety and checking the magazine. He held the gun as tightly as his lips, eyes narrowed and expression dark.

Some minutes later, Forgotten returned, gathered up Hendrick's smaller frame, and carried him off in the same direction he had dragged Fergus. He'd taken them to the abandoned meat factory where we'd interrogated Lampton; there, they wouldn't be discovered immediately, and there was no time for a burial. "Let's go," he simply said, and those of us who remained followed in silence.

I had known rage before, but never had I experienced the chill of true hatred, bitter and absolute. At that moment, I knew that I would never leave Priius. This city gets a hold on you. It's like an animal: it sinks its fangs in to the bone. And even long after you think you've healed, you always have the scars to remind you of the holes it left.

XXV.

At the exit to Old Hampton, I hung back, then hurried over to collect my things again. After pulling my pack back over my shoulders, I almost ran to catch up with the others, when a sudden thought struck me. Instead, I entered Fergus' shack. With as little to furnish it as mine, it was easy to locate the pouch he used to store his drugs and equipment; I stuffed it in with my belongings, then made my way back to the small group.

"We could move to Tobit," Peters was saying, as I walked up. They had waited for me, lingering in the shadows just beyond Old Hampton. "It's got plenty of rat-holes to hide in. A healthy immigrant population, too; Rothschild and I might not be noticed."

Forgotten shook his head. "It's imperative we remain in Priius: we need to be close by the enemy, so that we can constantly harry them. 'Strike like lightning from Heaven,' and all that."

"What about your papers?" I interjected, looking between Forgotten, Peters, and Rothschild. Milcher was watching for them slightly ahead, to ensure we weren't ambushed by any other Licenian agents. "I can't imagine you want them discovered."

Rothschild held up a briefcase. "All we need is here. The rest is inconsequential. Let them find it: it will terrify them. And when they are frightened," he grinned, "they will make errors." I had my own opinion on that, after seeing their reaction to being frightened. It seemed damned effective to me, all told.

"We can track down the other men one by one, if they don't scatter when they find out we've done the same," grunted Forgotten. "For now, though, It's just us. We might not be able to set up a permanent headquarters, but we'll need a meeting spot. Any ideas, gentlemen?"

I don't know why I suggested John's Kitchen. I hadn't been there in a long while, and while she tolerated me, I could hardly consider Mrs. Hughes a "friend." All the same, I had respect for her, and it had been a place of shelter for me in my first days in Licenia. Moreover, as I told them, it was nearby, unremarkable, and quiet. "It'll do," was Forgotten's assessment; there were no objections, so I led the way to Humboldt.

The marble floors and glass displays hadn't changed, but I had. I viewed them with a cynical contempt, sneering at the expensive clothing and jewelry displayed. Priius, the grand, gilded city, dressed in finery to hide its sores. It hadn't yet closed down, but there were few enough shoppers out and about that we weren't much noticed. Besides, other than Forgotten, we weren't a terribly remarkable lot. I'd wiped my hands on a handkerchief to clean them somewhat, and now, I hid the stains. Rothschild had a sling around his arm, but a casual passer-by wouldn't immediately think he'd been shot. And Forgotten's golden mask and crimson greatcoat are much revered by the people.

I pushed open the door to John's Kitchen, where Mrs. Hughes was just stepping out from behind the bar. There were no patrons left; she looked as though she were about to turn in. But the moment she saw Forgotten behind me, she ducked into the kitchen. I paused uncertainly, and had just enough time to blink before she returned, pointing a shotgun at us. Peters had already drawn his pistol while she was away; Rothschild, Milcher, and Forgotten ducked back out of the door, and I stood, paralyzed by confusion.

"Th' fuck are you lot doing here?" she hissed, hands as steady as any I'd seen, finger on the trigger. "I'm *done* with you. Now, you can just back out nicely, or I c'n end you." Peters said nothing, but neither did he lower his gun or retreat. In one of my more foolish moments, I stepped between the two, my hands held in the air. "Whoa. Hold on," I said, trembling slightly and heart beating rapidly. "This is my fault. I think I'm... missing something, here. But for God's sake, I've had enough shooting for one day."

Mrs. Hughes growled. "You're damn right you're missing something, Jackson," she grated, making no indication she wasn't prepared to shoot through me. "You have ten seconds to get your friends the hell out of here, or I start shooting."

I turned to Peters, and gave a slight nod. He hesitated, and Mrs. Hughes grunted, "Five." Finally, he lowered his gun and walked backward out of the room, closing the door behind him. As soon as he did that, I turned to Mrs. Hughes, somewhat calmer. "Okay," I breathed, "I apologize for whatever—"

"Shut up," she snapped, but at least she wasn't aiming at me, anymore. "I knew you'd fall in with those cunts. Fucking idiot. Why didn't you listen to me?"

I took a seat on one of the stools, watching her carefully. She was scowling, face flushed with anger I'd seldom seen in anyone. "I think I deserve to know what's going on," I murmured, as calmly as I could manage. "You clearly... know each other, and I've clearly screwed up, somehow. But if you care about protecting me—"

She sneered. "I don't. Get the hell out of my bar."

It was about then that I ran out of patience. "Goddamn it, I just watched my friend die!" I snapped, standing. "Every time I see you, every time you mention Old Hampton, you give me vague damn warnings. Now, I'm in deep shit, I just stood in front of two guns, and you're not even going to tell me why the hell you were pointing a shotgun at those men?"

Regarding me coldly, she set down the gun, folding her arms

across her chest. "You wanna know why, boy?" she asked, barely above a whisper. "Because I don't care to associate with cowards, hypocrites, and murderers no longer. I used t' be part of their sorry crew, and I got out years ago. I've left them alone, with the understanding that they'd do the same, and now *you* come bringing them right to my fuckin' doorstep."

That startled me, and I thought back. I'd never had occasion to mention Mrs. Hughes to Forgotten, nor had he ever made mention of her. Or had he? It came to me in a sudden flash. "The woman he mentioned," I breathed. "The one who was..." And I cut off there, blushing. "I'm—I'm sorry. I didn't know. If I had, I never would have brought them here. I can understand why you'd leave a place like that," I said, trying to bring some tenderness into my voice. "I'd leave, too, if I were a woman and I'd been raped."

Before I finished speaking, she was already staring at me, open-mouthed and through narrowed eyes. "You fuckin' asshole," she finally murmured, with a cold and quiet anger. "You think that's why I left? My life ain't defined by the actions of men. I left because I didn't agree with th' shit they were doing. What?" she continued, striding toward me. "Never occurred to you tha' I might have an opinion on plans to assassinate political leaders for some asinine fight for 'freedom?' Never occurred to you that if th' people are determined to remain 'asleep,' or whatever the hell he calls it, they deserve what they get?"

By now, she was leaning into my face; I regarded her in silence, feeling half ashamed and half affronted. "He says he has no room for cowards, but he don't mention he's one!" she growled. "When that bastard raped me, I managed to get away. I marched into Forgotten's shack and grabbed his shotgun, and he tried to stop me. Told me t' wait, t' consider, t' think about it.

Cut a man's ear off for cowardice, but let a rapist off scot-free. So I shoved him out of my way, found that bastard, and blew his brains out." She pulled back, turning away from me and grabbing up the shotgun again. That made me tense, but she showed no sign of turning it on me. "But I remained a while longer, for I was sure I'd have no more of those problems, an' I didn't. I reckon he was so ashamed of himself, rightly, that he never asked for th' gun back. Or maybe he just knew I wouldn't give it. But I left not long after, for I'd had damn well enough of Forgotten and his grand war."

A silence passed over us, then, and I regarded my lap for a time. "I see," I said after a while, hands folding together. "I can respect your decision. I... nearly did the same more than once. But I've seen what the government does, and I don't think I can stand for it any longer. They..." I swallowed heavily. "They took my friend from me."

She snorted, and turned to me again. "They took my husband from me," she grunted, "but that don't make it right to go killing the lot of 'em."

"Is that why you joined up with Forgotten?" I asked, finding it difficult to meet her gaze. "I'd imagine you'd need a place to stay. And he's very... persuasive. Especially when you're getting a home on his bill."

"I joined up for revenge," she shrugged, leaning on the bar. Though she'd always looked rough, now I could really see the toll age had taken. She was tired, weary, worn. "During that goddamn war, they took my husband from me. Dragged him off to some concentration camp, or something. Never saw him again; I reckon they killed him."

My heart skipped a beat. Leaning in, speaking quickly and excitedly, I asked, "His name—John? Dark-skinned? Educated?"

"He's alive, then?" She blinked. I expected to see some

emotion from her. If not tears, then perhaps anger, excitement. But she remained as impassive as ever. "Huh. Didn't do much t' find me, did he? Didn't even mention he was married?" My hesitation seemed all the evidence she needed, and she shrugged. "Figures. It's been a long time, boy. Wounds heal. And let me tell you something." Pausing a moment, she seemed to collect herself, closing her eyes and breathing deeply. "The problem with Forgotten? The problem with his war? No matter how much you've suffered, an' no matter how angry or hateful you are, you ain't different from nobody else in the whole damn world. There's others that've suffered more. There's others that've suffered less. That's not gonna change, boy. Not with war. Not with a new government, or a new revolution. That's fuckin' life." Reaching into her apron, she pulled out a cigarette, lit it, and looked at the floor.

I stood, and moved toward the exit. "You're wrong," I told her, though I lacked conviction. "There will always be suffering, yes. And war may not fix it, but it *can* be fixed. But we won't fix anything if we don't take care of the people responsible, first. That's what I intend to do. I don't care about what they did in the war, and I don't care about some great ideology of freedom. But I've seen suffering since I came to Priius. I've seen hatred, and now I've seen death, and I'm going to end it. No matter what it takes."

As I strode for the exit, I heard her voice from behind me: "Well, then, you'd better prepare for a lot more of it." Ignoring her, I slammed the door behind me, and glanced silently at the other four. Out into the night we strode again, though I had even more on my mind, now. Mrs. Hughes wasn't right about everything, I don't believe. But she wasn't wrong about everything, either. I knew it even then, but I thought I was prepared.

XXVI.

As night settled in, so too did the chill in the air. We turned our collars up, save for Forgotten, and huddled close in the back alleys of Priius, muttering to each other about where to go from here. Milcher suggested the factory, due to its abandonment, but the rest of us felt it too close to our erstwhile base of operations. There was more talk of going to Tobit, but Forgotten still insisted that we should remain somewhere in Priius, even toward the outskirts; having to take a bus to get to and from our targets might prove a liability. I remained silent, both due to a lack of ideas and because I felt no need to reveal what she had said to me. The animosity between them was clearly great enough as it stood, and no matter what I felt of her personal philosophies, I still didn't want harm to come to her.

Priius is a large city, as you know, and once you move past the urban centers, it sprawls out. There are few enough accommodations for the working folk, thanks to the way the moneyed classes ran them out in the "urban reclamation" projects that surrounded its designation as Licenia's capital. But still, we found some: tenements and hovels, old and half-forgotten, near the factories too important to relocate. We were all growing weary by the time we settled on a tenement on the far eastern edge of the city, where the older factories laid. The air there was thick and clogged, almost painful to breathe. It choked and sickened its denizens, but the rent was cheap. Forgotten roused the landlord from sleep and paid him a month's rent, giving a little extra to keep his mouth shut. And just like that, we had a new base of operations for our sorry party.

There were no furnishings there, so we resolved to take care of that the following morning; for now, we would sleep on the floor. There were cracks and stains in the walls and ceiling, yellowed with smoke and browned with water damage. It would have been small for a single person; for five of us, it was cramped. Forgotten removed his greatcoat and wrapped it into a ball, using it as a blanket. He still refused to remove his helmet, even in such intimate company. I thought him some sort of ascetic, determined not to show his face until his work was done. Paranoia had kept him alive this long, and I couldn't fault him for it.

Milcher used his brawny arms as a pillow, and laid down to sleep by the door. He still considered himself a guard, and I don't doubt there was guilt in his mind after the night's episode. He'd been quiet most of the night, his expression dark and thoughtful. Peters sat with his back to a wall, eyes closed and legs folded; when the settling of the building quieted, I could hear quiet breath from him, along with the tap of his cracked lips against one another. He meditated nightly, but it was the first I had seen of it. Rothschild moved to leave the room, and I followed him out, catching him before he could walk off.

"I don't intend to sleep tonight," I whispered to him, my eyes focused on his crooked ones. His good eye regarded me sharply, its glass partner never quite turning enough to match. However, he said nothing yet, only watched. "I'm in the mood for a hunt, and I suspect you are, as well. You've seen me work. You know I'm competent. I'd like to accompany you."

He chuckled, then inclined his head. "Clever fellow. I did indeed have something of a hunt in mind, for I suspect I know where Henrick received his intelligence. Come with me; we'll visit the shops and have a drink. I hope you slept well last night." With that, he slipped back inside for a moment, returning with his pack. "This has most of what we need. Do you have your knife?" I nodded, and he did the same. "Good, then. Hopefully, you won't need it tonight. All the same, best be prepared."

I followed him through the chill winds of Licenia's cool nights, forming a mental map so that I could find our new headquarters again. Where once, one might have encountered a single guard walking the streets at night, checking locked doors and running off vagabonds, there were several out, now. We were given a cheerful questioning about our intentions, and Rothschild faked a local accent as he told them we'd gotten off on the wrong stop. They laughed pleasantly, and directed us to the bus stop.

I'd expected him to lead me to the closed shopping centers of Priius, given his words, but instead we caught a late bus to Tobit, joining a handful of silent passengers who'd come from other towns. It was nothing like when I had traveled with the churchgoers; then, I had felt nostalgic and thoughtful, and I had been surrounded by cheerful chatter. In the light which shone through the bus' windows, I could see that our fellow passengers bore the same unhealthy pallor as that other group, even wrapped up as they were in their coats and scarves. They stunk of exhaust and sweat, clutching paychecks and bus passes in their weathered hands.

Rothschild and I left at the first stop in Tobit; I had seen the town before as night had begun to descend, but never in the dark of night itself. Flickering streetlamps lit the sidewalks and roads, but it lacked the neon glare of Priius. I was grateful for that much, at least. Still, several of the shops were open, not least the nightclubs which littered the more affluent, tourist-trapping sections of the city. To my surprise, it was to one such area which Rothschild led me. I knew better than to ask, though curiosity burned bright in my eyes as we entered a sporting-goods store. For a moment, I wondered if I was to purchase a gun, here, but there were no guns for sale anywhere near the cities. Those belonged solely to law enforcement, and only a select few, at that time. Instead, Rothschild had me try out an aluminum baseball bat, light and sturdy. I found a length to my liking, and he gave me an odd smile.

The cashier looked up as I approached, and gave me a practiced smile. "Good evening, sir," she mumbled, ringing up my purchase, the machine clicking with each press. I passed over a bit of cash, and she put it away with a ching from the lever. "Planning a bit of sport, sir?" she asked, as she handed over my purchase. "A bit of sport," I echoed, with a hollow smile. With that, we left again.

"Our lion isn't so subtle," Rothschild mused to me, as he guided me past the glittering lights of clubs and shops and into the darkness of the ratty quarters of town. "He makes enemies where he has no need, and intimate ones, at that. He leaves his allies as lost too soon, like the men who fled tonight. Many have left for good, no doubt, but some might have returned, had we stayed but a day. Still, I don't care to argue with him."

I kept one hand in my pocket, the other gripped on the shaft of my new bat. "He does have a certain... force of presence," I replied, occasionally tapping the bat on the stony sidestreets. Rothschild shook his head. "Not so much that," he corrected, "as that he's set in his ways. He bears no contradiction. I admire his goals, to be sure, and his prowess is undeniable. But he is a strong leader, not a wise one. I have no desire to lead, and I am content to do what I may to assist him." We were quiet a while, before I asked him what his stake in all of this was.

"Absolution," he replied, and I thought he'd leave it at that, for a time. "Forgotten, Peters and I all served in the war, as you know, and we are all three bitter from those years. I study people. It's why I am what I am. And I think I know their motivations." I'd never heard him so... chatty, but I'd never been alone with him, either. And perhaps he needed to talk, after that night. "Forgotten is hurt and angry. He joined the war thinking himself a liberator, but they turned him into a murderer, instead. I only worked closely with him briefly; he is a man of extreme determination and deep convictions. He is also a man of excruciating guilt, a festering self-hatred, and a shattered psyche. He became an officer after everyone around him died. His leg was in three pieces. They patched him up and sent him back."

He paused to enter a bar, emerging a few minutes later without remark. We continued our walk, and he continued his analysis. "I think you've spoken to Peters. He thinks that he can clear himself of his traitor's guilt by killing those who ordered the torture of his countrymen. I think he's lost in a country that hates his kind, and that Forgotten is the one person who's offering any sort of direction in a life of chaos. Like Forgotten, he has his ideals, and he is devoted to them. And like Forgotten, he's more of an ideologue than an idealist, these days."

"It doesn't sound as though you think much of our mission," I remarked, resting the bat against my shoulder and trying to read the signs of the buildings we passed. "What makes you hang around? Are you feeling guilty, too?"

He was silent for several minutes, and it wasn't until he entered and left a second bar that he answered me. "I was born in a country which no longer exists, across an ocean. It lost a war to Licenia. My family lived in extreme poverty; I had no stomach for it, and stowed away on a ship to the country I hate. As an illegal alien in this country, I joined the military for two reasons: so that I could receive my citizenship, and so that I could get the training I needed. At first, I thought I would move up through the ranks, and finally get into a place where I could sabotage the works." My eyebrows raised, but he took no notice. "Then, the Grand War broke out, and I thought I could act as a double-agent for Greenwood. But I would be helping one tyrant against another. Instead, I served as a spy for Licenia. And I did a good job, because I knew to bide my time."

"And then the war ended," I concluded, "and you were sent away again?"

"More or less, yes," he nodded. "For a while, I wasn't sure what to do: I considered working as a Licenian agent, and putting aside the memory of what they did to my family. Then, I met Forgotten again, by chance, while we were collecting our pensions. We talked for a time, and he confided his anger to me. I reciprocated, and became his collaborator. But I'm not concerned about freedom or justice," he shrugged, lighting up a cigarette and puffing on it. "I just don't have a taste for empires. Frankly, I think Forgotten will fail, and I'll disappear again. But if he does succeed, it will be a step toward destabilizing Licenia."

"So, what do you want, exactly?" I pressed, tapping my fingers on my arm. He was leaning in a third bar window, and didn't turn as he replied. "I want to destroy Licenia," he told me, calmly. "If Forgotten's method fails, then I'll find Parliament on my own. Every last one will fall by my hand, and I will then die with honor, having returned what they did to my homeland. It's not political. I just want to watch their cities burn in the same way that mine did, torn apart by the hungry hounds of their neighbors."

I watched him, finding no words to make response to that statement. He turned and smiled to me, nodding to the door of the bar. "Speaking of dogs, I believe I have located our mutual friend. Were you a wretched, mutilated traitor paid well by a government which might as quickly arrest you, you might find yourself with quite a thirst."

Curious, I glanced in the window while he walked inside. Seated alone at a table was a young man, a bandage wrapped around his head, where one of his ears had been.

XXVII.

I waited outside, watching through the glass as Rothschild entered the bar. There were very few people left inside; it looked as though it might close soon. He walked up to the young man, and took a seat across from him. Even through the grimy glass, I could see the fear of recognition in the deserter's face. He made no attempt to leave or fight, but the latter would have ended disastrously for the malnourished youth. They spoke for less than a minute, then the young man stood, trembling slightly, and began moving for the back entrance, Rothschild behind him. I did the same, slipping around the corner of the building.

"I don't know what you're talking about," I heard the young man say, holding up his hands. As I rounded the corner, I could see Rothschild with his arms folded, regarding the other man, who had his back to the wall. I felt no sympathy for him; if Rothschild's suspicions were correct, he had sold us out. It made sense; how else would they have found us so quickly?

"And I don't believe you," the spymaster murmured in reply. "Now, if you tell me the truth, I'll let you go. If not... well, I won't hurt you. But believe me, it's in your best interest to just answer my question. Yes, or no: did you or Talbot tell anyone about our headquarters in Old Hampton?"

"Fuck, man, I dunno what Talbot did!" he wailed. "You're crazy! Let me go!" Rothschild shrugged, and stepped slightly aside, so that I could take my place beside him, bat in hand. "I won't hurt you, either way," he repeated, "but I cannot guarantee that my friend will not. Stone, I believe you are acquainted with Jackson?"

Stone's gaze turned next to me, and he began pleading with me, now. "Jackson? Jackson. I know you don't know me that well, but—but we played poker that one night, remember? And

I know what happened with the explosion, and I'm sorry you got hurt, but holy shit, *don't kill me*." I was hardly in the best of moods at that point, and something about him annoyed me. I prodded him in the chest with the end of the bat, not hard, and grunted, "Answer the goddamn question."

He hesitated, then tried to bolt. However, with his back pressed against the wall, he had to make an awkward maneuver to evade us, and it failed: my bat came crashing down on his leg with a crack, and he fell, clutching it and crying out. It was the first time I had ever intentionally injured someone who wasn't fighting back. It felt strangely... empowering.

Stepping over him, Rothschild grabbed him by the hair and dragged him back where he'd been, shoving him against the wall. Stone kept the weight off his injured leg, panting and gasping while Rothschild pinned him by the throat with his uninjured arm. "Let me ask an easier question. There's no use lying to us. Whom did you tell?"

"You guys are fucking insane!" wailed Stone, thrashing about in his grip. "You broke my damn leg!"

"I'll break more if you don't start answering our questions," I growled, white-knuckled as I gripped the bat. "Two men are dead now. Their blood's on your hands. So if you want to get out of this alive, you'd damn well better tell us who you told. I don't want to hurt you, Stone, but by God, I will if I have to."

Stone's response was to grab and wrench Rothschild's injured shoulder. He cried out in pain, swinging for Stone's head, and missed. When the deserter tried to run again, my bat met him in the stomach. He sprawled out on the ground a good foot away from where he'd been standing, gasping and choking on the ground. While he coughed and sputtered, I knelt next to him, taking his pinky finger in my hand. Rothschild set a knee on his chest, his good arm shaking slightly as he gripped Stone's head. "Listen here, you little shit," he hissed. "One more antic like that, and you'll be walking to the hospital with ten broken toes. We're not going to kill you. But we'll fuck you up so much you'll wish we had."

Stone babbled incoherently until I started twisting his finger backward; it was reaching the point of tension when he yowled, "I told a city guard I had information! I'm sorry! I was angry and scared. He set up a meeting with a guy named... uh... named..." While he hesitated, I bent his finger a little more, and he writhed in pain. "God! I'm trying to remember, damn it! Keller!" I let go of his finger, and he breathed a sigh of relief. "His name was something-Keller, you crazy assholes. Now let me go."

I broke his pinky. He howled horribly, and I let him go. The door to the bar opened and shut; dropping Stone, Rothschild and I hurried off into the night. As we retreated, we heard his squeals of pain. He sounded like a pig, you know. I think he was one. A foul, filthy pig, deserving of slaughter. I have little stomach for traitors, and though you doubtless think me one, I beg to differ. For no-one who attempts to make a difference for the better is a traitor—misguided, perhaps, but not a traitor. The conformists are the ones who have failed their country.

I cannot say that it felt good to beat him, but it was satisfying. Cathartic, even. I regret it now, but at the time, it made me feel powerful; I could suddenly understand why sadists and brutes act in the way they do. Rothschild assured me, as we walked away, that I had done well. He knew our "names," such as they were, but could give no more information than that we had been in Tobit. Our descriptions, certainly, but he could have given those already. That night, with the thrill of "victory" coursing through me, I had no thought of consequence.

No buses were running by the time we arrived at the station; rather than wait overnight, we elected to begin the long trudge back to Priius. It was walkable, but it took several hours, when we had already been up all day. All the same, it gave us time to discuss our plans from that point on.

"I recognize the name 'Keller,'" he told me. "Very rich, very powerful family. They've got a town named after them, even. If not a member of Parliament, then no doubt connected. It's a shame he didn't recall the first name, but I'm sure I can work it out. People are much more predictable than they think themselves, you know, and in a city like Priius, privacy is an illusion. Everyone knows something about someone; it's a matter of finding the right people. And then, there are people like myself, whose business is information. We like to remain in contact," he chuckled.

By the time we were nearing Priius, the sun was rising, giving a crimson glow all about us. I yawned, eyes bleary, for I had been awake for nearly an entire day. Adrenaline had kept me going through much of it, but now, I could feel myself growing tired. A nearby streetlight quietly turned off as the light hit it; slowly, the neon signs all around did the same. We traversed the sidewalks of Priius as they grew thick with fellow travelers, though we were dressed rather less nicely than they were, and walked much more slowly.

Back at the tenement, the others had already risen. They were sore and stiff from having slept on the floor, and we had to wait for Milcher to move just so we could get in the room. "You two l-look like you've been dragged thr-through a wringer," he grunted, wiping his eyes. "G-guards didn't give you no troub-ble, did they?" I assured them they hadn't, and Rothschild looked around the room.

"Jackson and I hunted down our betrayer," he declared. "It was good luck, mostly: we found him enjoying his payment in a bar in Tobit. Stone, if you care to know. His leg is injured, if not broken, as is one pinky. Talbot may or may not be guilty, but if Stone told the truth, we have a lead on who orchestrated the attack. A man named Keller. If one of you gentlemen would look through the papers for that surname, I am going to sleep." And with that, he laid on the ground, not bothering to remove his clothing. I suspect he was used to such accommodations. Peters opened Rothschild's case, and began leafing through the papers. As for myself, I fashioned myself a sort of bed out of my packed-up clothing, and fell into an exhausted slumber.

I woke hours later, when the door closed and Milcher walked in, carrying a bottle of brandy. "I g-got what you wanted," he grinned to Forgotten, holding up four cups. "You sure y-you don't want any?"

Forgotten nodded silently, and Milcher set to work on pouring them. Rothschild, already awake, sat in the corner, regarding us all through half-open eyes. Peters and Forgotten were busy compiling all of the available information on Keller, though the former accepted a glass from Milcher with a rare smile. Milcher gave me one as well, and then held up his own. He looked around, a little shyly, and then cleared his throat. We all turned to watch, even Forgotten, while he composed himself.

"To Fergus," he said, speaking slowly and carefully, concentrating almost painfully hard. "He was a good man. And a good friend." He downed his brandy. Peters stood next; he might have been foreign to our country, but not to our customs. "To Rothschild," he declared, "without whom we might never have known we'd been compromised." He drank, and Rothschild stood. "To Jarkah," he solemnly intoned. "And to those who perished in its destruction." Though he had no drink, Forgotten stood next, before I could. "To Jackson. The newest of the five bravest men I have ever known."

I stood, holding my drink and unsure of what to say. As the

last to toast, I had the burden of coming up with the conclusion; I hadn't anything particularly grand in mind, at first. For almost a minute, I thought, before holding up my glass. "To Licenia," I declared. "Not to the Licenia that is, but to the Licenia that should be, and the Licenia that will be. To those who have given their lives in the pursuit of its liberation. To those who have worked themselves into dust in the pursuit of its greatness. And to those whose blood has been shed by the hands of its tyranny. We are damned today, that we might be saints eternally." I drank, and sat down again.

We were silent for a while, then Peters softly began to sing an old Greenwood folk song. None of the rest of us knew the words, but after he finished, we joined in a second round of it. I don't do it justice, and I won't sing it, but I remember the last verse well.

> "O, come, all ye children of war,
> Bruised and broken, bloodied and sore;
> Peace awaits a breath away—
> Sleep, and never face the day.
> O, come ye, and rest evermore."

XXVIII.

Five days. It was five days after we found out that bastard's name. Rothschild went on the hunt again, searching for information about our Mr. Keller and his involvement in the death of Fergus. I spent much of the time in a drugged stupor, in the belief that if I could obliterate my mind often enough, I could obliterate the memory of his face. But it was no use: it came to me every damned night afterward. I dreamt he was alive again, that it had all been some mistake. And every morning, I woke to remember that he was dead, unburied, lying in a meat factory.

The rest of us spoke little, save for hushed exchanges between Peters and Forgotten as they looked over the papers. Milcher did his best to cook for us, and the meals were passable, but nothing spectacular. The truth is, poor Milcher knew he wasn't as intelligent as we were. He never should have been part of that wretched company: he was as much a victim as...

He was a victim, anyway. We used him. We all knew he wasn't all there in the head, but he was a strong man, and loyal. Just like Fergus. And I suppose I saw him that way, in those days: a nickle-plated Fergus, not so fine as the original, but a surrogate of sorts. But that led to a foolish resentment, on my part: I wanted him to be someone he wasn't, to fill a hole which couldn't be filled. They held the same position within the camp, had much the same physique, and had—if you'll excuse my sentimentality—the same good heart. But the similarities ended there.

On the third night after my trip to Tobit, Peters led me outside, to chat a bit. In the cover of relative darkness, we took a walk through Priius' ugly side-streets, like two fine gentlemen discussing a business agreement. I suppose I was still something of an outsider, then: the new fellow. Forgotten, Rothschild, and

Peters all knew each other, at least to some degree, and Milcher wouldn't make a good confidante, for all his good intentions. That left me, and they needed someone to talk to. It's the only explanation I can come up with.

"Jackson," he muttered, never raising his voice above that quiet, rapid patter, "I have concerns. About you, that is. Don't take it harshly," he added, before I could voice my reply. "If anything, it's a compliment. We're soldiers. Forgotten, Rothschild, and I are soldiers, that is. Milcher isn't, but he's been with us for a while. And we don't entrust him with particularly sensitive work. But you." He stopped and turned to me for a moment, looking me up and down. I could see him knitting his brow. "You're a very ordinary person, Jackson. In a good way. You're a good man. An honest man. You lack the scars that come with warfare."

He fell silent, and my heart leapt into my throat. After all this, I wondered, was he going to tell me that I couldn't fight alongside the others? But he spoke again, resuming his walk. "I worry, sometimes, that we push people too hard. Too fast. We spent years planning. Gathering information. Gathering men. And gathering our courage. This is..." He took a breath, then released it. "Terrifying work. I haven't felt it since the war. It's not a common fear; it's more of a dread. You dread every fucking day. It's a fresh horror, wondering who you're going to lose. What new atrocities will be committed. And once again, I find myself on the side committing the greater number."

"It's for a greater good," I replied, in a quiet tone. "We're to rouse a sleeping giant. A few men have died, yes, but—they were the enemy. They're the oppressors. If we don't fight against them, who will? There's no-one who can defend our freedom—the freedom of Licenia—but us."

He gave me a long, searching look. I couldn't make out his

eyes, where we stood, but I could feel it, all the same. "Funny thing, Jackson. That's what they said of Greenwood, all through the Grand War."

We were silent for a while longer, circling around toward the tenement again. He broke the silence, eventually, placing a hand on my arm. "Don't take it harshly," he repeated, with a sigh. "I don't know you well, Jackson. I don't know anyone well. That way lies pain, especially in war. But I remember well what you said to me after we dealt with Lampton, believe me. And I worry, Jackson. I worry that you'll come out of this as broken as the rest of us. And you deserve better."

He lit a cigar, and gave me one, as well. We smoked for a time, leaning against a building and watching the cars shuffling by, around a corner. "I'm glad you're here, though. We need strong, clever men. Now, more than ever. Just don't ever lose sight of what you're fighting for. You'll become like them." He nodded at a passing regiment of guards, wearing the uniform of Licenia's military. "You'll become like us."

We went back inside after we finished smoking. I said nothing more to him. Each time I spoke with any of those three —Forgotten, Rothschild, Peters—I felt a keen sense of inadequacy and youth. They had been men, fighting and dying in a foreign land, while I was still a child. Now, I was supposedly a man, but I felt not much older than I did when I watched Forgotten on the television. The first color broadcast. It never seemed so real, back then.

Rothschild returned five nights after finding out that name, as I have said. He leaned against a wall after stepping inside, wearing an immaculate suit marred only by the sling around his arm. "Gentlemen," he muttered, twirling a cigar between his fingers, "I have an address. Keller."

We all turned to look at him, expectantly. He seemed

content to leave it at that: he light the cigar and started puffing on it, closing his eyes. "Well?" I demanded, lifting an eyebrow.

The spymaster regarded me, then shrugged. "I haven't cased the place yet. Considering the amount of wealth that family has, and our prior... exploits, I wouldn't be surprised if he has a regiment positioned all around the place. But it's 2460 Wells Avenue." He eyed me a moment longer, adding, "I'll inspect it tomorrow. Until then, stay put. Keller will be attending a funeral tomorrow; he might be more vulnerable on his return." He stripped, then laid down on a cot he'd apparently procured during his outing. "I'm going to sleep. It's been a long week."

Milcher moved to take guard, but I caught his arm. "I'll do it," I muttered to him. "You take a break, for once." The poor fellow had been standing guard all day, and it was showing on him. His eyes bore deep circles, and he walked with a stoop. Though he began to protest, a yawn interrupted him. We chuckled, and he shrugged, heading off to sleep.

I was quite certain that we didn't need a guard. At that point, if anyone had found us, having a guard wouldn't have saved us. It was just a formality, or perhaps a gesture to make us feel more like an organization, and less like five outcasts trying to pull off an impossible scheme. But I, too, had a scheme in mind: one born of the hot-headed mind of an angry young man. "Forgotten," I said, walking over to him as he was taking off his coat, "do you mind if I borrow your coat? It's cold out, you know, and I haven't..."

He stared at me silently through his mask for a long while, and I fell quiet, as well. I think he wanted to say "no," but couldn't quite bring himself to do it. When I glanced at his hands, they were digging deeply into the thick wool. Possessively. But I hadn't asked for his mask; that was the one thing he still never removed, save, I imagine, in absolute privacy.

He slept in the damned thing. Finally, he handed his coat to me, seeing that he was going to be taking it off, anyhow. "Keep it safe," he muttered, laying down.

I put it on; it enveloped me. He was just large enough that it slipped all the way down to my fingers, leaving a bit of sag around my shoulders. Although I looked more like a tramp in an ill-fitting coat, I felt like a child in his father's clothes. My hands felt for the fasteners, then slid them into place; it really was a remarkably warm coat. I grabbed a scarf, tying it around my face, and then stepped outside.

As chill as the night was, I still felt rather overdressed for the weather. All the same, I had a new identity: I was no street-bum, nor scoundrel, nor even a worker. Cloaked in that crimson coat, I was an officer of the military; for perhaps the first time in my life, a respectable sort of person. I spent the first hour of that night on watch, waiting for the others to fall asleep. Then, as silently as my boots would allow, I crept back inside. The others were all still, Peters softly snoring. I smiled to myself beneath the scarf, and grabbed the knife I had received from Rothschild—it seemed like years ago. And with that, I strode out into the night again, hands in the coat's pockets to disguise the way it covered my hands.

There was something thrilling in even the simple act of walking around the city: I felt like a spy from one of the movies I'd watched as a child. The streets were largely deserted, by now; other than the distant rumble of traffic, I heard only the faint buzz and whirr of neon signs, and the clopping of my own feet on the sidewalk. Once, as I passed through an alley to the main street, I saw a blur of motion to my side; in a quick motion, I drew my knife and turned to face it. But it was only a homeless man, clad in rags and holding up his hands. In the light from the streetlamp, I could see terror in his eyes. We said nothing; I just motioned him on, and he hurried away.

But fooling a wastrel was no test of my disguise. And so, walking the numbered streets in the plain light of Priius' night, I allowed any who cared to see me have a look. As I crossed a street, the light changed to green, but no cars dared move. Not even those behind me. The glow of ten headlights illuminated me, and all could see the coat. Not me: only the garment. But I suppose the garment is what they respected.

I approached a company of guards, and my heart leapt. This, then, was the true test. I lacked the helmet of an officer, and I figured there was an equal chance that I would be saluted or questioned. Narrowing my eyes, I avoided making eye contact with a single one of them. I was a man on a mission, and I couldn't be bothered with pleasantries. To my unspeakable relief, they gained that impression—not only did they leave me be, they stepped out of the way, saluting as I passed. I turned to give the last one a nod, and they resumed their march with pride in their step. A certain cynical amusement tugged at my lips.

As I approached the lower street-numbers, passing 3rd Street, I passed into a section of Priius I had never seen, before. There were actual houses, here: not penthouses, but huge mansions. Nobody had bothered to mention their existence to me when I'd asked about housing, because these were never for sale. They were family estates, more a bank vault than a living space. I consulted a city map, and located Wells Avenue. However, my passage into the district was stopped by a gate. A guarded gate, no less. This, then, was the regiment at which Rothschild had guessed. I prepared a story, decided I would tell them I had come in from the west on a private mission. But they simply swung the gate open for me with haste as I approached.

These weren't military men. These were ordinary civilians who had been dressed in the garb of the military, and set to

guarding the city. One, I noticed, even carried a pistol with him.
Expecting him to be the effective officer, I gave a salute, which
he returned with a trembling hand. Then, as easy as anything, I
strode into the richest neighborhood in the entire nation.

My mind reeled at the thought of what I had done and was
about to do. It would never have occurred to Rothschild to go in
through the front gate, and with this particular disguise, I would
disappear in an instant. All I had to do was give the coat back to
Forgotten, and I was Jackson again, not a Licenian officer. For
now, no-one gave me any trouble. With the greatest ease, I
found 2460 Wells Avenue.

The waste made me sneer. Doric columns of white marble
lined the front, while two huge, oaken doors barred passage
inside. Ivy grew along wooden supports placed along the walls,
and a paved walkway led to the front door. After ensuring that
none were passing by, I wandered up along the path, to test the
door. Locked. Around the house I prowled, checking every
window and entrance, to find them all locked. So much for the
safety and security promised by a gated neighborhood.

My heart began to race as I looked at a drainpipe. It led up
to a landing on the second floor, but would it support my
weight? What if someone saw me? What if there was no
passage inside there? I shook these thoughts from my mind, and
steeled myself, then ascended the pipe. My feet found purchase
in the stonework: laid out almost like a mosaic, there were
plenty of jutting angles and rough patches to support me. With
my hands and thighs clutching to the pipe, I shimmied up,
though the coat made this more of a difficulty than it should
have been. Finally, reaching the top, I leapt onto the landing,
hitting the concrete on my shoulder. It stung, but not badly;
brushing myself off, I tried the glass door leading inside. And
sure enough, I found myself in the dark of an unlit bedroom, with

the night's illumination casting my shadow inside. I closed the door behind myself, and crept silently to the bed, praising my fortunes in finding the correct room accidentally

He was a younger man, perhaps in his thirties. For some reason, that reassured me: here was no old man who couldn't have hoped to defend himself, but someone in the prime of life. Of course, I had no intention of giving him the chance. I raised my knife—and stopped. Fumbling in the darkness, hearing each sound multiplied tenfold, I searched for evidence that this was my man. Eventually, I found his wallet, with identifying information. Joseph Keller. I took the money, but left the rest, as tempting as it was. A famous corpse's papers would be of no use to me.

My chest heaved, breath rapid and shallow. My knife flashed in the light filtering in through the windows. I crept over to him again. Here, then, was the man who had ordered the attack on Old Hampton. Another piece of filth from Parliament. Another leech on society. Fergus' murderer, about to meet justice. Before I could think about what I was doing, I slashed his throat, sending blood pooling into the bed. He convulsed horribly, flailing about, staring wide-eyed and trying to scream. I shoved his pillow in his face, my eyes closed as I forced his weak body down. For a few moments, he continued twitching, the involuntary convulsions of a dying body. And then, all was still.

I felt nothing.

Neither remorse nor pity; neither disgust nor exultation. There was no satisfaction in this killings, despite the knowledge that I had avenged Fergus' untimely death. I stood over his bloodied form, clutching my dripping knife and staring at his lifeless corpse, but I felt no different than I had a moment ago. For some reason, that angered me: I felt slighted.

"Goddamn you," I breathed, before plunging my knife into

his chest with a cry of rage. "You murdering cunt! Rot in hell!" I fell on him like a madman, stabbing and slashing, leaving his corpse a tattered mess. "Fuck you, you... you..." But I trailed off again, glaring and panting. He remained as dead as Fergus. Nothing I did would change that. Nothing I did could bring either of them back. In confusion and frustration, I let out a cry of inarticulate fury—

—and stopped as I heard the faint cry of a woken infant.

I cannot explain what I did next. I fled blindly from the room, hurrying down the stairs with a noisy clatter, sure I was being pursued. I threw open the back door and fled, not bothering to shut it behind myself. As I ran, I shoved my bloodied knife back into its sheath, fleeing in the night for the better part of a minute before realizing that I had no pursuers. Slowly, slowly, I forced myself to walk as I had before, though my heart beat against my chest. I left through the opposite gate from that which I had entered, and circled back around to return to the tenement, my crusade complete.

XXIX.

I dared not turn on a light as I reentered the tenement, for fear that I would wake the others. Moving slowly, relying on memory and touch, I groped along blindly until I found my cot, where I laid down, using Forgotten's coat as a blanket. In that darkness, I could hardly see in front of me; still working by feel, I took hold of my kit of needles, and began the long, slow process of preparing the drug. After what I had seen that night, I needed to destroy myself again. I needed release from earthly concerns, into the swirling Elysium of mindless ecstasy. It proved a long, slow, painful process, during which time I pricked myself with the needle I know not how many times, and finally collapsed into a stupor after what seemed like hours of fumbling.

When I awoke the following morning, I was naked. I hung suspended, upside-down, from the ceiling. My hands were bound, my mouth gagged, blood rushing to my head in a singularly unpleasant way. A harsh, artificial light hurt my eyes; I could see nothing but two pairs of boots before me. Though I struggled and shook, I could manage nothing but to swing slightly in my restraints, grunting in fury and confusion. Through my bleariness, I was aware of a dull ache in my chest; this only added to my agitation, and I continued to struggle until I felt a single drop of blood hit my chin from above. Immediately, my struggling ceased, and I listened to determine what had become of me. Fortunately, I was not held in suspense for long.

The golden face of a lion slid down into my field of vision, to be met with a furious, accusatory glare. It regarded me with the same passionless snarl as ever, before growling at me in that horrid, gravelly voice. "If we were more than five," he told me, "you would be dead."

He straightened up again, and walked off behind me. I could

hear each fall of his feet, and idly wondered if he intended to stab me in the back, or perhaps treat me in the same way he had Lampton. Sure enough, his knife fell—but on the rope, not my flesh. I fell hard on my shoulders, landing with a grunt, and was soon squinting into the harsh light they'd suspended above me.

"Being a warrior makes you a light sleeper," I could hear Rothschild say, from the side. "And when I woke to find you missing, I set out to follow you. You're an easy mark, Jackson; you aren't paranoid enough." He chuckled once, infuriatingly, then sighed. "But you disobeyed a direct order. For this, you should be dead. But you are not, for two reasons." I had closed my eyes by this point, but I am sure he counted them off on his fingers. "One is that we are in poor condition, as a fighting unit. The other is that you are, to some degree, a clever man."

He approached me, then took a seat a little closer. I heard him lean forward in his chair, followed by the thump of a glass being set down. "You formulated a plan very quickly. You acted very efficiently, and somehow, you don't seem to have raised suspicions, despite walking right past the enemy in a coat which does not fit you." He snorted derisively before continuing. "Keller is dead, I am sure. I do not suspect you would have emerged unpursued, had this not been the case. It was not a bad plan; I will own that much. However, you are, by rights, a dead man. Never forget this."

Shortly after that, they unfastened my bindings, and gave me my clothes. I dressed, refusing to speak to any of them. Although Peters and Milcher had not said anything, I suspected they had offered little enough objection to this decision. Peters, at least, had likely been part of it. "I did the fucking job," I eventually grunted, without turning around.

"And you could have compromised us all in doing it," snapped Peters; I turned, surprised. Hearing him raise his voice was something new to me. "It's not about doing the job: it's about doing the job and getting out clean. You did—*this* time. And you might again. You might keep on forever, by good fortune. But good fortune is never guaranteed. It was a goddamn stupid thing to do, Jackson, no matter how good your plan. You *ask*. You talk to us about ideas you have. We discuss them, and we decide on a plan of action. Got it?"

I nodded, rather sullenly. It reminds me now of having been scolded by my father. "Good," he sighed, standing. "Then come with me. We're getting you a proper suit. God knows you deserve one, after what you've been through." This sudden change of tone nearly raised a question from me; he could see it on my face, and he shook his head. "You're overdue for this. You've done more than a lot of the others ever did. Consider it a uniform: you're part of our group, now. Officially. We've got enough from Forgotten's pension that we can afford this."

"Well," I said, trying to compose my thoughts long enough to make a better reply. I couldn't. "Alright."

Peters paused long enough to give me an odd look. "But if you ever do anything of that magnitude of stupidity again, have no doubt that we'll be taking it back, along with a solid layer of flesh."

It's relieving to reflect that I have had such solid friends during my stay in Priius.

You may have noticed that I wax garrulous—and at times, even eloquent, I'd like to think—while here with you, but the majority of my descriptions of my own sides of these conversation is terse at best. There are two primary reasons for this: for one, I have no love of quoting myself. The other is that throughout the majority of my time in Priius, perhaps even the majority of my life, I have been wandering about in a state of confusion. I fear I repeat myself, as always, for it's often hard to differentiate between what I have said and what I have thought. It might not be an overstatement to say that, until very recently, I was still a child. All my life, I have bristled at the idea that cynicism is the natural outgrowth of adulthood—

But I am no cynic. No. Cynicism is the philosophy of the weak, the bulwark of the coward. Am I jaded? Certainly. But never a cynic. Forgive me; where was I?

It is a wise child who remains silent. I was a ward in the care of the aged and weary men and women around me, clinging to one after another for guidance and support. From my parents, to Mrs. Hughes, to Forgotten, to John, to... Well. Until very recently, as I was saying, I have never had occasion to speak. It hasn't been my place: speaking should be reserved for those who have a purpose in doing so. I have found my purpose, and in my own roundabout way, I am relating it. I know that I'm eating away at the hours, but I assure you, we have the night and the morning beyond, should we find we have need of it. I know it's no fun for you, but believe me: I need this. I have to let out the words, lest they burst from me.

Peters and I had something in common, in that regard: neither of us were men who frequently spoke, but when we did, we spoke with a purpose. It seemed odd, almost surreal, to have him walking beside me in the broad light of day, when I had previously never seen him leave Old Hampton, save during our mass exodus. We wandered along the streets with our heads down and our hands in our pockets, though I glanced up each time we passed a member of the swollen town guard, to gauge his reaction to the man beside me. Almost without fail, they cast a suspicious eye on him; it burned inside of me, but I said nothing to Peters. In all likelihood, he already knew. C'est la vie.

The more we walked in silence, the more I found myself looking over at him; he took no obvious notice of my furtive glances, not even bothering to flick his gaze in my direction. A multitude of questions swirled in me, but too many of them were too dangerous to ask aloud. Eventually, if only to break what seemed to me to be a growing tension, I asked, "Why the help in picking a suit?"

He looked briefly irritated; I think he thought I was annoyed to have him around. He looked up at me with his lips slightly parted, then paused on seeing my quizzical expression. It took him a moment, but eventually, he muttered, "Because I know men's clothing."

"Oh," I said, and for a time, I said nothing more. A few cars rushed by us as we stepped into Franklin Square, fluttering the legs of my trousers and setting me to shivering. The others who wandered the sidewalks stared straight ahead, marching silently onward, only the sound of their dress shoes hitting the concrete to add to the city's cacophony. My mind began to wander—and, unsurprisingly, it wandered back to the night before, haunting me with the sound of an infant's cries and the strange huff of breath which accompanied Keller's last moments. "Where'd you learn that, then?" I asked, a little too sudden and a little too fast.

He shrugged, glancing to the side of himself which I didn't occupy. "I was an architect before the war, Jackson. I wore suits."

Even more than Rothschild—hell, even more than Forgotten —Peters never opened up to me. Maybe that's part of why I still hold him in high esteem: I never got to see as many of the ugly holes in him as I did the others. So you'll forgive me if I speculate a bit on him.

Here was a man who had a decent life. Rothschild and Forgotten—they were soldiers. From the moment they became men—too soon and too quickly, from what I understand—they did everything they could to thrust themselves into conflict and violence. I'll admit, with a bit of embarrassment, that I find it difficult to place his age, but I suspect he was older than Forgotten, and perhaps older than Rothschild. Not by much, perhaps, but by enough that he had actually set out on a career. Then came the war, and then came the draft, and he was catapulted headfirst into a conflict not his own. Initially, he thought himself in the right: it might not have been his first choice, but to fight for his country seemed like a noble end. From there, every moral, every value he'd ever held was brought under inspection. And the constant questioning, the constant process of turning everything over in his head, until he felt as though he might burn from the inside for want of answers, cooked him to nothing but a burnt, charred, hollow husk.

I'm calm. I'm calm. I'm sorry for my outbursts. I see—I see something of myself... It's inconsequential.

Peters took me to a clothing store. Not the most expensive, not the cheapest, but a good, solid clothing store. He helped me to find a white shirt, a black waistcoat, and a pair of slacks in my size—yes, the very outfit I wear now. He paid for it with some cash from Forgotten's pension, and that was that. I have nothing more to say of that day. I need another goddamn drink.

XXX.

Four days. Four nights. The steady stream of poison into my veins. Days of fasting, nights of ecstasy, lost in an apathetic stupor. The others judged me—I could feel it in their gaze, smell it on their breath. And don't think I don't smell it on yours, you bastard.

I'm sorry.

On the fourth day, I ran out. There had only been so much heroin left, and I used the last of it. Every time I was sober, the memories returned: I recalled the hot plunge of the knife into Keller's soft, giving flesh, the way it spread and gushed around the blade. I recalled the way his eyes shot open, mouth gaping like a fish on shore as he flailed and thrashed about. I could hear his barely-born child crying in the other room, calling out for the parents who could no longer run to comfort it. It made me nauseous. I still dream about it. I still remember, and I can never forget. I don't deserve to, and I don't want to, anymore. But all the same, I never forget.

They thought I deserved a break: I was new to the game, and I had only then made my first kill. So they let me huddle in the corner, where the light was blocked, curled into a tight ball on my cot or stretched out languidly, limbs splayed in all directions. While I erased, they planned. Even Milcher helped them plan. I have vague recollections of endless discussions that rattled around between my ears, loud and unwanted. Even during the days, I was too far gone to pay attention. I stopped eating regularly, subsiding on what Milcher gently forced me to eat. And then, a while after I'd run out, once I'd sobered up, Peters came over and laid a hand on my shoulder. It was night again, and I was laying on my cot, facing the ceiling, trying to ignore the craving I felt. But I was sober, and I suppose that's all he needed.

"We're going for a walk, Jackson," he told me. "Might take your bat."

He waited patiently—or at least with an air of patience—while I dressed, my hands feeling somewhat sluggish and lazy at first. I had hardly used them for the last several days, and I was out of practice with them. My tie was crooked, my shirt not tucked in just right, but I looked passable. While Peters tucked a small bag under his arm, I grabbed my bat. And we two alone set out, just like we had earlier in the week.

"Who's our mark?" I asked, as we wandered through the alleys and byways. There was a hint of rain in the air; it felt thick and heavy with humidity. "Torturer," he replied, as short and clipped as ever. He stopped abruptly as he began to round a corner onto the sidewalk, then pressed back against the wall, making as though he were lighting a cigarette; I hesitated, he glared at me, and I mirrored his action. Shortly thereafter, a city guard, portly and balding, wandered by. He took no notice of us, only whistled as he walked down the path.

It irritated me, for a reason I couldn't place. Something about his cheerful demeanor, and the knowledge that this was the enemy, bothered me. My knuckles tightened on the bat as I leaned around the edge of the brick, glaring at the back of that man's head. When I looked back to Peters, he was eying me quizzically.

Lowering my bat, I shrugged. "Doesn't it piss you off?" I asked, trying to make casual conversation. "The government keeps acting like nothing's wrong, but then it has these assholes patrolling the streets like they own the damn place." With a tone more petulant than aggressive, I added, "I wouldn't mind breaking a face or two. Show Beckstein what I think of his lies."

Peters continued staring at me for several more moments, before he surprised me with a response. "The fuck is wrong with you?" he asked, just before sliding around the corner and beginning the walk down the street. I hastened to walk up beside him on the right, somewhat blocking his dark face from the street's view. Though he kept his eyes focused forward, he mumbled to continue addressing me. "It's not like they want to be out here. Shit, *I* don't want to be out here. But keep the fighting limited to Beckstein, Parliament, and those who try to stop us from getting to them. Otherwise, there's not much to separate us from the dictator we fight."

"Yeah," I grunted, fumbling around in my pockets to withdraw a cigar. "Otherwise, you might torture people who torture people, because torturing people is wrong." I think it was my craving that had me in such a foul mood. I certainly hope it was. He had every right to punch me for that snide remark, but he refrained, instead stalking on in silence.

As we neared the gated community where so many of Priius' moneyed class lived, Peters ducked into an alley, beckoning quickly for me to follow. As soon as I did, he thrust a mask into my hands: the same crow's mask I had worn when Rothschild, Fergus, and I had kidnapped Lampton. Peters pulled on his viper's mask. And then, he reached into his coat and produced the pistol which had been used to murder Fergus. Leaning in, he spoke in a hushed, muffled voice.

"We need to do this fast, and we need to do this quietly. There are two guards by the gate. They're armed. There are more patrolling. I might be able to neutralize both at the gate, but the noise would draw the attention of the others, and I don't want to alert anyone else. The others aren't coming with us, because this isn't about Forgotten's goals: this is personal. This is for me. But you owe us for that stunt you pulled, so your ass is on the line, too." After pausing for a breath, he said, "What I'm going to ask you to do is damned dangerous, and it might not

work. If it doesn't, we run. If they yell, run. If they pull a gun..."
He shrugged. "Beat it out of their hands before they can fire."

The rest of his plan was... straightforward, to put it kindly. It
relied heavily on chance; too much for my tastes, in fact, but I
believe this was meant to be, if nothing else, a test of their
defenses. He'd brought with him a number of sizable rocks,
tucked into one of the inner pockets of his jacket; producing
several, he leaned out of the alley, gazing at the two guards who
loitered outside the gate. Then he hurled one at the lamp which
lit the street near the alley. It sailed wide, landing harmlessly on
the sidewalk. One more thrown hit the pole, producing a bright
ringing sound, and drawing the attention of the two guards.
Peters swore, and threw one more; this one hit its target,
smashing the lights with a spray of sparks and leaving us in
relative darkness.

We waited with bated breath in the alley while the two
guards at the gate hurried over. From the angle I was leaning
out, I could see them illuminated by the distant streetlamp, guns
drawn. These were no trained military killers: these were a pair
of young men who had been told to stand by a gate and shoot
any terrorists they saw. The sound of their footsteps stopped
not far from the lamp; in the dim light, I could still make out the
red of their uniforms. With our jackets closed, our white shirts
didn't stand out too well, and the black was difficult to make out
against the dark of the alley. I matched pace with Peters, who
approached slowly, his own pistol drawn. And by the time they
saw us, it was too late: we were within range to strike. My bat
met one across the side of the face, sending him sprawling to the
ground; he was unconscious, and likely had a broken jaw, but he
lived. Peters managed to grab the other's arm and jerk it around
behind the man, soon forcing him into a hold and choking him to
insensibility.

It felt strangely good, all told. But that satisfaction was nothing compared to the exhilaration that followed: Peters grabbed their guns, handing one to me, before searching the bodies for the key to the gate. It was large, and easy enough to find even by feel; soon, we were hustling through the gate and beyond, hurrying from shadow to shadow with only those masks to conceal our identities. He read each mailbox as we approached, eventually finding the one he needed. Through luck, perhaps, we encountered no more guards on the way. My heart was pounding, breath heavy as we approached the door. Then, without the subtlety I might have expected from him, Peters shouldered his way into it. Twice, thrice, four times, and it came loose, allowing us entry. Leaving the lighted streets behind, we slipped into the house.

We dared not turn on lights, for fear of them shining through the windows; instead, we crept slowly through the large, open rooms, over the thick carpet and through the winding mazes of wooden furniture. My knee once bumped against a thick, leather armchair; another time, my hand brushed the edge of a circular table. I had the pistol clenched in one fist, the bat in the other, and I doubt I would have been any good with either, had it come to that. The adrenaline surging through my body made thinking difficult; I felt as though my heart might burst.

We slithered through kitchen, sitting room, foyer, and dining room before finally finding his bedroom. The doors in the house creaked, and our footsteps weren't always light. Our mark—his name was never told to me—was still awake, and we could hear the creak of bedsprings and a gasp as we entered the room. I fumbled for a light switch, and flicked it on, to find a man and woman in bed, half-dressed, staring wide-eyed at the two strange figures who had invaded their home.

Peters pointed his gun at them, and I dropped my bat, doing

the same. My hands shook violently all the while, fingers twitching against the trigger in a dangerous way. They had the wisdom to make no sound; they merely capitulated as Peters quietly ordered them onto their knees, hands on their heads. The man placed his on a head of thin, blonde hair; the woman did the same on her ebony locks, both gazing at the floor with the grim certainty of death. Both faces were lined with wrinkles; he had a significant bald spot. Peters stared at them through the blank eyes of his mask, hands as steady as could be.

"I am a veteran of the North Licenian Army. I am not, however, a citizen of Licenia. I come from Greenwood, a country whose name surely evokes images of imperialists—or perhaps animals. Barbarians. Whatever the case, it is a name with which I'm sure you're quite familiar." The couple turned to look at one another, saying nothing. "I defected to join your country out of a sense of morals. I was met with torture under the guise of interrogation, to ensure that I wasn't hiding anything. I spent a lifetime in a prisoner-of-war camp, where my brothers-in-arms and I were subjected to inhuman treatments. Bound, gagged, stripped, beaten, crippled, killed. Kept in cages, like beasts. Made to lie in our own filth." He took a single step closer. "Now, look me in the eyes, you son of a bitch, and tell me why you voted against putting a stop to that."

The man looked up at Peters, too terrified to reply.

A silence ensued, for some seconds, before his wife made a sudden motion. I shouted for her to stop, but she didn't listen. She flung herself in front of her husband, shoving him down and shielding him with her own body. "That was twelve years ago!" she shrieked, clutching to her husband's shoulders and probably praying that her flesh would be enough to stop a bullet. "Stop! Just stop! It was twelve years!"

"Twelve years hasn't made these scars disappear!" snapped

Peters, his voice cracking on the last syllable. "Twelve years hasn't brought me back my cousin. Twelve years hasn't put an end to torture—and the next time Licenia goes to war, it'll be twelve *thousand* who never live to see the outside of a Licenian concentration camp. And in twelve more years, nothing will have changed."

"People change!" retorted the woman, turning around to glare through dampened eyes at Peters. "Are you the person you were twelve years ago?" She turned to face me, next: "Are you?" Looking back at the snake-headed figure standing over her, she lowered her voice, pleading instead of shouting. "People change," she repeated, arms shaking.

From below her, her husband croaked, "I'm sorry."

Another silence ensued; I kept my gun pointed, staring wildly from Peters to the two figures in front of us, wanting badly to shout at Peters to do something. He remained stony, though he turned his head almost imperceptibly to look at the man.

"I'm so sorry," he mumbled, quietly crying beneath his wife. "I never meant—I never meant to—" He took in a long, deep breath, composing himself long enough to speak. "It was war. You know that—you know that better than I do. And I thought we had to do everything, everything in our power... I thought I was saving lives. I was wrong; it was stupid. I know that, now. I know. And God knows I'm sorry. It's no comfort to you, I know. I know. I'm so sorry," he repeated, breaking out into fresh tears. "You're one of those... Forgotten people, aren't you? I was afraid—so afraid—kill me." Gently pushing his wife off of himself, he sat up, eyes closed. "Just don't hurt her. Please. I'm so sorry." He clutched at her hand, tears streaming down his cheeks. Quietly, so quietly that I could barely make it out, he whispered another apology, this one to his wife.

"I've tried to make up for it, but... I can't. I know I can't. I wish I could, believe me. Just don't hurt her. It was my fault. All our sins come back to haunt us. It's my time." He closed his eyes, and he gritted his teeth, waiting for the impact of the bullet.

"We're leaving." Peters put his gun down, and motioned me back.

"Leaving," I echoed, slowly reaching down to pick up my bat.

Peters gave a single nod. "Yes. We're leaving. Now." To the couple, he said only, "Don't leave the house until morning. We'll know. Don't call for help, and don't try to follow us." Then he slowly backed out, watching them all the way until he lost sight. They clung to one another, crying and shuddering. And as soon as they were out of our field of vision, Peters bolted, with me close behind.

We ran back through the gate, past the unconscious guards—for that entire exchange had taken little time at all—and into the maze of alleys that led back to the slums, all the way back toward the tenement. We had little regard for how conspicuous we might be; we merely fled from whatever invisible pursuit might be in tow.

"You should have shot them!" I hissed, as we neared the door. He opened it and walked inside, muttering to me without looking back.

"That's why your safety was on."

XXXI.

And then came the newspaper. We checked the newspapers regularly, since none of us had much of an inclination to wade through the hours of celebrity gossip and other entertainment "news" to get to what little real reporting there was. If it even merited that name. Much of the time, the only half-decent news revolved almost exclusively around matters of traffic, construction, and scientific advancements. The political news could be interesting, but centered largely on the lower levels of government. Never on Parliament. But, forgive me: surely, you read the newspapers. Or maybe you knew better.

Many of the dates I give as though with certainty are, more or less, estimates of the passage of time. It feels like many more days have passed than those of which the calendars assure me, and even my robust memory fails me as to precision. There are those few days, however, which are burnt indelibly into the paths of my brain.

Rothschild wandered into the tenement shortly after I woke, looking uncharacteristically solemn. Although he was never particularly jovial, he most often appeared to me as a man lost in thought, or else determined to complete whatever task he had at hand. Every once in a while, he would return from his latest escapade with a self-satisfied smirk, but seldom had I seen him disturbed. Though perhaps "troubled" is the better word: his brow was deeply furrowed, almost scowling, as he brushed by me to talk to Forgotten. After an exchange so quick and quiet I could make out none of it, the pair walked into another room, shutting the old, rotting door behind them.

While they spoke, I made breakfast for the lot of us. We survived on what we could buy on Forgotten's pension; I was loathe to use what money I had saved up, particularly if I ever wanted more heroin. Rothschild, I think, kept his account separate. He didn't seem like the kind to be reliant on others. As for me, I felt something of a need to be useful: perhaps it was because I was now the youngest among them, and probably in large part due to being their newest agent, but I could never quite shake the feeling that I was a child clinging to their legs. I wanted to be an ally, not a dependent. Cooking something provided... familiarity. It made me feel useful, at least for a moment. Even if my body ached for the drug all the while.

As I scraped eggs onto the rags we used in place of plates, I could feel a twitch in my arms. By the time I finished, and Peters and Milcher were joining me at the table, they were already starting to ache. My fingers trembled as I lifted the fork to my mouth, and I found it difficult to eat. It had been days since my last dose. My arm, hidden by the sleeve of my shirt, was peppered with holes. I didn't want to eat: I wanted to curl up on my cot, shoot up, and bliss out. It doesn't take much to get addicted, and it doesn't take long before the craving starts. And once it starts, you learn what Hell is. Had I been alone, I have no doubt that I would have just moved back to my cot, curled up into a ball, and willed myself to sleep. But even as sick as I felt, I was aware that I had two pairs of eyes on me. I ate mechanically, hardly tasting my food. The more I ate, the worse I felt. But I ate all the same.

Rothschild emerged in the middle of breakfast, but refused to answer any inquiries into the news. He scarfed down his portion of the slightly-burnt eggs I had prepared, then struck out immediately, having said nothing to any of us. Forgotten didn't emerge from his room, and only Milcher, carrying the still-warm eggs, went in to see him. Having finished my own breakfast, I wandered outside, hoping some fresh air would help the sweat which had broken out across my body.

The morning sun didn't greet me pleasantly. It seemed as intense as the summer's heat, and beat down on me with furious intensity. I wore the same shirt I had worn for the last several days, which stunk of smoke and sweat. My hair fell in greasy locks down my forehead, and my beard had grown wild. With my shirt sloppily tucked into my blue jeans, I wandered along the dingy streets of Priius' underbelly. Drawn and thin, weak and trembling, I had no particular direction in mind. All I wanted was relief. I think I knew I would find none, but I searched all the same.

I spent most of that afternoon wandering in a circle around the tenement. Every day that passed had been worsening my condition; I recognized that, now, but had no idea where to even start looking to buy what I sought. The more I thought about it, the more anxious I became; my pace quickened, and I glanced about myself in a fit of paranoia, sure that these silent streets hid assassins in every corner and alleyway. I'd brought my knife with me. I seldom went without it, in those days. The more I walked, the more certain I became that I would use it before the day was out—in hindsight, that would have been preferable.

Some time after the sun had begun its descent toward the peak of Candor Tower, my stomach began to ache more and more. At last, I could bear it no longer: I collapsed on hands and knees near an alleyway, and crawled into that shade to remain out of the public eye. There, between a trashcan and an abandoned bench, I vomited out what remained of my breakfast. It was agony—every time I thought I had finished, I just started heaving again. At last, nothing remained but the smell, and the sickening feeling of something in my beard. My sides ached, but the heaving subsided. I rolled onto my side, and laid there in the alleyway for some time, perversely grateful that the greater pain had stopped.

I spent what might have been an hour shuddering, huddled, on the street; in those alleys, which seemed far from the cold light of civilization, there were neither guards to rouse me nor vagabonds to rob me. Everything there was as still as death. Most of all, perhaps, me. My entire being ached. Everything, everything hurt. But eventually, mercifully, I was able to get up onto my knees. I didn't believe that the pain could worsen, and in that thought, I found the strength to rise. My legs shook and trembled, but I was able to make the long and grueling march back to the familiar tenement. Once inside, I said nothing to anyone. I simply curled up on my cot, careful to lie on my side for fear of choking on my own vomit, tugged the scratchy, woolen blanket I used up around my shoulders, and fell into a gainless sleep.

By the time I woke, it was dark outside, and I felt no better. The pain had subsided somewhat, but had been replaced by a permeating nausea. Everyone but Forgotten was seated in the ratty lawnchairs we used for furniture; there was an empty one for me. Groggily forcing myself out of bed, I walked over to it and sat down; across the room, Forgotten stood regarding a newspaper's front page.

"'A small organization of terrorists connected to the hanging in Priius' Franklin Square were executed today,'" he read off. "'Government agents previously located their headquarters on Old Hampton Street in Priius, an abandoned residential district in the historic heart of the capital.'" He read silently for a while longer, scanning down to the section for which he was looking. "'After laying in wait for the terrorists to return, government agents were able to capture approximately ten men, all of whom confessed to a series of political assassinations. Peter Garrivan, an officer in the Licenian Guard, said their execution should be the end of a recent crime spree in the nation's capital.'"

He let the newspaper drop from his gloved hands, which he then folded behind his back. It fluttered to the ground and scattered, soon trodden upon by his heavy boots as he stepped forward to address us. "Gentlemen." Although we had been silent already, the quiet which followed that single word was... terrible. It seemed as though all the world might stop for this grand and awful figure which stood before us, his crimson cloak and golden helmet gleaming in the flickering light. God, he was a sight to see. Even through the fog of my condition, I still found enough clarity of mind to pay him due reverence. He had a presence about him, as I have said. And like ecclesiastics before a priest, we all leaned in to hear what he would say next.

"They have killed our brothers-in-arms." He paused again, there, looking down for a moment. "They were bound, made to kneel before a wall, and shot through the head. One bullet each, in the back of the head. A quick death, yes. Some would say a merciful one. But not a death befitting a warrior, and by no means a death befitting a warrior who fought for the freedom of his countrymen." I swear there was genuine regret in his tone as he spoke, whether you believe me or not. "I have failed them. It was my intention—it was my promise—that I would find them and bring them back: both those who scattered during the invasion of Old Hampton, and those who were away on missions. However, I have..." For a short while, he trailed off, as though he lost his train of thought. "I have had other matters, pressing ones, on my mind. This is neither justification nor excuse: only explanation."

Slowly, he took a seat, pulling a pistol from its holster. He first ensured the safety was on, then sat and examined it, silent for a while more. Unlike the speeches I had heard him deliver before, his voice now was strained and quiet, almost tired. "The agents of oppression; the agents of lies; the agents of Beckstein and of Candor Network, have invaded Old Hampton. Our base of operations. The once-proud heart of a revolution." He let his hand, and the pistol it gripped, fall limp into his lap. "I have failed these men, and they have paid the cost for my actions."

I think he said, "Again." It was so quiet that I might have misheard.

"Rothschild brought this to my attention, and he has been invaluable in reconnaissance on Old Hampton today. Peters, Rothschild, and I have conferred, and devised a plan of action." He turned to me for the first time, with something of apology in his tone. "I'm sorry that our first major operation since your official induction into our ranks wasn't one to whose planning you were privy, but you understand that we are pressed for time and manpower. But, Jackson, Milcher, I have a question for you both." Leaning forward with his hands on his knees, back arched weirdly, the lion stared blankly into us. "Would you care to go on a walk with me?"

They gave me time to change into my suit, and once again, I found myself armed with a pistol. I took my knife with me, as well, as a precaution, but left my bat. All five of us struck out into the night, even Rothschild with his still-healing arm. He had brought more guns, procured at a cost I cannot guess. Five guns, forty-five bullets. For the first time, we were to see Forgotten in action. His greatcoat seemed to me almost to glow in the night's illumination; he walked before us with a purposeful stride, and with none of the limp that showed when he thought he was unobserved. I am young still, and was younger then; I could just fancy myself a soldier under his command in the Great War. It was inspiring. He was inspiring. In that moment, I would have gladly fought and died for him.

We walked all the way to Old Hampton; he knew the city well, as though he had traced its every vein. All the way there, we were unmolested: if I had commanded respect in his coat, he demanded obeisance. Whether it was something in the way he carried himself, or something in the frozen snarl of his mask, there was no question that this was a man with whom one would not trifle. There were only a handful of men still stationed at Old Hampton. Five, in all. I remember that number exactly. It was... convenient for us. They were lightly armed, and lowered their weapons to salute when Forgotten approached. He showed them something—I can only suppose it to have been some proof of rank—and told them to form up along the wall. All the while, I kept my shaking hand on the butt of my pistol, expecting any moment to be told to draw. My malady was forgotten in those heated moments, with my heart pumping in my ears and adrenaline rushing through me. It struck me like a blow when I realized we weren't there to fight these men.

I cannot know what they thought. I cannot know if they were military; I suspect they were merely the city guard, which had lately been given the uniform once reserved for the national military. Crimson. A wave of crimson lined up against the wall, surely thinking us to be some sort of special agents assigned to Forgotten's service. I cannot know what they thought, but I saw the horror in their faces as, in a fluid motion, he drew his gun and told them to drop their own.

Feeling as though in a dream, I drew my gun with a shaking hand, while the rest of us did the same. Not one had time to draw; they all knew it. These were no trained killers. They couldn't have fought us. We weren't there to fight those men.

"Kneel."

They did. They had no choice. They had no choice.

"Turn and face the wall. If you so much as look at those guns, you die."

They had no choice. We weren't there to fight those men.

He fired, and the first body jerked forward, hitting the brick wall with a sickening smack. Rothschild fired. Milcher looked at the two for a second, then aimed, pulled the trigger, and looked away before he could see the results. I froze. My hand shook violently. We weren't—

"Fire."

I couldn't. Barely a second had passed, but the two who remained already knew their fate. One began to twist around; I could see the action, as though time had slowed to a crawl around me. I felt giddy with adrenaline, processing thoughts and perceiving time in an alien, alarming way.

"Fire!"

He began to reach for his gun. We weren't there to— we weren't...

Peters had not yet fired. But he did, then. He fired twice, shooting both who remained in the head. Like me, he had hesitated. But unlike me, he brought himself to act when his comrades were endangered. Two gunshots, and the last two bodies slumped to the ground.

Crimson. A wave of crimson.

We weren't there to fight those men.

We were there to slaughter them.

XXXII.

Having fired our guns, we knew we could not linger long in Old Hampton. I remained numb, regarding the broken bits of skull that had been scattered across the ground. They were mixed with chunks of brain, flesh, blood, and hair; it's a truly gruesome sight, particularly if you aren't used to it. This time, my gun hadn't been on safety: I just hadn't been able to force myself to act. If not for Peters, I might have died for that inaction.

The others set about hastily, using matches and loose papers to set fire to what had once been our dwelling-places. The old, dry wood took easily, and each cabin went up like a torch. I, meanwhile, set to work collecting the guns of the dead, and rifling through their pockets for anything which might help. My stomach churned as I tried to avoid sticking my hands into the places where the blood pooled; I wasn't so much scavenging as trying to look busy. The ache in my bones was returning as the adrenaline wore off, and I felt sick—both physically and emotionally. I had killed in cold blood, before: why did this bother me so?

"If you're worried about getting your hands dirty, look at the blood already on them." That's what he said to me when he passed by. Forgotten, of course. I'm still not certain whether he referred to the literal blood that had stained my flesh in the course of my search, or the figurative; perhaps both. Both were certainly applicable. He knew I hadn't fired, and I expected to catch hell for it later. It was just another dread to add to my list, and went largely unnoticed: I had many already, too many to count.

Having set our beacons, we fled once more into the darkness, following the billow of Forgotten's coat. We had five new pistols, some more bullets, and a fair bit of cash—but moreover, we sent a message. "We can match your atrocities blow-for-blow," perhaps, or, "We've guns, too." I think we all knew, though, that at least the former wasn't true. Now, we were truly five, thanks to an indiscretion. Five broken men against an army. These weren't even odds for guerrilla tactics: these were hopeless, save in legends. Five broken men against an army.

I took no dinner again, that night; I wouldn't have been able to keep it down. Instead, I curled up on cot once more, shivering and twitching as I sought after sleep. My fingers clutched weakly into the wool, fingernails grown long and crooked, brittle and discolored. I shuddered convulsively, and twice retched, but had nothing to vomit up. Many times, I could feel myself drifting off, before another muscle spasm would jar me awake again. And shortly after I finally manged to drift off, doubtless to be haunted by what had become my regular night terrors, Milcher's voice invaded my sleep.

"Jackson." He was whispering, but so near to my ear that I couldn't help but hear. "Jackson, you aw-wake?"

I groggily muttered an affirmative, and rolled over to look at him. In the darkness, I couldn't make out his face, but I could dimly see his silhouette. He loomed over me, likely kneeling, with his hands on his knees. "Jackson," he repeated again, "w-was what we di-did there right?"

The question caught me off-guard, and I made no response, only blinked sleepily at him. He waited for a few moments, then repeated his question, quietly but insistently. "Was it right t-to shoot those men?"

"You just did what you were told," I slowly answered, sounding as unsure as I felt. It seemed a dangerous question, and I didn't know how to answer. It didn't help that I was wondering the same thing, on some level of my mind. "No-one can fault you for that."

At first, I thought that would satisfy him: he nodded, and fell silent, thinking. Just before I could roll over and try to sleep again, he asked, "But wasn't th-that what they were doin'?"

I hesitated again before answering, but could think of nothing better to say. "Just do as you're told, and nobody can fault you for that," I whispered back, reaching a shaky hand out to pat his leg. He started to make a sound of protest, but I interrupted: "Milcher, you're a good man. Loyal as can be. You keep on like that, and... and everything'll be alright."

After another moment's silence, he said, "Th-thanks, Jackson." He sounded truly grateful, as though I had put some great worry to rest. At the time, it made me feel slightly better about myself: I had helped ease Milcher's mind. Looking back, I should have known what was coming: more guards on the streets, tighter security, and more and more bloodshed. We couldn't have lasted long like that: striking out here and there, hoping that some politician would crack and let us know where we could kill him and all of his colleagues.

Were we not a fine microcosm of Licenia, though? When there's a problem, you shoot it. You get rid of it. Drown it in its own blood. We weren't so different from our adversaries: not with a million bullets, a thousand broken buildings, an ocean of blood and a mountain of dead would either of us realize that from no violence springs peace, and death does not beget life. It was funny, in a way: the grand freedom fighters were no different from the oppressors they fought. Wasn't it funny?

You aren't laughing.

I wasn't the only one who knew. In the early hours of the morning, when Forgotten took his meals and washed himself, I overheard him arguing with Peters. They were quiet, but not so quiet that someone listening hard couldn't hear. At first, I was inclined to go back to sleep, but after hearing the quiet fire in Peters' tone and the forced calm in Forgotten's, I laid awake and eavesdropped. Not every word was clear, but a few choice phrases stood out.

Peters, intense and insistent: "We have to end this."

Forgotten's grating voice: "We have to rebuild first."

Something indistinguishable, then Peters again: "...more of them can die? You know as well as I do—"

More unintelligible conversation, then a louder, more heated exchange: "That's out of the question."

"I'll do it myself."

"That's *out* of the question."

"This isn't the army, D..."

"Don't you dare call me that."

There was silence after that, followed by an even-lower murmur. I ended up falling asleep again, after a while, and woke later that morning, after the sun had risen. The craving was more intense than ever, and I felt sick to my stomach once more. My bowels proved loose, and after a painful bout, I felt almost too weak to eat. My strength waned and waxed as the morning continued, and I ate what was served me: my appetite in those days came in waves of voraciousness and apathy. Finishing a meal and keeping it down made me feel somewhat better, and I went outside to take a walk, bat in hand. After last night's adventure, I expected to find guards on every corner, questioning any who passed.

Peters was already outside, smoking a cigar and leaning on the wall. He puffed on what little remained with a contemplative scowl, and seemed to be muttering something to himself as though to memorize it. Although I was going to pass in silence, he called me over with a short bark.

"Hey," he muttered, pulling the cigar from his mouth and

taking a deep breath. I watched him with a mixture of curiosity and apprehension, while he studied my face and hands. I was pale, and the foul air of Priius had begun to affect me. Not so much, perhaps, as those who had ridden the bus to Tobit with me, but enough that it had just begun to show. Eventually, he looked me dead in the eyes, and said, "Get the fuck out of here."

I narrowed my eyes, irritated: my morning had already started poorly, not least thanks to a sleep haunted by the usual memories, plus some new ones. I'd been just about to do something stupid and rash when he elaborated. "Get yourself clean. Go back home. Work on a farm. Go to a university. Fall in love. Shit, I don't care what you do: just get out of Priius, and get far away."

That spooked me, as you might imagine: my anger turned to fear, and I asked what had gone wrong. Had we been discovered? Or was this because of my show of cowardice the night before?

"Everything's going wrong," he laughed. It wasn't a happy laugh, but it was one of the few I heard from him. "There's going to be blood, Jackson, mark my words. More blood than their God could wash clean, if he were to come down himself to do it. But you don't have to be part of it." He laid his hand on my shoulder. I twitched. "You've been through a lot, but you're not yet like us: you're not yet shattered. You might think that dramatic, but it's true. Forgotten, Rothschild, and I—even Milcher—we're in this too deeply to escape. There's nothing waiting for us outside of Priius' walls. But you have your youth. You're smart; act like it, and get the fuck out while you still can."

"So, this is what it comes to, then?" I asked, feeling unusually bitter. "I come along and hear pretty words that convince me to fight. And after I begin, I'm made to do things that I don't know are right or not. And before it's finished, I'm moved away too soon to even see the results."

"That's always what it comes to, in war," he mused, looking far past me, past years and borders. "But you won't want to be here for what's going to come. It's not cowardice: it's discretion. You have an out, and I recommend you take it."

"Funny," I said, "you sound just like everyone else I've spoken to since coming to this goddamn city: 'I'm not going to tell you shit, besides some vague warning, because I like you.'"

He didn't even look down at me. "I don't like you, Jackson," he muttered, dropping the stub of his cigar and rubbing it out. "But you're here, and you're in danger, and I think you deserve a warning. I'd rather not have you or anybody else end up like me: too stubborn to give up, but too battered to win. This fight is over; find another one. Consider me..." He paused, searching for the word. "...an Aesop. An Aesop's fable."

We parted ways, after that. I walked off in the first direction I turned to, still wearing last night's clothes, having taken the time only to wash the traces of blood off my cuffs and hands. I had no direction in mind: I just walked, seeing where my feet took me. And they took me on a walk, indeed: past an alley where one turns to find Old Hampton Street, blocked off by a police barricade. Past the glass displays of Humboldt Shopping Center, where, unbeknownst to me, Rothschild was blackmailing Mrs. Hughes. Past the giant screens of Franklin Square, where not a single display spoke of the guardsmen who had been shot, before: only a brief note that the fire had been extinguished without notable property damage. My legs led me all the way to Candor Tower, where I wandered inside, bat dragging along the carpeted floors.

The day secretary didn't greet me by name: I doubt she recognized me, in that state. She asked if she could help me; I told her she couldn't, and sat down in the lobby. My limbs splayed out in all directions, fingers still clamped around the shaft of the bat. I sat before the glowing screen, and let myself relax. But my mind wasn't on whatever show was on: it was far away, miles to the east, where my parents were probably wondering why I'd stopped writing. It was nearby, in the high penthouse where a crippled man and his family sat, wringing their hands and waiting for the strange men to break in again. It was a little further off, where an older couple choked down their fear each day to leave each others' sight. It was elsewhere, where an orphaned infant would spend its youth in the care of strangers.

With these things heavy on my mind, I left in the evening, having been deaf to the secretary's occasional, piqued questioning into whether she could help me. I wandered out as quietly as I had entered, no longer caring who stood behind the desk. That night, I walked in anger, deep and impotent, with no outlet.

It was far later than I had realized; late into the night, when even the traffic began to thin out. I was making my way through an alley, when a voice called out to me. I turned, to find myself face-to-face with a portly fellow, a man dressed in the regalia of the town guard. He had a pistol in a holster, but didn't know how to use it: it wasn't where he would be able to draw it fast enough. I didn't notice that at the time, though: all I could think was how familiar he looked. I have an excellent memory, from a misplaced file to a dropped screwdriver, and I don't forget faces easily.

"It's late, young man," he said, his hands on his hips.

"Yes, sir" I agreed, "it's late."

"Dangerous to be out so late, with these... these terrorists about, don't you think?" He read the news. He had seen their picture. Black waistcoat, white shirt, black slacks, black tie.

Young men, well-dressed but rough.

"Yes, sir," I agreed, "it's dangerous to be out with these terrorists." I knew his intent. He knew what I was, and he was taking too long to get around to it. It made me angrier than I already was. Irrationally, inexplicably angry.

He looked at my bat, his hand moving to rest awkwardly on the butt of his pistol. "Fine bat you've got there, sir. Planning a bit of sport tonight?"

"A bit of sport," I echoed.

"It's dangerous to be out this late." He was nervous. I could taste the fear in his tone. "Maybe you'd best just go home."

"You're right: maybe you'd best just go home, sir." I smiled with yellowing teeth, and gripped my bat harder. "Dangerous out, with these terrorists around."

He wasn't fast. I was. He moved for his gun. I swung. My bat hit flesh, and his head snapped to the side. He staggered. I swung. He fell. I kept swinging.

After the sodden thud of my bat had stopped, after he had stopped sobbing and crying out uselessly into the alley, I stood, staring down into his bloodied and broken face. It was shattered almost beyond recognition, now, the bones broken and warped, blood pouring down from where I had beaten his face until it was left in jagged fractures. I couldn't quite comprehend what I had done: I just stared for a while, my breath growing louder, heart pounding faster as the reality of my actions hit me. This was no longer a body; this was no longer a face. It was a yawning abyss, in which I saw nothing but the sneering face of...

I turned and fled, dropping my bat. I was clean, yet. Clean enough. The last bus was just about to leave, but I climbed aboard, paid my toll, and let it take me away to a place where I could, perhaps, disappear.

XXXIII.

Tobit had been my refuge once before: a place of solace from the day-to-day worries and mundane cares of the laborer's life. Now, this town of glitter and light would be my solace from myself, or so I believed. There was something wrong with me. I knew that much. Something had gone horribly, terribly wrong, and until it was fixed, I would have no more of Priius' cold streets nor the rolling hills of my hometown. Perhaps I would get a job, there: away from the tourists and profiteers, where the real folk lived. I intended to get myself clean of the drug, though I suspected that a dose or two might help with the pain.

This time, no arc of daylight nor blaze of sun waited for me on the ride to Tobit. I rode in silence along with a few other people, all weary and withdrawn. The moon tried to shine overhead, but still couldn't pierce the thick fog of light all around. I felt lost again, in the same way I had when first arriving in Priius. I'd lost sight of the stars, and without them, I couldn't find my way. All that remained was the road: I followed where it led.

There was a lady on the bus. I remember her because she reminded me, in ways, of Deirdre. The same dark hair, the same complexion. Young and plain, quiet. She had a child with her, cradled in her arms. It made me wistful, somewhat: at that point, I wasn't sure if I'd ever have the opportunity to have one of my own. Maybe I'd end up like John, a childless bachelor. A pang of guilt struck me as I realized I should have let him know that his wife yet lived; but I had had other things on my mind. Preoccupations. And the drugs hadn't helped.

The bus rolled up nigh midnight, and I shuffled off with a couple of others. While they wandered off their separate ways, I looked around, trying to find something that would distract me.

I still ached all over, and I continually checked myself for traces of blood I hadn't seen, before: had I cut myself shaving, had I taken a bad fall? How long until they found him there? How long until his family found out? How long until they took the time to hunt me down—or, worse, someone else?

The bars tempted me, of course. A few fingers of whiskey might help ease the other pain. But taking more drugs to get over the first didn't seem like an ideal situation, and I could easily waste what remained of my savings on alcohol. I would need shelter, of course, unless I intended to keep vigil the night through. As yet, I had no want of food: the way my stomach churned, I could hardly bear the thought of it. At once, I both yearned for and reviled human company: I had known nothing but the rough life of Old Hampton for what seemed like an age, with no-one to confide in, no-one to love. Fergus came to mind, and I...

Forgive me.

When I left the tenement, that day, I had intended to take a walk. And now, I decided to continue it, wandering along the sidewalks and keeping one eye on the alleys. Losing my wallet now would be the end of me: no identification, no money, and no fortunes. But beyond even that, one might serve for a sleeping-place, should the motels prove too expensive. All around me, I could see the glitz and glitter of tourist attractions, places where the upper classes could spend their money to feel cultured and as though they'd seen the world. I weaved through these brighter places to the poorer part of town, just as I had before. It seemed almost welcoming, now: a return to a safer, more familiar place. I passed by men from the other continent having a smoke, the homeless masses huddled together against the chill of the night, and the occasional drunken factory worker. Over the horizon of smaller buildings, I could make out a sign, flickering and half-dead, which called to me: "REST." God, how I wanted to. I wanted to rest forever, away from the world. For now, a night would suffice.

I stumbled in that direction, eyes focused always on the sign. It seemed to me as far-off as the moon: no matter how many steps I took toward it, it never felt closer. I didn't think anything could appeal to me quite like that: a shower, a bed, and privacy. The price no longer mattered; nothing mattered. If I couldn't afford it, I would simply have to break in. Indeed, I was so set in my direction that I almost knocked the poor thing over.

She was even more frail than before, her gaunt, skeletal appearance playing tricks with her age. Her limp, lifeless hair and protruding cheekbones gave her an air of aging, but the narrow swell of her hips, her malnourished, budding curves revealed the youth which had not yet been burnt out of her. She stood near the entrance to the alley, looking on the motel as hungrily—probably even more—as I. My steps paused as I drew near, looming over her whether or not I intended it.

A crumpled cigarette was clenched in her teeth, from a pack that I don't expect she bought herself. A pretty little thing, if she hadn't been so sickly, several years my junior but still old enough to be a young woman. Her tattered clothes, torn both from age and so as to put her moribund figure on best display, did little to protect her against the cold: she shivered even as she stared up at me with those sunken, frightened eyes. We regarded each other for a few moments, neither, I suspect, recognizing the other. I knew only that she was familiar, somehow; my world was not so large as I often believed.

"Are you lonely, mister?" Her tone had a sullenness, as though she knew she debased herself with the question. How must I have seemed, then: unwashed and reeking, half-feral for the wildness of my hair and talons? But, oh, her question struck a chord in me. For, as I have said, I *was* lonely: deeply, unbelievably lonely. I cannot call what I felt "lust," for I felt little enough attraction to this scrap of a girl. But then again, I suppose it was lust: lust for company, companionship. Lust for the humanity I had forgotten. And if I found my humanity in depravity, so be it.

"How much?" I asked, voice almost tremulous. All the while, I tried not to consider the enormity of what I was about to do. She gave me a price—far too low for what I was to take from her, as I recall—and I went inside to rent a room. The man at the counter gave me a key; I gave him my money, then went outside and fetched the girl I had rented.

I need not describe what I did with her in detail. Know only that it was simple. Bestial, in a way. There was no depravity in the act itself; that much was natural. The depravity laid in the circumstances, and in the partner I had chosen. I used her. I used her as others had; I used her as so much flesh. But in the exchange, I found nothing more than the banal scrape of flesh against flesh, a harried and hurried act which, thankfully, I could not bring myself to complete. Long before my time was up, I realized what I was doing, and began to cry quietly into her shoulder.

It might have been a sweet scene, if painted a little differently: the stoic young thing, born into this life of hardship, giving unsure comfort to a man taller, older, and stronger than she. Stronger in body, at least. I have no doubt that I frightened the poor thing then more than ever, sobbing like a child into her shoulder. After pulling myself away from her, I mumbled a hundred apologies, resting my head in my hands and covering myself with the thin blanket they had provided me.

After a time, I looked over at her. She remained bare, no doubt expecting me at any moment to get my money's worth

from her. Those deep, sorrowful eyes were locked on me; I
swear I could feel them. She seemed... she seemed so innocent.
I know she wasn't; she was born innocent, perhaps, but lost it
soon after. But if that thing, that broken-winged bird who had
known nothing but earth was not innocent, then by God, there
are none of us who are pure.

"I'm sorry," I told her, not for the last time. "You deserve
better than... I shouldn't have, and I'm sorry. Keep the money;
use it to buy food. Clothing. I don't know. Fuck, use it to get out
of here; use it to find yourself a proper job. There are
factories..."

"Not one will hire me." Her voice carried with it an
unexpected edge: the youth was tempered with a bitterness far
deeper and more justified than mine. She had been born with
an eye on Heaven, and that's a hard thing to fix.

I dressed, and asked her to do the same. But not to leave: I
had paid for her time as well as her... services, and as I told her, I
needed the company. She stood by the door, and I sat on the
bed, regarding my feet. We exchanged names: mine first, hers
after a period of hesitation. And from there, we spoke of many
things: of her dead mother and missing father, of the memories
she still had of the former. Her life and mine; my recent troubles
—though here I lied, so as not to frighten the poor girl with the
truth. That was wrong of me, really: she deserved the truth as
much as anyone. But, selfishly, I kept it to myself so that I might
keep her company, as well. I poured my heart out to her,
although her own remained so full that it amazes me it didn't
spill over. Quietly, and not without reluctance, she told me
something of her own story, though there wasn't so much to tell:
the child of a whore, who had taken up her mother's mantle
following her untimely death.

Her name was Katarina. It may not matter to you now, but

perhaps it will, someday. Born some fourteen or fifteen years ago; she had lost track of the joyless anniversaries. A frail, weak stick of a thing who bore an infinitely-greater burden than I, with infinitely more grace. And before she left for the night, that sad and wrecked angel gave me the scrap of a poem, which I have here in my pocket: it has not left my keeping since. A penniless mother read it, some nights, to her illiterate daughter; it helped, she said, to ease the pain, some nights. "You need it more'n I do," she told me, and slipped off into the darker places. Indulge me, for a moment: I suspect you may have heard this one before.

OF JUSTICE.

O unfavored, bastard child,
Whose sanguine flesh bears the marks of hatred,
Whose star-cross'd soul bears the marks of neglect,
Weep thou not.
For in your misfortune has been sown the seeds of strength.
Though your legs bear not the burden of your body,
Your arms have grown yet stronger.
There in filth and grime have they left you,
Struggling inch by inch,
Nail by claw,
Tooth by fang.
With words of scorn, they seek to bury you,
To rend your skin and still your heart.
But in their houses of languor and lethargy,
Where sound only the soothing songbirds,
They have grown weak and soft.
But you, O bastard child,
Unfavored son,
Unwanted daughter,

You have lived in the places where no God smiles down.
In chill and in fear you have trembled,
In dark and in pain you have stumbled,
In blood and in wrath shall you rise.
Though your legs lie mangled and broken,
You have crawled along the places men fear to tread.
And for that, you are the stronger.
Though now you founder,
Unsure of foot, untrained of hand,
You shall rise from the umber as endless light,
Blinding their eyes,
Searing their flesh,
Judging their acts.
Keep your good eye on Heaven, child.
Leave the weaker to wander the earth.

XXXIV.

Despite the comfort of the motel, I didn't stay more than a night. Aside from the pains which regularly woke me, I slept better than I had in months. I'm sure the cheap bed they gave me was nothing compared to what you're used to, but that night, it was heavenly. In the morning, I took a shower for the first time in far too long, before dressing once again in the same suit I had already been wearing. It improved the stench somewhat, but smoke, sweat, and sickness still clung to the fabric. After returning the key, I wandered into the streets. For the first time in a long time, I knew exactly where I was going.

I don't know if you can quite comprehend the peace which came over me as I walked to the station. My life had been uncertainty and turmoil for months; now, it seemed as though it might be coming back together again. Priius has been a sickness to me; it has poisoned my mind as surely as the smog poisons the factory workers who toil for its prosperity. I am no Luddite; still, I hold those squat, ugly buildings in some disregard.

After paying my fare and receiving my ticket, I boarded the vast train that would take me miles away—homeward. It was bound for Barbier, and from there, I could hitchhike back to Dalton, just as I had to reach Priius. They gently guided me to board the back of the train, where the less-fortunate passengers stayed. The accommodations were acceptable, by all means: I had a seat, and that was enough for me. I'll admit that some part of me wanted to see the rich part of the train, where I hear fine people eat fine food in fine trappings. But I was in no position to complain: it was clear from their demeanor that they were doing me a favor by letting me board. They didn't want me there, but I couldn't really blame them: I wouldn't have wanted someone like me getting on, either.

I spent much of the trip asleep, and the rest desperately hoping I wouldn't be ill in the middle of it. My guts cramped painfully, but otherwise behaved themselves, allowing me to complete that leg of my journey in peace. The others on the train didn't look to be much better-off than me: one man was missing a leg; another trembled uncontrollably the entire time, and the woman beside him was staring straight ahead with a grim expression every time I glanced in her direction. When I was awake, I spent my time either staring out of the window or reading the scrap of a poem, mentally filling in a few words that had been blurred from wear.

After several hours, the train rolled up in Barbier. Things hadn't changed, nor should I have expected them to. All the same, I didn't feel particularly nostalgic. Without stopping in at the shop where I had worked for a time, I bought a little food, and then set to making my way home. Hitchhiking is a little harder when you look like a starving madman, but a few kinder souls still let me ride with them. I chatted idly with the ones who wanted to talk, and left the others in peace, contemplating the road before me. More than one asked if I was ill; I told them I was, and I don't feel as though I lied.

I slept in the woods again, this time without a change of clothes prepared. I had left everything but my wallet in Old Hampton, so desperate was I to get away. They were only objects: objects, I could purchase later. Besides, I had some more clothes waiting for me at home; I tend to travel light, so I hadn't brought my entire wardrobe with me. The aches and the sickness continued all the while I traveled; those days were some of the worst, and I woke fatigued and aching every morning. When I could find no ride, I simply walked to the southeast, following the highways along which I had grown.

Night had fallen by the time I set foot in Dalton. That tiny, sleepy town seemed almost alien to me, now, so used had I become to the sprawl and bustle of Priius. Seeing the stars overhead was a welcome change; I had gazed on them often over the past few nights. I dared not smile yet, but there was a lightness in my heart as I walked through the old streets, past the drug store and post office, until paved streets gave way to dirt roads, and I had wandered past city limits. An hour or two more, and I was stumbling, half-limping from exhaustion. But I walked through a cornfield, amidst the packed soil and tilled fields. The lowing cattle seemed to welcome me home. I have no shame in admitting that I cried to myself when I saw my childhood home over the hill, my weary bones marching to the front door. After taking the time to wipe my face on my sleeve, for all the good it did, I knocked in three-beat measures until the door was opened by my startled father.

My parents and I shared a tearful reunion in the kitchen, all seated around the little table where I had sat since I was born. They were both dressed in their sleepwear, I in my wrinkled and dirty suit, while they asked me about my sudden reappearance and my lack of communication. Not knowing how much to tell them, I said only that I had been very ill in the city, forced to scrape by on the charity of others after becoming unable to work. True enough, in a way, I suppose. They insisted that I eat something: I did, gratefully, and we agreed to finish catching up in the morning, after they had completed the dawn chores. I was instructed to sleep as long as I need, and forbidden from exerting myself in my state.

The next few days were spent purely in recovery, for me. It felt as though when I wasn't sleeping, I was eating. I washed my clothes and put on some different ones, showering daily. My skin had grown rough and unhealthy, fingernails grimy and eyes sunken. Shaving made a grand difference in my appearance:

though it emphasized my gaunt features, it also returned a bit of my youth to me. My mother trimmed my hair, and my father promised to take me hunting when I felt up to it. I felt... normal. More normal, at least. The nightmares never ceased, nor have they yet; but day by day, I could feel my strength returning. Despite the horrible fits my withdrawal caused, I had reached a point where I could choke down three meals a day, and that helped.

After a week or so, I asked my parents for a pen and some paper, and set to writing a letter to John. The words didn't come easily, for I wasn't sure quite what to say: I apologized for my behavior on our last encounter, gave some bullshit explanation for why I had been so distraught, and made some gentle inquiries into his general health. After signing it, I began to fold it up so as to mail it, but hesitated. It took me a good few minutes to make up my mind, but I eventually added a brief post-script:

"P.S. Your wife has been spending a lot of time at John's Kitchen. It's in the Humboldt Shopping Center. You should go say hello."

My father drove me into town so that I could mail it, and we talked of the news since I had left. He told me how the livestock were getting along, and of the quaint goings-on of Dalton's citizens. It was nice to listen to it all, and have familiar names brought back to my ears. I asked after a few friends of mine, and he answered, but he was clearly anxious to hear about the big city.

"Priius is big, mostly," I said. "That's what most strikes you whenever you first get in. It's blindingly bright; I swear they've a TV screen on every corner. It's full of businessmen and some ladies, but not a lot of people actually live there. Only the rich ones—members of Parliament, and the like." I dodged a few questions about the "dangerous folk" who had been around there, claiming ignorance due to my illness. There came a brief, contemplative pause, and then I gave him an honest account of my time there.

"I didn't much enjoy Priius. It doesn't seem authentic, to me: people don't talk to each other. It's so consumed with economic progress that it leaves human progress behind. Once the initial awe wears off, you're left with a city bloated with traffic, polluted with light and sound, and lacking in culture. All the homeless people, all the crime, it's still there: they just shove them into the alleys and slums. Out of sight, out of mind." As we rolled up into the post office's parking lot, I concluded, "It's a city of steel-and-glass people."

I look back fondly on the days I spent with my parents. I could relax, at least for a while, and let them nurse me back to some semblance of health. The cravings and the pains lessened, now that I was eating regularly, sleeping regularly, and letting the remains of the drug work their way out of my system. And yet, I couldn't help but feel ultimately unfulfilled. Every hour that I sat idle, reading or even watching television, there came a nag at the back of my mind. I had left something unfinished. I had let someone down. And the night terrors never eased up.

It was a Thursday when I went to the church. They had no sermons on Thursdays, but I wasn't going to be preached at. I hadn't even intended to head that way, originally: I was taking a walk through the woods, dressed in a pair of blue jeans and a flannel shirt, and my steps led me to the well-tended graveyard which sat against their edge. I spent some time reading the graves and contemplating life, death, and all that came between. Then, the peal of the old bell caught my attention, and I turned to regard the worn old building where I had spent many a Saturday morning, in my early years. Religion had never been for me, in the past. But a momentary doubt wormed its way into my mind. Something long buried, long forgotten, which rose up again in my desperation. I realized, suddenly, what I wanted.

The chapel was dimly lit, the windows all shut. They left the door open; they always did, in case someone wanted to come by and worship in private. Many of the townsfolk did, I knew: I heard them speak of it in their conversations, of how they had gone to the chapel to pray for guidance, to beg forgiveness, to ask that a little grace be afforded them. Only the priest would be there, some days, and that old gentleman didn't judge. At least not aloud. Although I cared little for his craft, I held no animosity toward the man himself.

I called out into the empty hall, and received no reply, leaving me to think myself alone. There was nothing worth stealing, there, save for the offerings that they kept in the safe. I closed the door behind myself and wandered up through the pews, with a sense of unease following me. In the back of my mind, I couldn't shake the memory of the passionless recitations of scripture my young mind couldn't yet understand. It made me uneasy, like a trespasser in someone else's house. But there was no-one here to hear me. And so, I found myself standing before the altar, looking around in one last fit of self-consciousness before dropping to my knees.

I don't know what I expected to feel, exactly. I never felt as though I were good at praying; I mostly just spoke aloud to whatever might be listening, out there. With my head resting against the woolen cloth that adorned the marble slab, I whispered, "If you're out there, and you're listening—so am I."

From there, I spent at least an hour conversing with the empty church. What began an explanation of my actions and a request for forgiveness changed to a questioning, a challenging. As the minutes passed, and I continued to feel no different, a sort of jealousy took me. I envied the people I had grown up listening to, who could pray and feel the better for it. But for me, there was no comfort: a whisper became a mumble, became speech, became screaming devotions and denouncements, furious demands and desperate bargaining. But for all of it, nothing replied but my own echo.

It wasn't until the last reverberations had died out that I became aware that I was no longer alone. There I knelt, panting and sweating, wild-eyed and sore of throat—and a hand fell to rest upon my shoulder. I started, and whipped around to find the concerned face of the old priest, a man I had barely seen in a decade or so.

He asked if I had need of a confession. I hesitated, then told him that I did. He nodded, and took a seat nearby, while I propped my weary body against the altar, and took a deep, shuddering breath.

"I have killed a man," I told him. He seemed startled, but quickly regained his composure. While I watched him out of one eye, he nodded encouragingly, remaining silent. "Several, in fact. I have made an orphan of a child, and beaten a man to death in the street. I have been an accessory to the brutal torture of a public official. I have taken drugs. I have lusted after another man. And I have slept with a teenaged whore."

There came silence for a time, and I murmured, "I believe that's about it."

The poor old gentleman was frightened; there was no hiding it. In a tremulous voice, he asked, "Do... do you seek forgiveness?"

I turned to face him, giving a very slight smile. Not a mirthful one, for I wasn't truly amused. I smiled only because I had already known what I wanted when I walked in the door, and nothing that he could have said or done would have given it to me. "No," I told him, standing. "I seek understanding. Not from you, mind. I don't expect you to understand at all. But I think I know who should, now." I stuck out a hand, and he tentatively shook it.

"Thank you, sir." I smiled again, a hint more genuinely. "You've been a good listener. Just not the one I need right now."

Because that's you, isn't it?

XXXV.

I knew I couldn't stay. I suppose I always knew, from the moment I returned. After all, I had left once before; why should this time be any different? There was nothing for me in that town, and I had already begun to suspect that there was nothing for me anywhere else in Licenia. I am not an unintelligent man; unwise, perhaps, but not unintelligent. I longed for the kind of mental challenge which public schools and farming had never afforded me. Naively, I had sought that in Priius: I clung, tenacious, to the idea that I would "work my way up" even as John showed how foolish a notion it was. Had I remained there, I would have been, at best, a manager of the other janitors. To make money—more importantly, to be challenged—I would need to go to a university. And to do that, I needed money. A charming cycle, that.

Speaking of John, it was in my third week back home that I received a letter from him. It had clearly been penned hastily; the envelope was scarcely more than a scrawl, and it had neither a greeting nor a signature. Only the words, "Thank you," scratched nearly across the paper. I don't recall a time when I've felt better about my actions, even so belated an action as it was. For perhaps the first time since—well, you know since what—I felt as though I had made a positive difference. It's all I've ever wanted. It's all I've ever wanted. It made me feel *proud*.

I had begun to help out around the farm again, by the fourth week. Four weeks had made me respectable again, at least outwardly. My cravings had largely subsided, as well as the other symptoms. I had received a haircut, my beard was neatly trimmed, and I accompanied my parents to the Saturday sermons. I chanted out the passionless words with everyone else, and pretended that it gave me some comfort. There, my black suit fit in with the black suits of so many of the other men. There, no terrorists roamed the streets; no guards kept fearful watch over ignorant people. Never again would I have to raise a knife or pistol in defense or anger. I was normal. *Normal*, do you hear? But it couldn't last. I couldn't stay in that quaint, pastoral heaven.

Nearly a month after I left was when the incident occurred. Of course you remember this: I'll bet you were just as scared as everyone else when it happened. I remember it precisely: 11:29 p.m., sitting on the couch with my parents to watch the late-night entertainment. The variety show, which had been introducing a new musical group, suddenly cut out, replaced with the grim, sweaty face of Peters.

My heart stopped.

He sat, hunched over a chair, staring into the camera. For a time, he didn't speak; he glanced over his shoulder to the door behind him, which had been hastily barricaded and locked. Everything was slightly out-of-focus, and he seemed to be aiming the camera a little too low. My father tried to change the channel before I could stop him, but it was the same thing. From what little of the room was visible, he seemed to be in some sort of broadcast center. I recognized the red-and-gold furnishings behind him, and quietly admonished my parents not to turn off the television or say a word.

It took him a few moments to get settled, but once he did, he gave the camera a dark, slight smile. "Hello, Licenia," he said, as cool and quiet as I had ever seen him. "I am the person you least want to see. Because I am a reminder of your past. My name is Samuel Peters, and I am not a Licenian citizen." He paused here, to let that sink in. "I am, however, a Licenian veteran. I was born in Greenwood, but I defected during your Grand War. For this, I was tortured, both physically and mentally." He swallowed once, heavily; from behind him came a bang on the door, and incomprehensible shouting.

"But not by Greenwood. By Licenia. They had me detonate a factory full of innocent workers from Greenwood—people rather like many of you. I lost my cousin, and several of my childhood friends, that day. I am hardly the only one; any Greenwood prisoner-of-war would attest to the same treatment, were they still alive. They are forgotten, but I am their voice." There were only four men in the world, myself included, who might have understood his smirk.

"You live in a country without a strong central government, or so you believe. And that works splendidly in good times, but the times cannot remain good forever. When the wealth dries up, where will you find yourselves? Will you be sitting atop the money you, in your wisdom, have saved? Or will you be crawling to your government's table, begging for scraps they don't have?" During the next pause for breath, I noticed that he was breathing heavily, and the angle of his shoulder suggested he was holding something, perhaps his side. The barrel of a pistol came into view briefly, held in his other hand.

"I expect that you'll crawl after your government—but you won't find it. You see, Licenia, your government is very strong, indeed. And it doesn't want to be found. When was the last time you had an election? When was the last time you voted?" As my parents turned to say something to each other, I waved an agitated hand at them, blood running cold.

"I sit in Candor Tower as I speak. So, too, does your government. I am a member of a resistance group; you do not know our names, but you know our works. We are the Forgotten. We have failed in our mission, but I say this in the hopes that you will pick up where we have left off." From here, more bangs and shouts could be heard; he glanced over his shoulder again, and began speaking faster, more intensely. "You have all been made the pawns of tyrants. You have been continually deceived by Candor News Network. We have done our part: all of the men responsible for the torture of prisoners have been killed, many by my hand." He pleaded now, voice raising to a high, desperate pitch. "But I don't want to kill anymore. I am a man without a country, a future, or hope; only a past which I would sooner forget." There was fear in his eyes. He breathed quickly, and when he wiped his brow with one hand, it left a smear of blood. "I don't expect you to understand what I have done, Licenia, but I do suggest that you wake the fuck up." He spat each word, then gave a salute with the hand gripping the pistol. "Good night, Licenia."

With that, he gripped the barrel of the pistol with his teeth, wrapped both hands around the grip, and fired. His body jerked back, once, as his head erupted into a shower of blood, brain, and bone. The screaming from behind the door intensified, the banging knocking the door free of one of the hinges. His lifeless body slumped in the chair, dripping gore from his side and what remained of his head. The door came free. Several men in the attire of the military rushed in; one cried out. They were armed. One saw the camera. He swore. He rushed over. The feed cut out.

Although my parents were silent, I was not. I gaped for a few minutes, making a strangled, forlorn sound in my throat. Then, I sank my face into my hands, screaming and bawling. I cursed Peters, Licenia, Beckstein, Candor, God, Earth, and myself. I pleaded, bargained, and questioned the hissing, speckled screen before me. My parents tried to ask what was wrong, but I could make no answer other than a hoarse, bestial groan. The television's static gave way to the show that had been playing, and I stood to push it from its low stand, yanking the cord from the outlet and knocking the entire display on its side. After that, my parents managed to restrain me, holding me still as I shook and cried.

Our second parting was brief and solemn. After I had calmed down enough to speak, I told them only that I had to go: I had unfinished business in Priius. After I gathered my things, I dressed in that goddamned black suit again, and told them that I wouldn't be returning. I think they must have some inkling of what I am, now, but at the time they were too confused and distraught to understand. My mother cajoled me to stay, and my father tried to bargain with me, arguing that Priius was clearly too dangerous. I gave them each a last embrace, then set out again on the train to the capital.

There is nothing to say of the trip there. I spent it refining my hot rage into cold fury, planning my actions and trying to anticipate each person's reaction to my arrival. Forgotten and Peters' argument came to mind: Peters had likely acted without Forgotten's approval, and they might be in the tenement. But I could never be sure of that, nor could I anticipate what greeting I would receive, considering how I had fled. First, though, I would see John. And perhaps Deirdre, though it chilled me somewhat to think of my last encounter with her. Either of them, really. I had left manic and frantic; I had no intention of returning in the same manner. Deirdre was only a possibility. It's unlikely she had anywhere near the attachment to me that I felt to her. John, though... I felt as though I should see him. A bit of good news before my unpleasant task might help a bit to calm me. Fighting angry wasn't the way to do it.

A few days were just what I needed to construct my plan. I would visit John, to see how he and Mrs. Hughes were getting along, and to ground myself a bit. From there, I would locate Forgotten through whatever means necessary, and confront him.

It was time to end it. It was time to succeed where Peters had failed, and destroy Candor. Not the tower, but the network: the propaganda tool used to deceive and distract the public from the machinations of one Anton Beckstein. Don't think for a moment that he has faded from this narrative. I had no doubt then, nor do I now, that he had orchestrated much of Licenia's response to the liberation of Priius.

What remained was to find him. But he played at god, and gods don't like to be found.

XXXVI.

The evening is winding into the morning, now; I can tell by the clock. I suspect I've overstayed my welcome as it is, sorting through the trash of my memories and picking out what choice pieces I find. Does it seem a pretty reductionism to you? Does my tale seem to focus too much on what is wrong, and not enough with what is right? Maybe it does. But if you want to hear talk of the grandeur of Priius' skyscrapers, or Tobit's famous museum, you can listen to Candor Network. Although I have already made a sick web of justifications and explanations, qualifications and hedges, I will own that there are some good qualities to Priius. The music is nice. I hear the clubs are excellent. However, all the small niceties of my time here are irrelevant to the telling of my story: what matters is what is wrong. Fitting, then, that I should be the one to tell it.

I took a series of cabs from the train station, to Priius, to Candor Tower, no longer caring for the money I had saved. Money, I can regain; time, I cannot. Somewhere along the way, I found a payphone, and spent a dime to get in contact with Candor Tower. An operator connected me to their operator; from there, I was able to ask if John Hughes, in maintenance, was available. One more dime later, I was on the phone with him. It felt strange to hear the tinny reverberations of his voice through the ratty speaker, and I hadn't much more change; all I did was give him my name and ask that he be ready to meet me outside of Candor Tower within the hour. "I'm sorry I can't give more details," I told him, and I truly was, "but I'm in a hurry. I cannot stay in Priius long, but I want to see you before I go."

Only my suit jacket protected me from the cold rain which spattered down on the streets when I stood before that gaudy tower, glaring up at its monitors with hatred in my heart. It poured off of me in grimy sheets, and ran along the blurred lines of the street to my back. With my hands in my pockets and my shoulders hunched, I waited resolutely by the door, refusing to set foot in that building yet. Only John and my parents knew that I was back, and that was the way I desired it, for now. I could see Deirdre at the desk, through the glass of the doors. A keen sense of loss struck me: I suspected I had lost a friend. Had I entered then, would she recognize me? Surely, for I had not changed much, physically. But I feel so different now from how I felt in those earlier months, and I rather assumed it was reflected in my appearance.

Such thoughts were swept aside when John walked out of the building, holding an umbrella and peering over at me. "Jackson!" he exclaimed, rushing over to shake my hand. He grinned tremendously, and I found myself reciprocating it, clutching his hand in both of mine and giving a vigorous shake. "Hey, John," I laughed. "How the hell are you doing?"

"Fantastic, Jackson," he told me. There was joy in his eyes. It was beautiful. His dark eyes had been set straight, set to gaze on the horizon instead of the heavens. He looked so much younger than when I had seen him last, and I could feel the strength in his aging arms. "I'm sorry we parted on less-than-ideal terms; I owe you more than I can tell you." Although I tried to argue that he owed me nothing—quite the opposite, in fact—he shook his head, growing misty-eyed. "You were right," he told me. "I had given up the fight. What you said to me hurt, but... I needed that hurt. It made me stronger. I've been fighting, Jackson, ever since you left. And I did it: I got those tight-fisted bureaucrats to give me the promotion I've long deserved."

We shared a gay laugh, and I clapped him on the shoulder, telling him what an accomplishment it was. He hugged me, and I found myself returning the gesture, my anger forgotten for a time. "I'm sorry to have hurt you, all the same," I told him, stepping back. "But the past is done; let's talk of it no more. What of your future, John? Where do you go from here?"

"Off to my wife's kitchen," he grinned, before his face fell somewhat. "I do owe you thanks for that, as well. Innumerable thanks. I don't know how you found her, or how you found out, but—thank you. Come with me; I asked the night off early. We can go see her together."

I nodded, shivering slightly as I recalled my last meeting with her. I'd had no strong desire to visit her since then, nor did I suspect that she much wanted to see me. "How's she doing, then?" I asked, holding the umbrella for him and keeping it over his head.

"She's changed," he mused, after a few moments' silence. "She's angry with me, and I suppose she has every right to be. We both forsook the other for dead, and we've drifted in the years that followed. Neither of us have... moved on, though, and that gives me hope." He turned a smile on me again, nodding slightly. "All the same, I can't help but be a bit worried. She always seems... guarded. Cautious. It's as though she's hiding something from someone, but I'm never sure what. And she keeps that gun at the ready nearly at all times, it seems." With a slight sigh and a shrug, he continued, "But the guard keep a thick patrol over by Humboldt, it seems. I can only hope she'll be safe. There've been more killings, you know. The city's gone insane." He shook his head, while I did the same.

I know these streets well, now, and had no trouble guiding John through the thicket of traffic, toward the side-streets of Humboldt. The situation had obviously declined since I left; beyond the haunting memory of Peters' last words, I saw graffiti in a number of obvious locations, along with a thicket of guards in all shapes, sizes, and ages working to wash it clean. All of them were armed. All of them were insufficiently trained, I expected. Bringing in the military would have scared the populace, and hadn't the terrorists been dealt with? So many had been captured; only a handful could remain. I knew better than they could have. And, more importantly, I knew better than they where to find the remnants of these terrorists. Or, at least, so I believed.

"What drives a man to do that?" John's words cut into my thoughts and made me look over at him. He was frowning slightly, rubbing his chin and regarding the pavement. "What makes him so angry, so... broken that he can just shoot people, without blinking an eye?"

"Vengeance, mostly," I replied, keeping my voice and gaze low. "Haven't you felt angry enough to kill someone, before? Maybe in the internment camps."

He shook his head. "No. Not really, at least. I was angry: I wrote, when I could find paper, and more than once, I tried to rally my fellow prisoners. But if it came right down to it, I don't think I could have actually killed someone."

I shrugged, and we walked on. The streets grew crowded, as we continued, until we were wading through a small sea of people. I felt uneasy: Humboldt had never been so busy as that night. A flash of blue light caught my attention, reflected off of a shop window from around the corner. The murmur of the crowd became distinct over the rush of traffic, and upon rounding the corner, the two of us could see a line of police holding back a sizable crowd, Humboldt's entrance taped off to allow room for an ambulance to pull up.

"Oh, God," I breathed, as I saw the first stretcher. "God, no." It was a request, not an exclamation.

Rothschild's foreign face was easily distinguished, from his pale features to the glass eye which never quite followed his real one. He was dressed in a black suit, his arms laid limply beside him. It gave an appropriately-funereal pall to his bullet-riddled corpse as they wheeled him into the ambulance.

We pushed our way to the front, with me more or less dragging poor John to the tape. I shoved aside any who wouldn't move, my eyes wide with horror. Rothschild was dead. Rothschild, whom even Forgotten seemed to fear; the spymaster of our company, and the snake in Licenia's boot.

Next were several members of the guard, all clearly dead. Except for one: he twitched and shuddered against the restraints of the stretcher even while they loaded him into the back of the ambulance and sent it off to be replaced by yet another. Then came Milcher, that great, loyal man. A croak escaped me as I saw his face, and I began to tremble violently. Only distantly aware of the crowd, now, I reflected on my last words to him. I thought I had given him comfort, but I had brought only death.

I do seem to be rather good at that, don't I?

There was no time to mull it over or analyze at the time, but I have my suspicions regarding their death. Rothschild had known for some time that Forgotten would fail; he had told me as much. And from there, he said, he would forge his own plan. He had come to Licenia from Jarkah to join its military, climb its ranks, and then betray it. He had served in the war as a double-agent and spy; his entire life had been built around deception. Mrs. Hughes had once been part of the company of terrorists; perhaps he thought he could sell her out for a pat on the head. And Milcher... well, he was just doing as he was told.

When they wheeled her out, I turned to John, to see his stricken face go pale. The rain fell in grimy sheets, running along the blurred lines of her face. It pooled and eddied in the street below, dripping crimson on stone. Before I could stop him, he ran toward her, pulling down one of the stands of caution tape and flying straight into the arms of the guard. "That's my wife!" he screamed. He shouted it over and over, struggling against two of the guards as they tried to restrain him. "That's my wife! That's my goddamn wife! That's my wife, you bastards!"

They shoved him down, and one clubbed him with a baton to get him to stop fighting. I wanted to rush in, to save him, to throw them away. But I was one man, and they were many. Nothing I could do would have helped him: I could only watch as he was cuffed and dragged away, crying and bellowing to the night sky.

You know, what alarmed me most in the minutes that followed was myself. For I felt no anger. I felt none of the fury and hatred which had consumed me in the moments after Peters' death. I shed no tears, for there were none left within me. Instead, I was given some small glimpse into what he had become.

I have seen more death in the last year of my life than any human should be exposed to in a lifetime. I have endured some small portion of the spectrum of pain, and yet not come out the stronger for it. I have witnessed the senseless deaths of innocent people, and the senseless death of innocence, from both ends of the gun. I am broken, now, perhaps beyond repair. No longer do I feel that I can lay claim to humanity; I have forsaken it for something greater: an ideal.

Like Peters, I am now an Aesop's fable for you. It's all I can ever be again. An Aesop in broken glass.

XXXVII.

I wandered through the crowd, brushing past the silenced bodies which clung like leeches to the spilled blood. From now on, I realized, I, Jackson, did not matter. There is nothing left to me.

Scientists say that the universe acts like clockwork, with everything conforming to predictable laws. There is nothing random on any level which affects our cognition; we are, they say, fleshy machines. To be anything else would require a randomizing agent, or some sort of free will. The only possible device I can imagine which would supply that is a soul. Being clearly lacking in that department, I can only conclude that my actions are the culmination of the interaction of particles and waves created at the conception of the universe. You could say, then, that I was destined to sit here, now. If I am wrong, then I suppose I will answer to God. However, it doesn't seem as though God wants to be found.

We are, all of us, taught the tale of men and women who sought out God. Whether through the construction of grand monuments, the invocation of spirits, or some display of skill, no attempt has succeeded; it shows itself only when it wishes to, and seldom directly. Instead, we are told, it acts through agents. And only when it deems us worthy are we allowed into its realm. All those who attempt to circumvent that are met with the void, punished for their hubris.

We have discussed philosophy enough, today, I know; I know, too, that I am no philosopher. But what I'm getting at is that, across all the cultures with which I am familiar, deities work to hide themselves away from their followers, save when they bear some mask. As I walked through the night-crested alleys toward the tenement, I reflected on all which I have just said to you, and more. Two grand moments of serendipity came upon me, then: there was a chance—only a chance—that I had discovered how to locate the men who would be gods. And like so many of their predecessors, they would experience a fall from grace for their hubris.

The door to the tenement was locked, so I simply shouldered my way into it; the rotten wood gave way easily enough, though not without noise. Within seconds, Forgotten was there, aiming a pistol at me. "Jackson," he muttered, startled. "You could have knocked."

I said nothing, for a moment: only regarded him coolly, waiting for the gun to be moved away. The tenement seemed so strange, with only the two of us in there: almost spacious. Empty. My hands were clearly empty, so I felt no need to raise them; I asked only if he was going to shoot me. "Not yet," he grunted, stepping aside and gesturing toward the room he had taken as his own. "Step inside. I'm curious to know what you've been up to, lately." I did as he bade me, stepping inside and sitting down at a small table. He followed, closed the door behind himself, and sat opposite from me. His knife had been plunged into the wooden table between us; as he sat, he plucked it free, idly toying with it. I was reminded of our first meeting.

Rather than answering his question, I relaxed in the chair, resting my hands on the surface of the table and folding my fingers together. We both waited for the other to begin speaking; eventually, I gave in, and began. "Peters was right, you know."

He didn't look up. "Peters is dead."

"So is everyone else," I shrugged. "Your revolution has failed. What do you do now? Where do you go from here?"

I'll admit that I was surprised when he laughed. It was nothing more than a bark of laughter, as he plunged his blade into the table. "My revolution hasn't failed; it's only been delayed again. This is just another setback: I've always found more angry young men willing to serve with me. Peters was an unfortunate loss, but I've had worse." Glancing up, he added, "Besides, you're back. Care to tell me where the fuck you went?"

Rather than answering his question, I tried again. "You've 'had worse.' 'Another setback.' How many times have you tried before, then? I get the feeling my arrival wasn't simply a fortuitous circumstance."

"It was and it wasn't," he hedged. "It was coincidence that you arrived when you did, but you're right. I'll be honest with you: I've tried twice before. Peters and Rothschild were with me, then, as well; I couldn't have asked for more loyal lieutenants. This time, the casualties were higher. But I've started from nothing three times, now, and I see no reason I can't start once again. I'll just have to wait for all this to die down." He waved a hand toward the window.

"You could have ended it." Regardless of whether or not he wanted to meet my gaze, I stared at him, my gaze as cold and dead as his own. "Well, perhaps. You might have ended it, I should say: you could have supported Peters. If Beckstein is, as you say, the ringmaster—"

"He is. Rothschild has assured me of that. He bribed, cajoled, and threatened his way to power in the shadow of Candor. After you disappeared, I even managed to get one representative to admit it before he died."

"Rothschild's dead, you know. I saw the corpse dragged out of Humboldt."

"Shit." For an instant, I wondered if I could get any emotion out of him. But I had seen it in the past; I knew it was there. I simply shrugged, and carried on.

"I don't think you want it to end, though." That got him to

look up at me. The lion's head seemed toothless, now. He had been presented to me as something unto God: his was a domain one did not enter without permission. I have, however, little enough love for gods. "I think you're afraid of ending it— because when it's over, what are you?"

He rose from his chair, just slightly, and gripped his knife's handle more tightly. "This is not an avenue of conversation you want to pursue, Jackson."

I smiled. "I have been quiet for a very long time. It's my turn to speak. Now, I don't think you want to end this revolution, because I know what they did to you in that Grand War: I know what you became."

"You don't know *shit* about what I went through in that war," he hissed. "Shut the fuck up, or I swear to God—"

"That's what you've become," I continued. "Anger. Aggression. When you left for that war, were you a man, I wonder? Because I don't see a man before me." Fear prickled at the back of my mind as he drew himself up, but I grated out each word. "I see a mask. I see a trigger. I think they stripped you down to nothing but those two things, and you're afraid of losing them." He pulled the knife from the table, and I tensed. "You're afraid that if you stop fighting, there'll be nothing left of—"

He shouted over me as I spoke. I took little heed of what he said: only waited until he was finished before resuming.

"—there'll be nothing left of you. So you're afraid to end this revolution; you're afraid to end the violence, because a trigger is worthless without a gun to fire, and a mask is useless without a coward to hide behind—"

He tried to lunge over the table at me, with a cry of fury; however, I had anticipated something of the sort. Indeed, it had been my goal all along. In fury, I found my true self; in fury, I would find his, as well. Shoving the table against his gut, I knocked him back against the chair, where he toppled, hitting the wall. From there, I stood from my chair, picking it up. Before he could struggle to his feet, I cracked him across the helmet with it, sending him sprawling to the ground. Although he tried to pick up his knife, my boot found his hand; I stomped and ground until his fingers gave way, then took the knife for myself. When he tried to grab my leg, I kicked him in the face. Fighting's much easier when you're clear-headed: with a few more well-placed stomps, he was left gasping for breath as I took his pistol for myself.

"And if you're too much a coward to end this," I breathed, "I will." With those words, I stole his face.

I don't know what I expected to find under that helmet. Once upon a time, I might have expected an angel; some messianic figure sent to Priius to free us from oppression. In that very moment, I suppose I anticipated a scarred and broken thing. And, indeed, his throat bore a line of burns and scar tissue. But his face...

He was just a man. He was just a very ordinary man.

From there, with a knife ready in one hand and a pistol ready in the other, I left that broken thing in the tenement, cursing me with every last ounce of breath he could summon. He lives yet, for some definition of the word—but I doubt he'll ever return to being a man. Regardless, he fades from the narrative, as so many others have. There's very little of importance left, save for three of us.

The cover of night shrouded me as I made my way toward Franklin Square for what I can only hope is the final time. I had already put on Forgotten's helmet: it smelled of sweat, but fit fairly comfortably, even if it did reduce my peripheral vision. I have always had something of a flair for the dramatic, I suppose. And so it was that I stood before the banners and televisions of

Candor Tower, where lately Peters had sent his message. It was time to send my own.

I strode right through the door, my mind racing as I tried to think of where a god would hide himself in a tower like this. On the very top? No. Too exposed, and too cliche: a clever man builds a fortress, not a tower. The middle, perhaps. As I walked, I made no great attempt to hide my armaments, and so I heard a woman's voice by my side: "Sir, Candor Network doesn't allow for the carrying of firearms by anyone except authorized security personnel. I'm going to have to ask you to leave." It quavered slightly, but the words were resolute. Slowly, I turned, to see Deirdre there.

Some sort of shame came over me: unbidden, the memories of my evenings spent in her company as she worked came to mind, and I concluded that I didn't want her to see what I had become. I would rather she think me a madman, due to our last encounter, than a monster. I lowered my voice a bit, and did my best to address her with neutrality. "Ma'am. I can't say that I give a damn about Candor's policies."

She raised her chin, tossing her brown hair out of her plain, round face. The gaze she turned on me was strikingly contemptuous, without a hint of either the compassion to which I was used, or the fear I had expected. "If you don't leave, I'll call security," she warned me. She stooped slightly to one side, her hand beneath the counter, presumably on a button.

My prior attraction and fondness for her slid to the background as I raised my gun, aiming it at her chest. "If you press that button, security won't come faster than a bullet, ma'am," I replied. "You've nothing to gain by it. Just back away, and I won't hurt you."

I suppose I should have known: she always stood her ground. It's part of why I liked her; she had a fire and an independence which is beaten out of most women, in these days. Without another word, she pressed the button. Alarms began to sound throughout the building; there was no hiding it. I glared at her through the slits of my mask, and she returned my gaze without so much as a wince.

My finger twitched slightly. I could feel the trigger begin to slide back. There she was: one of the few people I had met who had shown me compassion in Priius. One of the few who stood by her principles. One of the few deserving of respect. And I was about to shoot her.

I lowered my gun and turned away, rushing to the elevator in the hopes that I could make it up before security found me.

After pressing the buttons for every elevator, fortune smiled on me: one had been waiting in the lobby. I stepped inside and chose the highest floor, hoping it would give me time to consider where to begin my hunt. I racked my brain, trying to think of any evidence I had discovered; any clues.

It was serendipity; I can only assume that some mixture of adrenaline, cleverness, and luck led me to think of it. As I thought back over all my time working as a janitor in Candor Tower, all the rooms I had cleaned, one stuck out to me.

"We don't go in there," Milcher had told me, when I tried to enter the shower while Forgotten washed.

"We don't clean that room," John told me, when I started toward the room wedged between four offices.

I remembered the room; I had passed it many times while I cleaned. I selected the button for that floor, and waited for fate to take root. If I was right, I was also damned lucky. If I was wrong, I would likely die, for I would never be captured alive.

Twice, the elevator stopped, and the doors slid open to some contingent of guards. Time seemed almost to slow, to distort: as my heart pounded in my chest, I experienced a sort of sickly hyperalertness, raising my gun. I fired. I pulled the trigger until they weren't there, anymore. And then I continued on my way.

I know you remember this next part, but it seems a shame to abandon my tale before it's complete. We have time, after all; I think you can afford me a little more of it before we have to go.

It's such a small room; by necessity, of course, trapped between four larger offices as it is. It has neither windows to the outer world, nor televisions. Only two armchairs, a table, a small bar, a desk, and filing cabinets. Modest, really, for the dictator of a country. It's not what I expected when I broke the door in, but that's the point, isn't it? Any other time, I never would have looked there. Neither, evidently, did the guards who were hunting for me. The alarms have ceased, now. We're alone, you and I.

You know, it's almost funny: after all the murders we committed; all the bombs we planted or tried to plant; all the violence conducted before I ever arrived, finding you was as simple as going where I was forbidden to go. I owe you some respect, as well: not once have you interrupted my tale, nor have you sought to deny the claims I bring before you. You have indulged me thus far; it seems rude now to ask that you indulge me a few minutes longer.

When I walked in, you met me with a remarkable calm. Were you expecting this end? Did you fear that, in the end, all your guards, all your hunts wouldn't be enough to keep something from slipping through? You're not stupid. Far from it: you're one of the cleverest, most intelligent men I've ever met. And one of the most unflappable; not many would answer a gun at their chest with a philosophical argument. You knew what I was from the moment I walked in; the black suits, meant for anonymity, have had something of the opposite effect. And you had a pretty argument ready.

I won't say that it hasn't swayed me, to some degree. It's pleasant to think that all your bribes to the warmongers were in the hopes of ending the war, not prolonging it. And you have my sympathies, as far as your motivations lie: had I spent years building on a company on reporting on the horrors of war, only to find that it had borne the opposite effect, I suspect I might have despaired as well. No-one can blame you for feeling that the masses are too ignorant and apathetic for self-governance; it's an ancient view, and not without justification. You owe your life, right now, to your polemics. But don't mistake my acceptance of them for agreement. Whatever your motivations, your actions are my concern: you admit that you have manipulated a nation, but you have yet to show real remorse for your actions. That, Beckstein, is why I sit before you today.

It's funny, you know: you're supposed to be the good guy, here. You're pious. You care about your fellow man. I doubt very much you've ever laid a hand on someone in anger. You're almost everything I'm not: I'm an angry, violent, atheistic husk of a thing. And yet you're the villain of this story. I don't know: I just think it's funny how things play out, sometimes.

Ah, but you aren't without your vices. All our sins come back to haunt us, and you are no exception. I suppose that I'm proof enough of that, but there are more specters of your past waiting to greet you. You see, Beckstein, I know something you don't know: I know a little whore selling her body in the streets. And I know who her daddy is.

I can see by the fear in your eyes that you remember. What was it, then? A night of loneliness, some fifteen years prior? A celebration of your company's success? True love, maybe? But you used her and left her, like all of the men before you—only, you left her something to remember you by. No, no; I don't believe for an instant that you knew yourself to be a father. You aren't that kind of man, are you? After all this, you're probably one of the most respectable people I've ever met. I only wish it could have been on better terms. Really, I do.

I bring this up for two reasons: one is for her sake. She deserves better than what she received. Better than to be dragged along those dark places, with her eyes set on Heaven. The other, though, is for your own sake. You know who I am. You know where I grew up, and you would not be hard-pressed to find my parents. After all of this, they're among the last four people in the world who matter to me. I'm going to be leaving this shithole of a country, this city of broken glass. But I'm going to let you in on a secret. Listen closely.

I will always haunt Licenia. And if I find that John, Deirdre, or my parents have been harmed—if I find that even one more innocent is caught up in this, I will manifest. Fergus, Milcher, Mrs. Hughes: none of them should have died the way they did. There's precious little left in the world which I can claim to love, and I will protect it more fiercely than you can imagine. So let me make this abundantly clear: if you so much as touch any one of them, you will never escape me. I won't kill you, no. But don't think for a moment that I will hesitate to kill everything you have ever loved, and force you to watch. You will kneel, in darkness, trembling, and beg for death to my shadow. And when I can see that you are truly penitent, that you wish for nothing more than the void, I will deny it to you.

In a moment, you're going to join me in a trip to your broadcast station. You will not call out, nor will you warn anyone of your current situation. Once there, you will record a confession of what you have done, to be broadcast on repeat on every goddamn channel. If what you have done is so shameless, then you have nothing to fear. Otherwise, I recommend you leave before the public remembers the last time it had a parliamentary election. You will do all of this, and you will do it truthfully, or by God, I will paint these walls with your blood.

But don't worry, Beckstein. It's not your fault. None of this is, really. You couldn't have helped it. You were blind. I suppose we all were, really. Forgotten was blinded by hatred, and for that, he lost everything. You were blinded by an inability to trust in people, and for that, you gave up the fight for candor. And I... I was blinded by loyalty. And for that, I have lost myself.

But it's alright, Beckstein. After all...

It's a rare man who isn't blind.

About the Author

Adam Proctor was born and raised outside the city limits of a rural Tennessee town in 1994, and has been writing since shortly thereafter. Currently, he is in the midst of pursuing a degree in economics. He is a voracious reader, whose collection tends toward the 1880s to 1920s. In addition to writing, he also sings and plays the piano, and has self-published several hours of original piano music.

www.ingramcontent.com/pod-product-compliance
Lightning Source LLC
Chambersburg PA
CBHW031106260626
47172CB00001B/241